AS LONG AS
YOU LOVE ME

AS LONG AS YOU LOVE ME

MARIANNA LEAL

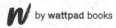 by wattpad books

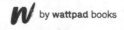 by **wattpad** books

An imprint of Wattpad WEBTOON Book Group

Copyright © 2023 Marianna Leal

All rights reserved.

Published in Canada by Wattpad WEBTOON Book Group, a division of Wattpad WEBTOON Studios, Inc.

36 Wellington Street E., Suite 200,
Toronto, ON M5E 1C7 Canada

www.wattpad.com

First W by Wattpad Books edition: September 2023

ISBN 978-1-99077-834-6 (Trade Paper original)
ISBN 978-1-99077-835-3 (eBook edition)

Library and Archives Canada Cataloguing in Publication information is available upon request.

Printed and bound in Canada

1 3 5 7 9 10 8 6 4 2

Cover design by Carina Guevara
Author photo by Vic Cavalieri (@weirdowithluv)
Typesetting by Delaney Anderson

A mi familia.

CHAPTER ONE

What can be sown in the streets of Venezuela is death.

Someone said this at my brother's funeral with the kind of acceptance usually preceded by a sigh and followed by, "Qué se puede hacer?" Like we were talking about losing a contest rather than normalizing the fact that venturing out in the streets might mean returning home in a casket.

My body trembled during the entire service, but my chin didn't waver, and my eyes were dry. I was so full of anger that my insides were a volcano about to erupt, ready to wipe away civilizations. In that moment, it was my civilization I wanted to clean the slate of.

How had we got to this point? How was I the only one bursting at the seams with anger like lava and ashes? Wasn't anger supposed to be one of the early stages of loss? And yet everybody around me either cried or shook their heads, murmuring about how young he'd been, so full of promise.

Mami sobbed. Ever since we'd received the news, she had been unable to draw a breath that didn't come along with a fresh wave of tears. Papi's face was stern, which probably added to Mami's sorrow. My brother, Carlos, had died fighting for the opposite political side from Papi's. Our father loved Carlos with every fiber of his being, but he'd never really moved past the disappointment of Carlos not sharing his support for the revolution.

Meanwhile, my twin sister, Coralina, clung to her boyfriend, Rodrigo, with a grip that would probably leave a bruise. She was stuck in a combination of shaking her head and crying, bewildered that her brother would give his life in protests against the chaos our country had descended into.

And then there was me. I had dressed in all black for the funeral service, and the color seeped into my heart, inflaming me with the same rage Carlos had felt that fateful morning. It had already been close to two months since he'd last been able to go to class at university because the teachers were on strike. A bunch of his friends and guys from other schools had agreed to protest downtown, close to the main newspaper of Maracaibo. I'd helped him prepare bottles full of vinegar and cut up rags from old T-shirts so he could protect himself from the tear gas sure to hit them.

Almost as if I'd *known*, I'd clutched at his hands at the last minute and wouldn't let him go.

"Yo también," I'd said, gripping him tighter. "Let me join you."

Carlos's dark eyes had twinkled. "I never would've imagined a day would come when you'd want to skip school."

To emphasize his point, he'd looked down at my school uniform. I'd woken up as soon as Papi had left for work at five-thirty in the morning, got dressed, and sneaked out of my room to wake Carlos up while Mami and Cora still slept. The plan had been that after Carlos left, I'd wake them up with breakfast and act as a smokescreen for Carlos.

His joke had made me wrinkle my nose. I was the most responsible sixteen-year-old I knew, and never had I skipped a single day of school. I was the best student in my class, so advanced my teachers always told Mami it was a shame they couldn't accelerate my education.

And yet that day I didn't care. I didn't want to let go of my brother. I wanted to cling to him, school record be damned.

He flicked my bangs the way he knew annoyed me and gave me a hug. "Leave the ugly fighting to your champion, mi princesa. One day we'll be free, and I'll give you this kingdom again."

I remembered rolling my eyes and saying he was so corny. I remembered watching his back disappear around the corner outside our apartment as I closed the door.

That was it. Carlos was gone. I would never see him again, hear his obnoxious laughter, bury my face in the crook of his neck when he hugged me, watch him banter with Cora until her face turned red like a tomato.

And I'd had a hand in it. I'd prepared him for the final joust. I'd sent him off. But it was my country that had killed him.

The biggest question I asked myself was how we could possibly move on from this. How could we pick up our lives as though Carlos was no more, or had never been, when any one of us could be next on any given day?

How could I move on? At least the answer to that question was easy. I couldn't.

Coralina cried herself to sleep that night. Her top bunk shook for hours with the force of her sobs until eventually they ebbed away and her breathing evened. I still shook, my eyes open so wide it was painful. My roiling heart threatened to explode, but blinding terror paralyzed me. The terror of what my parents would think once they knew the role I'd played in Carlos's death. Terror that tomorrow it could be Mami or Papi or my sister or my best friends or myself. Terror that came with knowing I had to face a lifetime, however long or short, without my brother.

I kicked the blankets away from me and shot to the bathroom, bile rushing up my throat and out my mouth. In the aftermath, I felt hands rubbing my back, and dizzy and weakened, I found the blurry face of my mother.

Finally, the feelings came out in a word vomit that made little sense. She never stopped rubbing my back or caressing my hair, even as I told her what I'd caused, what I'd almost done—and finally, a day after Carlos's funeral, I started to weep. That was when Papi joined us and things got even worse.

"Que hiciste *qué*?" His scream echoed against the bathroom tile, hitting me harder every time it bounced back into my ears.

Mami shot to her feet and got in his face, her voice raised as high as her temper. "Don't you dare! Don't you dare blame Catalina when you know who did this!"

His face had gone almost purple when he retorted with, "You're right, this isn't Catalina's fault but Carlos's!"

Mami raised her hand and slammed it across his cheek with all the force of her grief, making him stumble. Behind him stood Cora, who also had just witnessed a scene that had never happened in this family. Silence fell over us that night like a heavy blanket that drowned out laughter and chatter forever.

The Diaz Solis family had long struggled with the ideological differences of each of its members. Papi had always been a supporter of the government, even when the policies stemming from its revolution made his business falter. Cora, the quintessential daddy's girl, went along with whatever he thought. Mami had always been the ni-ni of the family, ni esto ni aquello, going to herculean efforts to stay neutral and maintain harmony even though Carlos and I were firmly on the opposite side.

But the night after Carlos's funeral was when my family broke. That was the moment I understood that without Carlos, I had no place in it, and no future in a country where my life was worth less than the cost of a loaf of bread.

Months later, as I received my high school diploma from the Catholic school all three Diaz Solis siblings had attended, I decided the only way to live was to leave. I discarded my plans of enrolling at La Universidad del Zulia, my hometown's university and the one Carlos and my parents had attended, and started looking into programs abroad. I'd saved some money working part-time at Papi's company, and I spent it all on the extensive paperwork required to apply for studies abroad.

A year later, I had an acceptance to the University of Central Florida, in the US, with a partial scholarship. I did all of this behind Papi's back, knowing that he'd never let me go.

But then I needed to get a plane ticket to Caracas to get my visa stamp.

"No," Papi said at once, tossing aside the stack of bank notes he'd been counting on the kitchen table. He rose from his chair, probably with the single-minded purpose of getting a better angle to blow my eardrums with shouting, but Mami turned around from the kitchen sink with the same fire in her eyes she'd had the night after Carlos's funeral.

"Yes, she's going."

I was torn between jumping in the middle to keep them at bay and the opposite impulse of running away and locking myself in my room.

"How can you be fine with losing a second child?" Papi asked her, and Mami shook her head.

"We're not losing her. We're *saving* her."

The next day, I traveled to the capital to get my visa. A month later, I rode on a bus for eight hours to get to Bogotá, Colombia, where I flew out to Orlando, Florida, to start my new life. As the plane lifted off the runway, I was full of hope like I hadn't felt in my chest since the day Carlos went ahead of us to heaven.

I would get a chance to actually live, to build the life my home country had denied my generation.

CHAPTER TWO

PRESENT

The phone buzzing in the cubicle next to mine made me grind my molars.

After a quick sip of bland coffee that didn't calm me down in the least, I returned my attention to my screen. Metal Systems, the engineering company I was interning at, was in the middle of a massive construction project. I had to make sure every drawing was in the system and, if not, I had to upload them. If they were unavailable, I was in charge of finding out why and making them available. The latter portion had potential for excitement if it meant I could march up to the engineer in charge of that component and demand that the drawings be created stat.

But so far, the only excitement had come from Gabe's phone incessantly buzzing with notifications.

As it went off again, I glared over at my nemesis of almost four years, Gabriel Cabrera. We had the same boss to impress, but he clearly wasn't focused on work. I cast him a look that conveyed my exact level of annoyance.

The road to the American Dream was crystal clear for me.

First, I'd come into the country to do my bachelor's in mechanical engineering, and now that graduation loomed closer, my next step was renewing my visa to find a job that could keep me here, away from the Venezuelan Nightmare.

This plan was the fuel that kept me going even though I was pretty sure the task Jeff—my internship supervisor—had assigned to me was unexciting admin work. I couldn't help wondering what he had assigned to Gabe. Snooping shouldn't be hard in an open office, but Gabe's screen was angled away from mine, and he typed so fast I couldn't imagine his assignment was boring like mine.

The moment I stumbled upon a drawing completely missing in action, my own phone vibrated. Mami's name lit up on my phone screen, sending my heartbeat from normal to about-to-run-out-of-my-chest.

Chatting with anyone back home was . . . not exactly pleasant. Most of our conversations were strained under the pressure of keeping them light when all we wanted to do was complain about the worsening situation: the fact that a paper cut was enough to kill someone with the way the healthcare system had collapsed, or the interminable lines to find basic goods at prices so steep that years ago you could've bought a house with the sacks of bills people had to bring to buy flour for arepas.

Or the fact Mami was alone in a household where two out of three residents believed the slogan "the country is truly ours," in tatters as it was. I toed a fine line between letting her manage the brunt of Papi's and my sister's beliefs, trying to save myself, and succumbing to my own need to commiserate with someone about how misguided they were.

Because Mami was the only one I could have the semblance of a conversation with. I had barely exchanged a word with Papi in the almost four years since I'd left. He still couldn't forgive me for betraying him. As for my twin sister, Cora, if she wasn't talking about politics, she was prattling on about Rodrigo, her boyfriend since high school. He was now a political activist in a student party affiliated with the government's, and he kept roping Cora into their activism.

The worst part was how none of us wanted to talk about Carlos. Just mentioning his name brought back a rush of grief and hurt that hadn't ebbed away since the day we'd lost him. His death hovered over our conversations about the nightmare back home, making it much starker. Making me even more glad I wasn't there.

My phone rattled against the desk once more, and I told myself I was at work. It was a legitimate excuse to not pick up right away. Once I made it home tonight and called Mami back, she would most likely rip me a new one. But I preferred that over having to deal with all the turmoil talking with her would bring while I was still at the office.

Gabe's phone went off again, and like magic, so did mine. I made the mistake of meeting his eyes just as he turned his device upside down.

"What's that? An angry boyfriend?" he said.

"No," I huffed and volleyed back, "What's that, then? An angry girlfriend?"

"Yeah, actually," he replied before going back to what I now imagined to be a heated discussion with Liz. From what little I'd seen of her, she could be, uh, *intense*.

His pretty face darkened with a frown. It was an expression I'd never seen on him before. A strand of his jaw-length hair had escaped his low ponytail a while ago, so at odds with the perfectly ironed shirt he wore for the office. But I shook my head because I wasn't about to give an ounce of pity to the Campus Babe, as people called him. Girlfriend problems were exactly what he needed in order to grow up and past his womanizing ways.

Jeff's head popped in from the hallway. "Hey, guys."

Gabe and I jumped in our skins, but it wasn't as though using our phones was against the company guidelines. Except I couldn't calm down when Jeff said, "Can you follow me for a quick chat? I have some news I'd rather you hear from me right away."

That didn't sound good.

Gabe and I left our phones behind and followed our supervisor. Was Jeff quitting? Or being assigned to a different team? Were Gabe and I going to be left hanging? Or worse, fired?

And if that happened, well, shit. I'd have to start looking for a new place to intern in the hopes of being kept full-time after graduation. But if push came to shove, the OPT permit that allowed me to work while on a student visa was still valid for about two months. After that, I would renew it while looking for another company. And if that didn't pan out—

No. I shook my head hard. I was starting to catastrophize again. Maybe the reason for this impromptu meeting was nothing terrible.

Jeff took a seat at the head of the table and gestured for us to join. I noticed he motioned for Gabe to sit at his right, even though I was technically closer to that chair. Whatever. That didn't necessarily mean anything, right?

"Okay, so good news and bad news rolled into one," Jeff said, running his hand over his bald head. "Head count has been approved in the department."

Gabe and I puffed our chests like peacocks about to fight for a peahen.

"Wait," I said, deflating a little. "What's the bad news?"

Jeff cringed. "Only one full-time employee position got approved."

I clamped my mouth shut tight so I wouldn't scream that the position should be mine. I was more hardworking, focused— desperate. I'd already gone through the pains of getting accepted by this team. I wasn't about to let all that effort go to waste and have to start again somewhere else.

Besides, Gabe was a guy. Men ruled the engineering world. It wouldn't be difficult for him to find alternatives. I wouldn't be surprised if he was already getting recruiting calls from other companies. Maybe he'd even lied earlier when he said his phone kept buzzing because of his girlfriend.

Before I got ahead of myself, I asked point-blank, "Who's getting it?"

"Why only one position?" Gabe asked at the same time.

I felt him glance at me, but I kept my eyes firmly on Jeff.

Our boss sighed. "Well, we're not exactly putting out the best results this year, what with the delay of two projects and all. One head count is all management approved."

This time I sent Gabe a glare as a knee-jerk reflex, but I cooled it down because I was trying to stay professional.

"In that case," I continued, modulating my voice so it didn't sound anywhere near as unhinged as I felt, "what will be the selection criteria?"

"Performance," was Jeff's response.

My rival pressed him for further clarification. Jeff said many words that explained nothing further, leaving a whole lot of space in my mind to be filled with wild ideas of how to earn the spot.

When Jeff left the room, I folded my arms and lifted my chin, sizing Gabe up as though I could figure out his weakness. "This position is mine, and you know it."

"Think whatever you want, but in the end, I'll be the one on top." Gabe gave me the most annoying smirk.

I walked out. When all was said and done, I was the one who would win this. He didn't have the work ethic I did, even if he had twice the brains—which no one would ever catch me alive saying. He wouldn't be a stumbling block on the road to *my* American Dream. Gabe Cabrera was going down.

CHAPTER THREE

Defeating Gabe was easier said in my mind than done in reality.

If this were a popularity contest, I would one hundred percent lose. Everyone loved Gabe. From Jeff to our colleagues, from the other interns to the higher-ups.

Speaking of Gabe, some of his fans waited by his desk. A couple girls who interned in the accounting department lit up like fairy lights upon setting eyes on him.

"Gabe!" One of the girls called out his name with obvious joy.

I blew a sigh that sent a strand of my hair flying and said to myself, "Paciencia."

Gabe tossed another little smirk at me before sitting at his chair to hold court like the king of the interns he was.

Unfortunately, flexing my patience was part of the life I was building for myself. Not only was I alone in another country, miles and miles away from what remained of my family and everything I had grown up with, I was also studying and working in a language I hadn't quite mastered yet, enduring all the mocking associated with pronouncing it with the hard vowels and consonants of my own.

But I had to contend with this guy both at work and at school.

They had better not flirt for hours by my desk, or else I wouldn't get any work done before it was time to leave for class.

Meanwhile, even as they chatted, Gabe was the picture of a hardworking intern, a keyboard warrior making his way through the maze of emails that piled onto the battlefield that was every day as a TPM intern. The technical project management team, a subgroup in the engineering department, was the frequent recipient of all the flying debris post turds hitting the fan. If our supervisor walked by now, he would still know Gabe wasn't just spending his time flirting with the girls in the office, because he was honestly great at work.

The twitching of his lips gave him away, though. The attention must be giving him the warm and fuzzies.

Since the girls didn't speak Spanish, I whispered to him, "Haz que se vayan."

That tore his eyes away from the screen. "Why? Jealous?"

"Asco." I wrinkled my nose against the bad taste that filled my mouth. "More like I need to focus on work. You know, the thing we're supposed to be here for?"

The twinkle in his eyes made me grit my teeth.

It was the same one he got every time he bested me on an exam or assignment. The one that always came along with the little smirk and lifted chin he gave me right now, as though issuing a challenge that needed no words. The patented *look at me, I'm better than you* Gabriel Cabrera expression.

But he was wrong. I didn't care if he had hordes of girls falling at his feet. He gave me the look simply because this whole thing distracted me. And damn it, I was behind with my task, *and* class would start soon.

"You can come too, Carolina," one of the girls said.

The surprise invitation rattled my brain. What had they even been talking about?

Right, some party at a sorority house. My favorite place in the whole world.

I made a sour expression. Fortunately, I had my back to them, and I was able to put on a serene façade when I responded. "My name is Catalina, and thank you, but I have plans this weekend."

The three of them gave me the same look of incredulity.

Yeah, my plans consisted of catching up on my assignments and maybe hanging out with my only two friends. So what? They were valid plans, especially because they were *mine*.

Throughout my college experience, I'd had many barriers to making copious amounts of friends. The most obvious one was my struggle with the language. Back home, I'd taken a lot of English courses that had given me a foundation. Now, after almost four years of being immersed in it, I was fully fluent. Except sometimes my tongue still tied around the hybrid vowel sounds native speakers used so freely. And when I got excited, it could be really hard for them to understand me.

Additionally, I wasn't interested in going to parties or in joining sororities or clubs. I was here to study like my life depended on it. Because it did. I didn't care if my peers saw me as an antisocial pariah with no personal skills if it meant I could secure a good enough job to keep me firmly on this side of the border.

Gabe glanced back at the girls. "Anyway, Liz and I will definitely be there."

Their expression fell a little at the reminder that he was taken.

A little sigh escaped from my lips. I wasn't like Gabe, who could perfectly balance school, work, and a social life. That last one was easy for him, since he drew people in with his charisma and ridiculous good looks. But what irritated me the most was that he didn't have to put a lot of effort into the first two to excel.

Back in the first semester of freshman year—and this I could only admit to myself—I had been as drawn to him as anyone else. He'd had a sort of bad-boy air as he sat in class, looking bored for all intents and purposes, not even picking up his pen to make notes. Then the grades for our first exam came out, and even though I'd busted my ass studying freaking calculus *in English*, he'd scored the highest in our class.

I'd been second, by a good margin.

When he'd caught me gaping at the calculus teacher's announcement board, Gabe had said, "Better luck next time, Cat."

The condescension, the nickname—or perhaps the botching of my name—had evaporated what little interest I'd had in him, and he'd become persona non grata ever since.

My alarm went off. Even though I wasn't anywhere near done with the task, I started shutting the computer down and packing my stuff to go to class. I popped by Jeff's desk to officially clock out. Since he was in a teleconference, I mouthed that I had to go, and he gave me a thumbs-up.

Gabe still chatted with the other interns. I didn't bother mentioning he'd be late for the most important class of the semester, where we'd be assigned the senior design project that would make or break our final grade before graduation. Did it make me petty that I wanted a head start over my rival to get to class and pick the best group first? Sure. I didn't mind, though.

I juggled my backpack and lunch bag as I power walked to the exit. At the door, I realized I'd tucked my ID into my backpack and wasted a bunch of time digging for it. I pushed the door open with my shoulder, and suddenly it gave as someone behind me held it open for me.

The gratitude faded from my lips as Gabe hovered over me. His amused expression sent my blood boiling.

"I see what you're trying to do. You're too transparent, Kitty Cat," he said.

I pursed my lips but otherwise didn't acknowledge him while I headed towards my car, an Acura that had been in its prime in 2005 and I'd bought for five hundred dollars. So far, I had probably spent twice as much on repairs, but until I got that full-time position, I couldn't afford to buy a better replacement.

One of the car's many quirks was that the front doors didn't open. Opening the rear passenger door, I threw my stuff into the farthest end of the back seat, then hauled myself into the car headfirst. I could feel Gabe's stare while I maneuvered to the driver's seat from the back, contorting my body so one leg and arm made it first. I was in such a hurry to beat him to class that the gear stick stabbed against my ribs, which hadn't happened often the past few months. I twisted to get my hips through the space. When I finally lowered myself into the driver's seat, I was so sweaty, I had to roll the window down. Manually.

Which also put me face-to-face with my tormenter.

The sunlight made the honey in his eyes almost iridescent as he leaned over my open window and said, "You know, most people don't have to bend like they're in Cirque du Soleil to get into their car."

"Most people's car doors work." I gritted my teeth. My grip on the steering wheel turned into a vise with the effort of not launching my fist at his perfect nose.

"You don't say." The tilt of his head made a lock of dark hair escape the weak hold of the back of his ear. "I could help you repair it. My cousin Manny works at an auto body shop, and he can give me a steep discount."

I hated when he was nice and rubbed in how charming he was.

"I'm okay, but I'd be much better if you'd let me get going," I said, and he leaned away, hands raised in a sign of peace. I gunned the engine and drove away. Even as his figure grew smaller in the rearview mirror, I was aware of him watching.

By the time I got to campus, my hair was a nest atop my head, and my blouse was soaked through with sweat. The blast of air-conditioning in the classroom made me shudder, but I welcomed the change. My car was an oven in the summer, and two years of owning it had turned me into an overbaked bun.

I spotted my targets sitting together. Adrian and Jasper weren't exactly my friends, but the two guys were good people and, more importantly, good students. Taylor sat with them. The four of us should be set to nail the senior project.

"We're in this together, right?" I said for a greeting, plopping onto the seat beside Jasper.

He offered me a fist bump, saying, "Obviously."

"We're gonna kick so much ass, no one will have any left to sit with," said Taylor, which made all of us laugh. She and Maya, my roommate, were my best friends and the ones who had assumed the responsibility of keeping me sane all these years. If Taylor was on the team, she'd make sure I didn't become Projectzilla in the process.

The professor walked in, and silence settled over the lecture hall. Just minutes into the lecture, though, the front door burst open and produced Gabe Cabrera. He had an iced coffee in one hand and a hot one in the other.

"Sorry, teach. The dean intercepted me for a quick chat." He placed the hot coffee on the professor's desk. "Here's a late fee."

Ugh, what a suck-up.

Professor Jones narrowed his eyes, but instead of a scolding, he said, "Thanks, Cabrera." And then he turned back to the class like nothing was amiss. "Anyway, as I was saying, this will be a group project all through the semester. A simulation of the work environment, if I may."

If the group had to be more than four people, I would have to find some other decent candidates who wouldn't drag me down. I turned around, zeroing in on a couple of other good students. Gabe caught my eye as he took a sip from his drink. I ignored him.

"The groups will be as follows," Professor Jones continued, picking up a piece of paper from his desk. It took me a while to process, but he was indeed reading names in a specific order. Almost as if . . .

As if *he* were the one determining what the teams were. I sat up straight, clutching my desk. My heart picked up more speed than my Acura could as Professor Jones's choices caused waves of despair or joy around the room.

"Catalina Diaz," he called out, with a pause I found too dramatic for my liking. My ears rang over the next names he called.

Wait, who had he called out before me? Were they also part of my group? Did I get stuck with the worst students of my grade? Was he done with my group?

Vaguely, I heard him list a few familiar names, one of which made my stomach lurch. "There you have it," Professor Jones said, setting the paper down. "I'll tack the full list on the board outside and email it after class. Now, let's focus on the project requirements."

The derailment of my plans tore my concentration to shreds. The queasy feeling in my stomach grew as class finished and Taylor turned to me. "Are you going to be okay? The group we got is kind of . . ."

I scrambled along with everyone else to wait as Professor Jones hung the list outside. It took some pushing and elbowing to make it to the front of the group. My eyes scanned the list three times, until it finally sunk in that Gabriel Cabrera's name had been called out before mine, and that I'd be stuck doing this project with the rival I was supposed to be defeating.

I stabbed the ice cream like I wanted to kill it. Maya and Taylor watched me shovel out about half of the pint at once and bite into it with more force than necessary.

I'd gone home after the news, changed into shorts and an oversized T-shirt that had more holes than Swiss cheese, gathered my hair into a mop above my head, and raided the ice cream.

"How is it possible that life gives a person exactly what they don't want *every single time*?" I asked them between bites of chocolate ice cream so thick I might as well have been eating a frozen bar.

Taylor's ice cream was beginning to drip from her spoon. Maya didn't bat an eye, though. As my roommate, she was used to worse messes from me.

"It's not that bad," Taylor said with a shrug, finally giving up on her treat and putting it on the coffee table. "At least you have me in the group."

"Yeah, but *he's* there too."

A corner of Maya's lips lifted. "Gabe's not bad—as a person. As eye candy, he's exceptional."

"I'm definitely not going to complain about that." Taylor sighed and flopped back on the couch, spreading her arms like an eagle. One of them landed on Maya's lap. "Too bad he has a girlfriend."

I choked. Among spluttering obscenities in my mother tongue, I managed to ask her, "So, what—you'd date him if he were single?"

She shrugged. "If he stayed single for more than a minute. Or if he didn't date, I don't know, only the hottest girls ever. Maybe I should just ask him to hook a girl up."

"I think everyone on campus who likes guys has had the same idea at some point," said Maya as she inspected her nails. "Including me."

The laugh that escaped from my throat was so ugly I barely recognized myself. It was the laughter of someone on the verge of greatness or disaster. Both would have been fitting if either of them had ever dated Gabe. First, it would have been a great achievement to nab him. Second, it would mean he'd developed a taste for intelligent and good-natured women. From what I'd seen so far, his track record consisted mostly of gorgeous but mean girls—case in point, his current girlfriend, Liz. And third, it would've ended in disaster anyway, if one were to go by the constant turnover in his dating pool.

"You're kidding me, right?" But I didn't wait for either of them to answer. Shaking my head, I added, "Enough that I have to put up with his obnoxious face at school and at work. If either of you turn into his arm candy, I will riot."

Maya went back to filing her nails. Being the healthiest person in the room, she didn't need empty calories to cope with her day. Her words, not mine. She had no issues spending calories on giving me the side-eye, though. "Maybe life's giving you a sign because he sure does take up a lot of your attention."

"What are you trying to say?" I challenged.

Taylor's face also transformed into her signature *let's tease Catalina* look. This look had an extra glint that her other smiles didn't possess. "Do you maybe . . . like Gabe? Are you jealous of his girlfriends?"

It was as if I'd sucked a lemon. In my soul.

"Okay, that's how I know you guys have lost the plot. Maybe we should go to church this weekend." I made the sign of the cross and shuddered.

"The hypothesis has merit," Maya said, spoken like the future medical researcher she was. "I mean, the statistical sample size of times you've spoken shit about him is, to simplify, *huge.*"

I rolled my eyes, about to say they were exaggerating, but the looks on their faces said that nope, they weren't.

I sat back for a moment, eating my ice cream and trying to think about the last time I'd brought up Gabriel Cabrera before this conversation. Yesterday, I'd complained he'd had a higher score on a report than me, even though he'd barely shown up for lectures. And two days before that, he'd made me look like a clown in front of our supervisor as he'd pointed out a key piece of information I had totally missed from our monthly status report. I still couldn't get over the gloating smile on his face. And then there had been that time last week, when his girlfriend, Liz, had dropped by after work and made a big deal out of him and me leaving the office at the same time. The word *cheating* had been bandied about too easily for my taste, when all Gabe and I had been doing was talking about a joint report we had to make for Jeff.

I had seen him break up with flings for less, so it was kind of a surprise they were still together, which meant—

"Oh my word," I said, sitting up straight. "You're right."

Taylor's eyes positively lit up. "That you like him?"

"No," I scoffed, unfolding my legs out and standing up. "You're right that I talk too much about him. I must excise him from my vocabulary."

Maya's smirk made a return. "Easier said than done."

As I put my half-finished pint back in the freezer, I thought about those words and recognized the truth in them. It was the same thing as telling a Venezuelan household to quell any conversation about politics, because that talk made everybody sick to their stomachs. Except the daily doses of negativity were the drug we couldn't be free of.

Talking shit about this annoying guy was the drug that had replaced all that. I couldn't talk about Venezuelan politics with Maya and Taylor. I occasionally told them how terrible the situation was, and they commiserated, offering emotional support and distraction, but they didn't *understand*. They hadn't lived what I'd lived, what I'd left behind. They didn't have scars so deep they mutated the fiber of their very being.

But talking shit about a boy was something we could all empathize with, including Taylor, whose heart had been broken by boys as well as girls.

I flopped back on the couch and picked up my laptop. "Okay, I promise I'll try to find more topics of conversation."

"Uh-huh," quipped Maya. She was about to say more when someone knocked on the door. Since she was closest to it, she got up and looked out the peephole. Her sigh could only mean one thing, and she confirmed my hunch by saying, "It's my fool of a brother."

I tossed my laptop aside and sprinted for my bedroom. There was no way I could let Malik see me with my cheese-holey

T-shirt and ratty shorts. As his voice drifted into the apartment, I threw myself into my closet in search of something more decent. I ended up in an oversized sweatshirt with the UCF Knights logo on it that I'd bought at Publix, and I almost made it out of my bedroom before I remembered the state of my hair. Ripping out the hair tie almost made me bald, but I arranged my long hair in a way I hoped made me look effortlessly cute, like I just got up from a nap. At nine in the evening.

Whatever.

My face flamed as I greeted him. "Hey, Malik."

The smile that lit up his face almost melted my legs.

"Cata, I was wondering where you were."

I had to ask my heart to be still. How could Taylor's hypothesis that I liked Gabe exist when they both knew I'd harbored the biggest crush on Maya's brother ever since I'd met him?

As if she knew exactly the kind of direction my thoughts had careened in, Taylor said, "Malik brought food."

"From my mama," he said, sorting through a bunch of plastic bags he'd placed on the kitchen counter. One container came out, followed by a second, a third. Soon there was a whole pile. "You know how she is."

I glanced at Maya, and yep, like every time this happened, she was embarrassed. She had this notion that by coming to college she should be entirely self-sufficient, but her mama disagreed, especially since she lived just half an hour away. To mama Muriel, her two college kids would always be her babies. And by association, their friends would always be her babies too. Which was why, at least once a month, she cooked enough food for an army, and I got to enjoy Malik's visit to bring it over.

And I got *my* eye candy.

I sighed, trying to not make it obvious I was staring. The Thomas siblings were, without a doubt, stunning. Maya turned heads everywhere she went with her medium Black skin, bouncy curls, a smile that deserved commercials, and an impeccable sense of fashion. Malik was the male version, taller, with more muscle and even darker skin. He was the most beautiful man I'd ever seen with my own two eyes—even better looking than Gabe.

And naturally, I turned into a fumbling fool every time he was around. "I . . . uh, yes. I like what I see." Heat traveled to my cheeks as all eyes fell on me. "The food, I mean. Thank you. Or more like thank mama Muriel."

My friends looked like they were on the verge of exploding in laughter, but Malik took my mess of a sentence in stride. "I'll make sure to pass along the message."

My heart beat faster than a quarterback who had just fumbled the ball in front of thousands of spectators. "Bye," I squeaked out and dashed back to my room.

Oh. My. Word.

What a dork. How could I show my face to him ever again?

I banged the back of my head against the closed door. If only it were Malik everywhere in my life instead of Gabe . . . Then I'd be better used to seeing him up close, and he'd also see me in better moments, where I kicked ass in class or took names at work. Also, when I was dressed like a decent person.

Who was I kidding? If Malik were my competition in class, I'd be inclined to let him win just so I could see that wide smile of his that made me feel butterflies in my stomach. And if he were at my internship, I would get absolutely nothing accomplished.

But maybe Taylor was somewhat right. Maybe life hadn't put Malik in that position so I wouldn't tank in my academics. Maybe I should be thankful it was Gabe instead—who I wasn't attracted to in the least—and that he motivated me to go above and beyond.

Competition was a way better drug than politics or love anyway.

CHAPTER FOUR

I was almost done reviewing the tedious list of documents in the system. After three days working on it, I'd only found two interesting cases I'd have to chase. I debated whether to send some emails about them, but the clock showed it was well past seven in the evening. What my body showed in turn were the signs of exhaustion.

Leaning back in the chair, I stretched my arms and shoulders to loosen the kinks I'd developed from sitting in the same position all afternoon. A groan tore out of my throat as my back made popping sounds.

"Ma'am, this is an office."

I jolted so hard it almost toppled my chair. Beside me, Gabe giggled as if his joke had been oh so original. He didn't even pretend to appear bashful when I set a hard stare on him.

"Note to self," I said aloud. "Today is not the day you commit murder, no matter how much you'd like to." I spun to face him. "Why are you even here this late?"

"I could ask you the same question, but I won't, because the answer is probably the same." He stuffed his company laptop in the cabinet under his desk and locked it.

I mumbled, "And what's that?"

Maybe I should wait until he packed up and left, so we wouldn't leave the office at the same time. But my eyes were bleary, and my stomach rumbled too violently to hang around long. I scrambled to my feet, trying to beat him instead. Thank goodness our team wasn't meeting for our first senior design session tonight and I could just head on home, slip into pajamas, and stuff my face with homemade arepas.

Gabe paused, gathering stuff into his backpack. The corner of his lips lifted just enough to irk me. "Working hard to nab that full-time position, huh?"

My silence spoke volumes. If only he couldn't read me like a freaking book.

"After you, Kitty Cat." He motioned towards the hallway of empty desks.

I gritted my teeth. "First of all, I know the way. And second, don't call me like that. In fact, don't even talk to me at all." With that, I turned and headed through the maze of desks towards the lobby.

His steps followed closely all the way. "Isn't that kind of an extreme reaction to a bit of chivalry?"

Chivalry was opening the door for someone else, not what-ever that was back there.

I kept that to myself, though. The last thing this conversation needed was more fuel. I hurried my pace until I reached the empty lobby. The night guard was probably walking the perimeter. The door slowed me down, and I pushed it open with my shoulder. I made a point of slamming it shut in his face and grinning when he almost smacked into the glass. It was a refreshing change to be the brunt of his glare instead of the other way around.

Night had begun to fall, the gradient of purple hues in the sky replacing the receding oranges and pinks of the day. My Acura waited under a tree, surrounded by empty parking spots. I didn't glance back to see where Gabe had parked his car; as long as it was far from mine, I didn't care.

I did my gymnast routine to make my way into the driver's seat and breathed out a sigh. My brother's picture smiled up at me from the dashboard, where I'd taped it up shortly after I'd bought the car. I took several deep breaths, just trying to calm myself down enough to head home.

Traffic wouldn't be so bad at this time, and the thought cheered me up. But then I turned the key in the ignition and nothing happened. Sometimes I did it wrong, though, so I tried again. Nothing. And one more time for good measure.

My car was dead.

"Mierda."

I let my forehead fall against the steering wheel. Why couldn't I catch a break?

All the pressure I had bottled up in my chest bubbled up with tears. I had been so strong at work since Jeff's announcement, just focusing on making myself so essential they had no option but to hire me. And that meant working overtime, like today, and pushing my study time until much later in the night. Between that and the barrage of texts I got every evening from Mami, I wasn't sleeping enough to be fully functional. This setback was the last thing I needed.

I smacked my hand against the steering wheel. The horn didn't even go off. Instead, my mouth did. "You piece of—who

said you could die, huh? I'm the one who feels like dying, yet
here I am! Couldn't you just die at home?"

The rapping of knuckles against my window startled me. I
swiped my hands at my face to clear the tears. I didn't want the
night guard to see me melting down.

But it wasn't the kindly old man who watched the building
after everyone was gone. Of course not. It was Gabe.

There was nowhere for me to hide, so I rolled the window
down. He leaned over the opening. "Are you crying over boyfriend issues or car issues?"

The urge to tell him to screw off was very strong. "Go away,"
was what I managed. I might be a bitch, but I was a classy bitch.

Gabe rolled his eyes. "Look, I'm just checking in to see if
you need help."

"I do, but definitely not from you."

He recoiled as if he'd been punched, and his pretty face
darkened more than the sky behind him. That was the final hint
he needed to pick up and leave me alone. He turned and headed
over to his old but functional red Jeep, and I watched him drive
away with renewed tears in my eyes. I was ashamed of my reaction and even more that he'd seen me in such a low moment.

Somehow, all through my college career, Gabe had seen all
my worsts. Every bad grade, every awkward social exchange. Like
he'd paid for front-row tickets to watch me fail in my American
excursion from the comfort his American passport gave him.

I sat alone in my car for an hour, scrolling through Mami's
text messages and wondering what to do about being stranded
with little funds in my account to fix the situation. If I texted
Taylor, she'd for sure pick me up, but she'd text Maya, who in
turn would tell Malik. And he was the next to last person—after
Gabe—I wanted to see me in any sort of trouble.

Another rap at my window made me scream. I squinted against the darkness around my car, since my eyes had grown used to the brightness of my phone screen. Two shapes loomed outside of my car, and my heart picked up speed. I fumbled with my door lock, which was a futile exercise considering no human could get the door open, anyway. But if they broke the window to rob me, or worse, I didn't have much protection aside from my purse and the extra pair of shoes I had under the passenger seat.

"Get out of the car," a familiar voice said, but I was too petrified by the scenarios running through my head to connect it with a name and face. "I brought my cousin Manny to take a look."

"Gabe?" I whispered.

Why was he back?

"Hi!" The other guy waved. "Can you please pop the hood open so I can inspect the engine?"

"Uh, yeah. One sec." I fumbled with the knobs on the side under my steering wheel until I found the one. Gabe joined Manny at the front of the car, which made it easier to breathe.

Manny asked if I was okay when the car shook, but it was just me twisting and stumbling to the back seat. Gabe must've known exactly what I was doing, because he started laughing. They sounded so different already, a nice guy versus the arrogant one who hadn't wanted for anything in life and found it funny when people's car doors didn't work.

Huffing, I opened the back door and stepped out of the cloying heat of the car, following the light from a lantern they'd hung from the open hood. Gabe had rolled up the sleeves of his shirt and was passing tools to his cousin, who was deep into inspecting something.

Okay, so Gabe was helping a little. A lot, actually, by bringing someone who seemed to know his way around cars. I wasn't used to this version of my nemesis.

"Why are you helping me?" I asked, looking at his profile while he watched his cousin work. "This isn't a ploy to get me to relinquish my bid for the full-time position, right?"

Gabe blew a raspberry. "Not everyone is as mean as you are, Kitty Cat."

This time my cheeks heated up. I didn't even feel angry at his irritating nickname when I knew I'd acted like a damn fool an hour ago. I cleared my throat and said, "Thanks. And I'm sorry about how I, uh, lashed out."

His eyebrows went up, and for once he had nothing to say.

I swore to myself it would be the first and only time I was in a position to feel gratitude towards him. After this, Gabriel Cabrera was definitely going down.

CHAPTER FIVE

The dump that was my car lived to see another day, and so did I, after thinking I could expire from the embarrassment.

I now owed Gabe Cabrera. Ugh.

The thought roiled my insides as I walked up the lawn, heading for the machine shop at school, where we were going to make the first manufactured test models for our senior design project. This year we had to build a hybrid electrical and human-powered one-seat vehicle from scratch. A.k.a. a fancy bike. We'd divvied up the different systems of the vehicle among the five people in the group: Taylor had the transmission; a guy named Tom, who was an okay student, was in charge of aerodynamics; another one, called Brandon, had the entirety of the loads calculation; Gabe had the engine and battery; and I had the chassis.

I didn't know if I could trust the work Tom and Brandon had started this past week, because I didn't recall them being on the honor roll like Jasper and Adrian, but the rest of us would kick ass. I couldn't wait until we had the car assembled and started testing and fine-tuning it. Excitement gave me an extra pep to my step.

"Liz, wait."

The annoying voice stopped me mid-stride. I zeroed in on the bane of my existence and his girlfriend heading in a path that would intersect mine. I scrambled to hide behind the thick trunk of a tree to wait for them to pass.

My last encounter with Liz wasn't something I looked forward to repeating. I understood that she was jealous, especially having a serial dater for a boyfriend, but there was no need to call me the names she'd spat in my face or threaten me with violence because she imagined Gabe and I were having an office affair. Girl was wild.

Liz stormed across the campus with wide steps meant to leave him behind, but he caught up at a jog and tried to hold her hand. She smacked it away.

"No, I'm sick and tired of this," she shouted, as though the students milling about absolutely *had* to hear her drama.

A tiny voice in the back of my mind said this was none of my business. A louder one said if they didn't want it to be everyone's business, they'd be having this conversation in private. It was a shame I didn't have any popcorn in my backpack.

Gabe ran a hand through his hair. The dark brown locks were slightly wavy in a surfer dude type of way, even though we were an hour and a half from the beach.

His eyes were set on Liz under eyebrows scrunched up with devastation. It was a look that would wreak havoc on a lesser girl. "Please help me understand why you're so upset, because I'm coming up blank."

Liz threw her hands in the air. "I want to spend time with you, but I can't! If you're not in class, you're at work with that bitch. And now you have a project with her? You've got to be shitting me. Just come right out and tell me you're cheating on me with her."

My body vibrated with the desire to throw one of my steel-toe boots right at her face. But I forced myself to take deep breaths and stay rooted in place.

"Again with that?" Gabe released a sigh that deflated his posture. "I've invited you over and over to hang out at my place after class, but—"

"But what?" she cut in, flipping her long hair behind her shoulder. "You want me to hang out with you at your *family's place*, with your mom who absolutely hates my guts? Why don't you get an apartment I can crash at, or better yet . . . why don't we move in together?"

The way his face contorted was a work of art. It was as though he was choking from eating raw garlic.

"C'mon, you're exaggerating. If you get to know my mom, she's not that bad."

I noted he'd evaded two topics deftly. The first one was the fact I was neither a bitch nor his paramour, for which he deserved my other boot thrown at his pretty mug. The second was that he'd completely bypassed the point about them moving in together. Color rose on Liz's light skin, and I figured this last piece would be the one she'd spit back at him.

Instead, what came out of her mouth was, "And why would I want to get to know her? It's not like I ever want her to be my mother-in-law."

The breath I sucked in was so big, it seemed to halt the breeze.

Everything stood at standstill as the words sunk in on Gabe. A complex display of emotions flashed across his face. His square jaw set tight with anger, to the point I worried he'd crack the enamel of his teeth. His fists tightened, and even from five meters away, I could see the white in his knuckles. The scariest part was how his eyes blazed. The sunlight hit his honey eyes straight up, but I watched in real time how they darkened to molten chocolate.

"We're over."

"What?" Liz recoiled as though the possibility that those would be his next words had never crossed her mind.

I pulled up the collar of my black T-shirt and bit into it to hold back the laughter. This was so much better than the telenovelas I occasionally caught up with online.

"You heard me." Gabe's voice was flat like a plank that he dropped hard on her. "Get another boyfriend who can shape his life around yours."

He turned around, and Liz tried to grab him, babbling and repeating the phrase, "But babe," which he ignored with a very dry, "Good luck." She stood there, watching him walk into the same building I needed to get to. I'd be late, but the last thing I wanted was for this girl to see me going after her now ex. She was the kind who saw two innocent things as connected and part of a big conspiracy against her. As much as I couldn't stand Gabe, I'd always wondered how they'd even got together when every other girl I'd ever seen hanging from his arm acted like he was a celebrity.

When she finally turned around, I caught the red cheeks and nose typical of tears. I wiggled around the tree so she wouldn't see me while she passed.

Finally, I made it to the machine shop, where, effectively, I was the last one in.

Gabe rolled his eyes at my entrance. "The queen is here. We can finally start to work."

I gritted my teeth and told myself to bite back the insult threatening to spill out of my mouth. After all, he'd just broken up with his girlfriend.

But nah.

"Oh yeah?" I asked while flipping him the bird. "You're always late to everything, and this time you just lucked out getting through the door a minute before me."

His eyes narrowed and made me catch on to what I'd said. It sounded like I'd been close enough to keep track of his timing versus mine. Which indicated I might've seen what I certainly saw.

Time to change the topic. I rummaged through my backpack and pulled out the printed drawings of my chassis design, spreading them over the workbench as everyone gathered around. There was significant noise in the shop as some other students worked on various projects. I spotted a couple that clearly were from earlier semesters, machining screws from stubs of aluminum. In a different area, Adrian and Jasper cut sheet metal. They waved our way, and I sent them a friendly nod before pulling my attention back to my group.

They picked up my drawings. I folded my arms as they inspected them. They were flawless. I'd asked Jeff if it was all right to run my designs using the company's software, and he'd agreed. We'd checked the calculations together, and my design was simple, effective, and very light.

"Aluminum piping." Gabe lifted his eyes from the paper. "Are you kidding?"

"What are you talking about?"

He gave me a look as though I was the one who had no clue.

Brandon raised his hand as if this were class and said, "Uh, welding aluminum isn't easy, you know?"

"Or cheap," added Tom, stretching his face into a grimace. "If we use the budget the school gave us for the project, it'd pretty much go up in smoke just making the chassis."

Taylor came to my rescue before I bit their heads off. "Yeah, but if we don't make the chassis with aluminum, the vehicle will be too heavy. Or we'd have to sacrifice the fairings and lose aerodynamics."

That settled over everybody like a cloud. The final examination didn't just account for the design and manufacturing of the vehicle but also its performance. I'd overheard another group a couple of days ago discuss building their chassis out of plumbing piping. Cheap, light, and somewhat durable—unless their engine overheated in the height of Orlando's summer heat. Or unless another car crashed against theirs. Not that I was planning to install spikes on the wheels of ours, but still. You never knew.

"I can do it for free," I said with a sigh. All eyes turned to me, and a specific pair of them narrowed. "You don't believe me?" The question was rhetorical, as the answer was patently clear. "Fine."

I headed over to the discarded junk bin, where I found a two-inch aluminum pipe someone had burned from one end. I gave it to Taylor and asked, "Can you saw it in half, sand down the edges, and bevel it a bit?"

"Yes, ma'am." She saluted.

While she did that, I went over to the attendant to request some welding equipment. They didn't have pure argon, but a mix with helium would work just fine. The TIG welder was busy, but the MIG machine was free, so I checked it out along with gloves, a mask, and other tools. The attendant helped me drag everything to the workbench, leaving me to set it up as Taylor finished with the piping. All throughout, the three guys followed, and I didn't miss the ironic tilts of their mouths.

I rolled up my sleeves because things were going to get really hot in here. After putting on my gear, I secured the two pieces of piping with a press attached to the workbench, turned on the ventilation, and dropped the visor of my mask down to get to work.

It was over in a flash, figuratively speaking, because welding aluminum well had to be done a lot faster than with steel.

Papi had taught this to Cora and I at his shop when we were thirteen, well after Carlos had gone through the lessons. Our friends from school were going to after-school lessons; meanwhile, we did metalwork at the family's company. He'd even taken us along for jobs in remote areas of our home state when oil piping broke and had to be repaired. Nothing amped up the adrenaline quite like oil pouring down on the soil from a pipe that had burst. Or even worse, if the oil poured straight into the lake. Obviously, Cora and I had asked Papi to teach us how to weld underwater, but that was where he'd put his foot down. Instead, we'd picked up skills that to him were basic but that people actually had to be formally trained in.

It had been a while since I'd thought about Papi in a way that didn't fill me with dread.

I turned the machine off when I was done and didn't even need to remove the mask to know I'd made a perfect seam. I lacked the American certification, but I could do this for a living if push came to shove.

Rivulets of sweat dripped from my forehead. I wiped them with the back of my arm and asked, "Any other issues with my design?"

The shock was painted clearly on my classmates' faces. Brandon shook his head, and Taylor started laughing.

"Oh, we so got this," Tom said with the widest grin I'd seen on a human.

Then I made the mistake of looking over at Gabe. The heat from the welding torch paled compared with what was in his eyes and my body's reaction to it. No matter how much I dabbed at the perspiration trickling down my skin, I *knew* that if Gabe had ever looked at me that way before, I would have burned.

I did my best to ignore him through the rest of the session, but his proximity was suffocating. My only consolation was that soon he'd get a new girlfriend, and I could go back to pretending he'd never made my insides feel like molten lava.

Taylor and I left the machine shop together, heading to the cafeteria. I must've been really out of shape because a half hour of welding had rendered me exhausted. Even worse, I could detect my own stench. When I finally grabbed a cold bottle of juice, I chugged it bottoms-up like it was alcohol and I was determined to lose consciousness.

My friend whistled as she watched me. "How did you learn to do that? Because it was really hot—and I wasn't the only one who noticed."

"Drink like a sailor?" I asked, wiping my mouth with the back of my hand. The question made her snort.

"No." She jerked a thumb in the direction we'd come from. "Weld like a pro."

Technically, I was. At least by the number of hours I'd spent being Papi's apprentice.

I shrugged and chucked the bottle in the trash bin. "Back home, my dad owns a metalwork company, and he provides welding services to the industries around."

"And you just . . . picked it up?"

That made me laugh because this wasn't like watching

Mami make mandocas and knowing how to replicate the recipe thereafter.

Cora and I had learned because we liked what Papi and his employees did, and we wanted to be a part of that. In contrast, Carlos had never cared about machines. He'd leaned more towards Mami's educational background, the human sciences. He'd been studying journalism. I remembered being a kid and hearing my parents whisper about how their kids had their roles switched around. All along, Papi had wanted Carlos to take over the company after he retired. Instead, his twin daughters were the metalheads, in the non-musical sense. In our last year of high school, Cora and I had decided to go into mechanical engineering together and work at Papi's company after graduating. The plan had been to start from the bottom until we learned the business inside out and became worthy successors.

That was basically the only thing we'd ever agreed on. We didn't like the same music genres—Cora was into ballads and anything that played on the radio. She liked dressing up in the latest fashion, using makeup to enhance the very same features I didn't care about, and going to the gym regularly. But most of all, she liked her political activist boyfriend.

I didn't.

Not only did ballads make me gag—I'd used foreign hard rock as a tool to practice my English and escape from the world around me—I had no time to focus on my appearance when I was too busy trying to secure myself a future away from there. And I certainly had no time for distractions like boys.

"Of course not," I said, bringing my focus back to my friend. I shuffled my feet after her towards the door. "I learned from my dad since I was a tween."

"Gee, all I learned from mine was how to drive."

"And barely." I elbowed her side.

She winced, and color rushed up her cheeks. If ever there was a car in the streets of Orlando that looked like it belonged to my hometown, it was hers. She'd put more dents in it than should be legal.

"Yeah, well. Sometimes the roads get tight," she said with a chuckle. And then her arm lashed out, bringing me to a dead stop. "Oh, shit, what do I do?"

"What?" I craned my neck to catch what had caused her reaction. And then I saw her ex walking towards us, headphones in place as she listened to something playing on her phone, her attention glued to the screen. She hadn't caught sight of us yet. "Okay, what do you want me to do? I can shove you into the bushes, or I can pretend to be your girlfriend to make her jealous."

Taylor snorted and ran a hand through her pixie haircut. "Thanks, but I should probably face whatever happens."

"Very mature." I shrugged and put a hand on her shoulder. "But you don't have to be."

She cracked a smile despite the anxiety lining her eyes.

Amber and Taylor had been dorm neighbors in the first semester of freshman year, and that span of time was all they'd needed to fall in love. It had been smooth sailing through the second semester until small differences started to get in the way. Taylor hated the show *Friends*, and Amber's catchphrase was that she couldn't be friends with someone who hated *Friends*. Taylor was vegan, and Amber was a southern barbecue type of gal. It all came to a head when Taylor got a tattoo on her forearm that said *forever*, dedicated to Amber, who hadn't liked it one bit.

"Forever" lasted three more months. By the start of sophomore year, they were broken up, and halfway through, they were dating other people.

Taylor got a boyfriend who was a year older. Ben was a sweet guy, but he didn't make my friend's eyes shine quite like before. After he graduated, they parted amicably. Meanwhile, Amber was in her second relationship after Taylor, and, rumor had it, the other girl might become another ex soon. Which was probably why Taylor appeared half eager, half scared of Amber noticing her.

A little gasp escaped from Taylor when Amber finally did. Their bodies moved towards each other as though drawn by magnets. Taylor looked back at me, asking for permission, and I waved my hand magnanimously. Who was I to deny her wish to collide with her ex like a train wreck? Having Cora as a sister, I had learned that trying to prevent other people's drama was impossible.

"Wish me luck," my friend whispered, and I sent her off with a smile.

It wasn't that I wanted her to fail. On the contrary, I wanted her to be happy and find someone whom she could also make happy in return. But I didn't want her to hurt anymore, and her ex was really good at that.

Watching them, I wondered if all of this was worth it. The drama, the pain, the uncertainty of wondering if you were offering your heart to someone who maybe wouldn't handle it with care.

Nah. Not for me.

I turned towards the parking lot. The night was unseasonably hot and humid, which was a portent of an awful drive home. But once I got there, I would enjoy the shower and air conditioner for the pieces of paradise they were. After, I had a lot of studying to do if I wanted a perfect GPA this semester as well, and—

My phone vibrated in my pocket.

I counted until twenty seconds had passed and the caller didn't give up. The only person who could be that insistent was Mami, and I had already blown her off last time. I would have to pick up her call right then and there. Calls in my pressure cooker of a car were impossible, and once I got home all I wanted to do was wind down. So I sat on the grass, feeling the dampness seep through my jeans.

I took a deep breath and clicked on the green button to answer the call. "Bendición," I said right away, and Mami blessed me back.

It felt strange to have a conversation in Spanish with someone who had my accent. We made it a point to speak on the phone at least once per week, and I felt silly that the way she spoke—that I spoke—now gave me a shock compared all the English I spoke every day, or the Spanish with people from all over Latin America.

"Al fin contestas, mija," she said, chiding me for taking so long to answer with the kind of sigh that usually spelled trouble. "Cómo has estado? Cuéntame todo antes de que me saques una excusa de que tienes que irte."

At the last second, I managed to morph the laugh that almost came out into a cough, though we both knew I wasn't fooling her. Every time we talked, it was as if my body was there, holding the phone and saying words into it, while my mind was already moving on to the task I'd been wanting to do when she called. And she and I both knew it.

I pulled my knees up to my chest and forced myself to stay rooted there, using that sensation to ground my mind. Sitting on the campus grass and looking out at the streetlights that illuminated the straggling students coming in and out of the cafeteria reminded me that I was here, she was there. The problems back there couldn't necessarily reach me.

So I told her everything, just as she'd asked, including the big chance I had to make my internship a full-time position. In turn, she mentioned it was getting harder to find black beans in the supermarkets, but that she'd traded some toilet paper for queso de año. She guessed right that I grimaced at the mention, knowing I'd never liked that cheese.

"Cómo están Cora y Papi?" I asked, even though talking about them was tricky. The silence on her end went on so long I almost thought the call had dropped, until the sigh came again.

"Deberías hablar con Cora estos días."

Something about her voice made me sit up in alert. "Todo bien?"

"No lo sé."

I tried to calm down. Why would I need to talk to Cora? Carlos had been the sweet, steady one of us three. The one who made sure everyone was comfortable and had what they needed. The one who would have made the best parent. Despite whatever stereotypes middle children had, I was the responsible one. But Cora was the drama queen of the Diaz Solis siblings. A paper cut was enough to send her into the deepest throes of agony. Mami's warning tone didn't necessarily mean something was terribly wrong with Cora.

"Okay, ya la llamo." I said, a statement Mami agreed to right away. We cut off the call, and I scrolled through WhatsApp until

I found my twin's chat. The last time we'd texted had been about a week ago. Things couldn't possibly have changed much since then, but we never knew with her.

I pressed the call button and waited.

And waited some more.

My jaw tightened. The fact she'd let her phone ring for five continuous minutes could mean either she was mad at me and was ignoring me or she was tied up with something and couldn't talk.

I disconnected the call and dropped back on the grass, staring up at the fading light in the sky. I grunted at the few stars, annoyed at how bright and happy they looked when all I wanted was to kick something. And then the stars grunted back.

I startled because of course that couldn't be possible. A glance around confirmed the source of the noise wasn't the sky but the boy sitting like ten feet from me. And of course, it was Gabe Cabrera.

CHAPTER SIX

"Are you stalking me?"

He did a double take, as if noticing me for the first time. We weren't the only students strewn about the grass watching the sunset, but he could've chosen to sit literally anywhere else.

He rolled his eyes before fixing them on his phone screen. Then he tossed it on the grass like it was the source of all his problems and hadn't cost a cool grand.

"Trouble in paradise?" I asked, failing to not sound happy about the fact that, for once, he wasn't a ray of sunshine.

"I guess," he muttered loudly enough to reach me. "Life's hard when two women hate you at the same time."

Obviously one of the women who hated him had to be Liz. But who else could possibly have that same level of anger towards Gabe? No one but a girl who had been his side piece, having found out her status when Gabe's castle of cards fell apart.

At the strong whiff of telenovela drama, I impulsively said, "So that's why Liz broke up with you, huh? You actually were cheating on her, and now you're in trouble with the other one?"

Gabe's eyes narrowed to dark slits.

Ah, shit. I wasn't supposed to know about that.

I bit my lip, wishing I could take back the words, but it was too late, and I was coming up blank with damage control methods.

"You were the eavesdropper behind the tree?" Gabe flopped on his back. "Great."

I folded my arms. "I'm not going to apologize. You both were having a sensitive conversation in a public place."

"Yeah, but most people would've moved along."

"Not if they didn't want to become a scapegoat again. Remember last time?"

Gabe's face scrunched up. "True, she's always been a bit too jealous."

A bit was putting it mildly.

"Anyway." I pulled myself up and patted my jeans free of grass clippings before shouldering my backpack. "I'm gonna leave you to wallow in your two-timing mess. Bye."

He cracked up. The intensity of his laughter stopped me dead in my tracks.

I turned to find him curled on his side, absolutely losing it. I was torn between running away or asking if he was okay. He saved me from the embarrassment of either option by wheezing, "Stop, stop. You keep saying I'm some cheating jerk, and no. That was my mom on the phone. She's the second woman not so happy with me right now."

The skeptical look I gave him had him scooting over to show me the call history. Huh, it looked like his mom had been calling all night. How could I use that information as ammo?

I figured I might as well ask. "Why would your mom possibly hate you?"

Gabe tucked his phone in a back pocket. With the movement,

a few strands of his loose chocolate hair fell forward, and some grass fell off it. He mussed his hair, getting rid of any extra blades, and combed it back before glancing at me again. I'd secretly always wondered if his hair was as soft as it looked. My fingers itched, and I stuffed them in my pockets.

"Because," he said with a sigh, "with the breakup, I had to cancel my plus-one for my brother's wedding, which according to her has to be the most perfect affair in generations of my family. And I can't possibly show up without a date when everybody else in the bridal party has a plus-one."

The skepticism was back. "You're kidding."

"I wish." The self-deprecating smile was unfamiliar on his face. Maybe Gabriel Cabrera didn't have a hundred percent perfect life. Maybe it was just ninety-nine percent perfect.

"Then just find a new girlfriend. It's not like you're going to have a shortage of applicants for the job." I motioned all around us in a sort of the-world-is-your-oyster manner.

Gabe scrunched up his nose while looking down at his scuffed-up safety boots. "I don't really want to ask a new girl out to my brother's wedding, you know? It would kinda send too strong a message."

Ah, yes. I could see the issue. A fanciful girl could start imagining that such a date was a portent of wedding bells for herself with Gabe the Campus Babe. What a problem to have.

"Bueno," I said, shrugging. "You'll figure it out."

But before I turned away, his voice rang with vehemence. "Unless."

That one word made a tingle run up and down my spine. I looked at him over my shoulder. "What?"

"Unless I ask the one girl who would never, absolutely by no means, look too much into being my date."

Our eyes remained locked for longer than necessary, as if neither of us could actually believe what had just happened. It was clear he was referring to me, and yet my brain was having a hard time processing the words that had come out of his mouth.

My brain broke, and I started to laugh.

"It's perfect. It's not a rebound, no false expectations." His eyes lit up like there was enough electricity in him to power the entire campus. "And I get to find a better way to ruin Chris's wedding that won't blow over easily."

"Excuse—what? Habla en español o inglés, mijo, que lo que dices no tiene sentido."

Gabe chuckled, running a hand through his hair as his pretty head prepared machinations. "I mean, I guess I could just show up to all the events sans plus-one and it would attract Mom's attention for a bit. But I need something bigger to really keep her focus away from my brother and his bride. You could definitely help with that."

"Let me give it to you in Spanish: no. I knew you were annoying before, but I didn't know you were plain evil." I started to leave, but he kept pace with me easily.

"I'm not being evil. I'm trying to save this wedding by ruining it." I slashed a stare at him that had the unintended effect of making him smile. "The problem is that my mom doesn't approve of Chris's bride, Ellen. And I love Ellen. But if I don't do something, Mom herself will ruin the wedding for real, just like she did with my older sister's."

I stayed quiet for a few paces, even though I was intrigued by someone else's family drama. It certainly beat rehashing my own over and over.

At the parking lot, I asked, "Is your mom one of those over-protective parents who can't bear her children flying the nest?"

"No, unfortunately she's just racist." That made me stumble, and Gabe grabbed my elbow to steady me. I looked up at him, emitting so much *what the hell* energy that he continued. "My brother-in-law is Black, and Ellen is Korean-American."

"Oh." I cringed. "Your mom needs to be stopped."

"Exactly. So, are you in?" Gabe rocked on the balls of his feet.

I noticed he hadn't let go of my elbow and freed myself with a little tug.

"And what would I get out of this?"

"A few free meals?" He shrugged, and I started to walk away. His footsteps followed again. "C'mon, there has to be something I could give you."

Was it just me, or was there some hidden innuendo behind his words?

I gifted him one of my patented eye rolls, about to ask what I could possibly want from him. And then I had an epiphany.

There *was* something. Gabe was my biggest rival both at school and at the internship—and I *needed* that job.

I stopped abruptly. The words about to tumble out of my mouth would be wild, and yet they were exactly what I wanted from him. "The full-time position," I said. Every muscle in my body grew taut as if bracing for the laughter sure to follow.

But it didn't come. Instead, Gabe tucked his tongue against his cheek, a sign he was mulling this over more seriously than I'd expected.

"Está bien." Gabe gave me the same look I'd caught on his face as he'd watched me weld. A more intense version of when he gloated about getting a better grade than me—as if this time I was the exam he'd aced. "Be my pretend girlfriend and help me ruin my brother's wedding, then the full-time job is yours."

"You'd . . . give up a job for that?" I blinked hard at him.

Gabe stuffed his hands in the pockets of his jeans, shrugging. "Family's the most important thing for me, and I'm all out of options there, short of mooning everyone at the ceremony."

My brow furrowed. Were Gabe Cabrera and I complete opposites? Here I was, desperate to get this full-time job that would keep me away from my home country and my family—all for my own sake. But I shook the uncomfortable feeling in my chest when I reasoned that the scales were not the same. My life would be at risk there, just like my family's lives were. If I could bring them here, I would, and getting that job and the security of a work visa could be a first step to doing that.

So, really, I was just putting on my oxygen mask first before helping them. And if the oxygen mask happened to come via Gabe's absurd plan, so be it.

I stuck my hand out, and when he shook it, I said, "Deal."

CHAPTER SEVEN

The next morning, Maya smacked me upside the head. It was like looking at a carbon copy of her mother, with her eyebrows pulled back to reveal her wide, dark eyes beaming in menace at me. Her lips pursed as if barely holding back the epithets she wanted to throw into a new remix of my name. More importantly, the strength in the palm of her hand would make sure the back of my head smarted for a couple of hours.

"What the heck was that?" I jumped to my feet, not to fight back but to put distance between us in case she wanted to pick up the chancla. Then I remembered she wasn't Mami.

Maya raised her hand but didn't move closer. "Is there something wrong with you?"

"Not before you rattled my brain just now, no."

"Do you think that's the right way to get a job?" Her voice lowered into something close to a growl. "Because a man gave it to you?"

A flash of heat went off in my body, except it wasn't anger. When she put it that way, it sounded like I was lessening my own accomplishments, as though they weren't enough to get the job. As though only because of Gabe taking himself out of the running could I truly land the position. I hadn't worked as hard as I had for four years to get a job out of pity.

However, pride was nothing compared to the *need* to stay in this country.

"Technically, Jeff is also a man, and he'd be my hiring manager," I said. She continued giving me a look like she was pondering whether to inflict more bodily harm, so I raised the palms of my hands. "Okay, I get it. Trust me. It's not super ethical, but this works out for the better. I don't have to crush Gabe in cutthroat competition, and I still get to stay in the US. All I have to do is go to a wedding with him and done. Can I go back to eating my cereal now?"

When no immediate reaction came, I figured the worst had passed and joined her back at the table. The cereal in my bowl was turning soggy the longer I stared at it, though. My stomach had clenched after being forced to face the moral implications of what I had agreed to do.

I rubbed the back of my head while I chewed on over-soaked Special K. It wasn't like I'd stop being an excellent performer at work just because the position was almost mine now. After all, something left-field could happen—like maybe the bosses would decide to rescind the department's new head count. That was why I still had to make sure I was the best possible addition to the team.

"Are you sure, though?" Maya asked suddenly, stopping half-way to lifting her spoonful of Cheerios to her mouth.

While chewing, I asked, "About what?"

"That all you have to do is attend a wedding?" Maya set the spoon down with gravitas. "What if he has something different in mind? Like you acting as an escort with certain benefits?"

The food lodged itself in my windpipe. I made a mess of the table as I coughed it out. Despite being first aid certified, Maya did nothing to help me. I had a feeling she was enjoying the impact of her words.

"Bet you hadn't thought of that, huh?" Folding her arms, she sat back to observe my struggle with a little smile on her lips.

"That's impossible," I shouted after I was able to cease wheezing.

She lifted a shoulder and tossed her curls over it. "Is it, though? We're talking about Gabe the Campus Babe. Latin Lover Bae." I cringed. I'd never been a big fan of that last nickname, it's such a stereotype. "I mean, with just a few words he got you to agree to a ridiculous scheme like this without even revealing the full extent of his plan. Who's to say he doesn't have some ulterior motives of his own?"

"Okay, first of all," I cut in with a huff, "I'm not easy. Second, he came up with this exact strategy because of the universally known fact that I hate his guts. Third, it all seems to be because of his family issues, and who am I to care about those motives?"

Especially when I kept trying to run from my own family drama.

Maya leaned forward as though we were talking about a secret conspiracy. Even went as far as curling her finger at me. I leaned forward with some reluctance, and she said, "Yeah, but what if he wants to ruin the wedding by causing a scandal with you or something?"

It took me a few seconds to work out a scenario where this could happen, but eventually, I could picture it in my mind. Me wearing a barely-there dress, drunk in the middle of the dance floor, making out with Gabe as if no one were watching. That would be a way to piss his mom off for sure. Gabe was used to girls going wild just for a date with him. I'd once heard that two girls came to blows at a party for a turn dancing with him. Wouldn't he enjoy putting me in a position where he could humiliate me like that?

Maya had a point. I couldn't allow that to happen.

I lifted a palm. "I'll just have to draft an agreement with him about dos and don'ts. And might as well add in there the reassurance that he'll remove himself from the running for the full-time position."

My friend cringed. "Not quite the conclusion I wanted you to reach."

I finished my cereal and put the bowl in the sink before grabbing my backpack and the secondhand jacket I'd wear at work, where there was air-conditioning. Taking a moment to smooth out my creamy blouse from Target that made me look more put together than I was, I told her, "An immigrant's gotta do what an immigrant's gotta do, me entiendes?" And added a one-shoulder shrug for emphasis.

She sighed. "I just wish it were another way."

"I'll take the one way life gives me."

As I drove to the office, my own words rang in my head. If I played this right, it was a massive opportunity.

Everything at work would continue as usual, except now I wasn't completely at Jeff's or Gabe's mercy. I had a card up my sleeve. So what if my competitor had given it to me? It wasn't my fault he valued this job placement so little. It wasn't a crime to solidify my position.

That was my thought process while I was in the copy room photocopying documents to apply for my OPT extension. Gabe walked through the hallway with a cup of coffee. I latched onto his sleeve and dragged him into the room with me. The copy room didn't have a door, so it wasn't like someone could come in and think we were doing something not safe for work. It was also less suspicious than walking into a meeting room with just Gabe.

"Buenos días," he said while maneuvering the near-over-flowing mug away from his crisp white shirt. With the tight fit over his muscles, any spill was bound to burn his skin. "To what do I owe this pleasant surprise?"

I jammed my finger on the start button to scan my transcripts, then turned to give him my full attention. "We need to talk about last night."

His eyes danced like I'd said something naughty. Which would be precisely the impression of any possible passersby. I stuck my head out and saw no one up or down the hall.

I pointed at him. "Wipe that annoying grin off your face. We need to draft the rules of engagement."

Gabe took his sweet-ass time blowing steam off his coffee. The smell made my stomach rumble, and I debated whether to snatch the mug from his hands. But I didn't really want Campus Babe saliva anywhere near me. Who knew which places his mouth had been on or under—okay, gross. I lifted my eyes to his, and the amusement there had turned into something worse. Like mocking.

Maybe he sensed that I was on the verge of violence, just like Maya with me this morning, because he asked, "What do you mean?"

"We have to make it clear that this is all pretend." There was a stack of blank sheets of paper on the counter behind the copier, and I'd come with a pen in hand to tick items off my to-do list. I grabbed all the materials I needed for a contract, and as the header I wrote, *Agreement Between Catalina Diaz and Gabriel Cabrera.* "We're going to jot down what we can and cannot do, and what each of us is getting out of this deal."

"Do we have to?" Gabe asked with a grimace, but one look from me sobered him up. "Right. So, what do you have in mind? Because clearly you've thought about this way more than I have."

That sounded like an insult, but I was the bigger person at that moment, so I let it go in favor of getting what I wanted. I scribbled the goals in a quick chicken scratch. Gabe would get to piss off his mother and ruin his brother's wedding. I would get the full-time position. When I presented it for his approval, he just nodded.

"And now the most important parts." I cleared my throat and took a deep breath to say, "There will be no PDA, definitely nothing beyond that, or any situations where I can possibly be humiliated. I'm not here to be your Fifty Shades of Toy if that's what you had in mind."

The mug slipped in his grip, but once he'd recovered from the initial shock, he started cackling like a hyena. It was early enough in the office that most people were still sleepy and not in conference calls, which meant his obnoxious laughter rang all through the place. However, I didn't want to catch anyone's attention, so I jumped and put my hands over his mouth.

Which naturally made the damn mug tilt and pour coffee over *me.* The hot liquid seeped through the front of my blouse faster than I could react. An inhuman sound came from both of us.

Me, I could understand. I was the one with a stinging burn and a soiled blouse. Gabe put away the mug and, in his haste to prevent the blouse from sticking to my skin and worsening the burn, he tore the would-be contract from my hand and stuck it right down the collar of my blouse. We stared at each other, breaths ragged and eyes wide.

"Tell me you're okay so I can start laughing," he said in a whisper.

I punched him in the shoulder, which likely did more damage to my hand. "You have no idea how much I hate you."

I assessed the damage. Pulling the blouse away from my skin helped to cool it down. The sheet of paper also kept the sticky heat away from my skin. His hand had brushed my bra as he'd jammed the paper in. Even worse was the fact I couldn't walk around with a wet, brown stain that showed my underwear for the entire office to see.

I tried to blink away the prickling sensation in my eyes because I did not want to make this moment more memorable for him. As though nothing were amiss, I grabbed another sheet of paper and started jotting everything again.

"Seriously?" he asked, snorting.

"Yes, seriously. I don't care about the blouse." I glared at him from the bottom of my heart. "I want this job. No, I *need* it, and I'm going to make sure I get it. Now sign this."

Silence hung between us for a long moment.

Gabe folded his arms. "Now wait a second, how is there going to be no PDA when you're going to be pretending to be my girlfriend?"

"No one said anything about pretending to be your girlfriend yesterday. This was supposed to be just a date." Good thing I was drafting this contract, huh? Maya would have no choice but to be proud of me.

He tilted his head and took a step forward. We were so close I could see the dark brown flecks in the honey of his irises. For a terrible second, I thought Gabe was angling to kiss me, but that made no sense. We were in the office, for goodness' sake. The contract wasn't even signed yet. But if I jumped back, it would show he had an effect on me, and maybe that was the point of his little game. To push for PDA. So I stayed rooted to my spot.

The little smirk that stretched his lips made knots of my thoughts, making me fear he could read them.

"Ah, but you see, a simple date won't cut it." The coffee on his breath fanned over my face, and the fact I wasn't revolted definitely was revolting. His voice went really low and sent a shiver down my spine. "This is a big affair, the wedding of the decade in my family. There will be dinners, rehearsals, the bachelorette party, the wedding itself, and the reception."

"That's not what I signed up for. This was just supposed to be a date."

His eyebrows went up, but the act of innocence fooled no one. "No, I said you'd be my date—pretend girlfriend was the term, actually. Besides, didn't you say you wanted this job above anything else?"

My jaw was so tight, at this rate I would run out of enamel at the tender age of twenty-one, and it would all be thanks to this nonsensical boy.

"Fine. I'll be your pretend girlfriend for all of those things. But I stand by the rule that there cannot be any humiliating situations. I'm not going to show skin or act like someone you picked up from OBT," I said, referring to the Orange Blossom Trail's reputation as Orlando's red-light district.

"Sure," he said offhand.

"And you have to share with me what your big plan is for actually ruining the wedding. I must have a say on it, since it's going to be my face in the pictures too."

"Once I develop said plan, you'll be the first to know. But

you have to act like a convincing girlfriend, and that will imply *some* PDA." Gabe punctuated the sentence by drawing closer. He let a lock of my waist-length hair slide between his fingers, filling my stomach with butterflies.

I tightened my fists, barely keeping them at my sides instead of connecting them with his face.

PDA with Gabe, Everyone's Babe, was not something I'd ever contemplated. Just thinking about him in those terms had always given me a rash. But now he stood flush against me, and my body had an entirely different reaction from what I would have expected. The heat of the spilled coffee had dissipated, only to be replaced by his warmth seeping into me, melting my bones and raising gooseflesh all over my skin. His eyes were hooded, and the angle of his face cast shadows on them that turned them a molten milk chocolate.

This was how he ensnared his victims, huh? And now he was trying to seduce me into being next.

I took a step back so large I slammed against the idling copier. With horror, I saw that I'd left a large coffee splotch over the front of his pristine shirt. If I'd feared being caught before, now it was simply a matter of time. Unless I ran home.

"Okay, fine," I said, now in full panic mode. I picked up my papers and pen and held them up against my chest, hiding the mirroring stain. "I'll send you a contract draft to sign this afternoon, but now I have to go."

Gabe took a step back and stuffed his hands in the pockets of his trousers. The pants were snug around the thick muscles of his thighs, which I had no business looking at. He was on the verge of laughter when I met his eyes.

"Looking forward to it."

Trágame tierra, I thought to myself.

Just as I was rushing out of the corner, he called, "Oh, and Kitty Cat?"

I glared at him over my shoulder. "What?"

He cupped a hand around his mouth so he could hide his lips, which formed silent words that said, "Nice bra."

If this deal didn't kill me, I would definitely kill him.

CHAPTER EIGHT

My face peered out from the laptop's screen, except it was different. Cora and I had stopped looking identical after Carlos's death. Once, we'd had the same softness around our eyes and lips, but mine had been replaced by the hard lines of someone who had lost too much too soon. I knew Cora had suffered the same loss, but her innocence in the matter no doubt contributed to the fact that she could still smile all the way to her eyes.

Right now, though, her expression was a lot more like mine.

Even though her hair was perfectly coiffed with thin strands of gold dyed across the extensive mass of it, her face artfully made up with the same delicate sense of a beauty magazine, she looked a lot like me. And that could only mean Mami was right. Something was wrong with Coralina.

"I've been calling you," I told her in English.

Mami had insisted on us learning English since we were kids, which at first Papi had refuted. It was Carlos who'd convinced him, half-jokingly, that it would be a good idea to learn the "imperialist" language so we could understand their rhetoric firsthand. With that in mind, Papi had enrolled us in private English lessons when we were starting high school, without knowing it would open a path for me to emigrate years later.

Cora had continued practicing it with me—not because she was finally coming around, but because this way our parents couldn't overhear our conversations. And that wasn't any sort of guesswork from me; she'd told me so herself.

Thus, she replied in English. "Yeah, I've been busy."

I let my eyes roam over her and said, "With what? Buying winter clothes for air conditioners that don't work?" I vaguely pointed at the turtleneck sweater she wore. It had to be baking her.

My hometown of Maracaibo was considered the hottest city in the country. Everyone outside it joked that it was the coldest city, solely due to the prevalence of air-conditioning everywhere—at home, schools, shops, and certainly in our cars. Ever since the electrical supply had become so unstable, though, the city had gone back to the oven it typically was, and its inhabitants were its sourdough bread rolls. Seeing my sister in such a stifling piece of clothing was the most ridiculous sight I'd seen all week, and I'd had to endure Gabriel Cabrera's face up close, so that was saying something.

"Excuse me," Cora said with a little sneer. "This is all the rage here, you know? I bought it at Zara. Only the people who can afford to keep their air conditioner running dress like this."

Never mind, it could get more ridiculous after all.

"Is that what has you so upset?" I asked, running my hand through my dark hair as it air-dried. "The fact you have to dress like you're in Europe so people think you're high class, even though you're sweating your makeup off?"

I could see her process through the barrage of words. When she eventually got the gist of it, she flipped me both birds.

"No, I'm upset because you keep ignoring me."

I raised both hands in the air. "I've been calling you for days, and you're the one who doesn't pick up, who's ignoring who?"

"Yeah, but I texted you on WhatsApp, and you didn't reply," she said, reaching closer to the camera to bare her teeth at me.

I checked my message log, and sure enough, there were five texts from her over the course of the week, and I'd missed them all. Scrolling through, I didn't see anything that would raise the red alert I had detected in Mami's voice the other night.

Anyway, since I was clearly in the wrong here, I had to proceed with caution.

I set my phone down and said, "Sorry, I guess I've been too caught up in everything that is going on."

Cora snapped her jaw shut and then opened it, her dark eyes dancing with the clear idea of giving me a piece of her mind. In the end, she went the same route I'd taken and asked, "So what's going on, then?"

A rush of heat traveled up my spine and settled in my chest. If I told her everything that had happened recently, I ran the risk of giving her enough fodder to make a whole-ass telenovela out of it, which was the last thing I wanted to reach my parents. And yet I kind of wanted to see her eyes light up with something silly that took her mind off whatever had her in a funk.

That was what I was debating when Maya burst into my room and announced, "Get ready, bitch. We're going to a party."

This made Cora gasp with delight. "You are? I knew it! There was a fun person stuck inside of you all along."

"Girl, you're looking gorgeous." Maya laughed and jumped on my bed to greet Cora, who was certainly her favorite Diaz twin.

Cora tossed her mane over her shoulder and batted a hand. "Nowhere near your goddess levels, though."

"You guys are making me gag," I said deadpan. "But also, I haven't agreed to go to any parties. My party tonight is in my pajamas, making the final touch-ups to my chassis design—"

My sister cut me off. "Bo-ring. Your chassis is going nowhere until you put it together with the rest of the car."

"Exactly." Now emboldened by my fun-loving sister, my roommate bounced on the mattress. "Instead, you should take yourself out with me and Taylor to a party full of hot boys that will take your mind off metal chassis and center it square on their flesh and blood chassis."

They made me want to laugh, but I knew if I did that, they'd take it as my defeat.

"I'm not interested in machines with chassis made of bones. The flesh and blood would be more like the doors and windows of the car—"

"Por favor para," Cora said, raising a hand.

Maya's eyebrows went up. "Not even if I tell you that Malik is coming?"

I froze.

Cora squealed. As much as I tried to not give her fodder for her drama, it had slipped out last year that I kind of had a thing for Maya's brother. Who could help it when he had only the most beautiful chassis and doors I'd ever seen, with perfect aerodynamics in the front and the rear—and was, without question, the ultimate ride?

My entire face flamed as Maya and Coralina enthusiastically began to plan the outfit I should wear. Then Taylor showed up, confirming that the plan had been agreed upon before I even knew about it.

"Show him what Mami gave us!" Cora exclaimed, barely containing her excitement. "And don't forget to tell me tomorrow if you at least manage to make out with him."

I couldn't take any more of her teasing, and with a dry, "Chao" I shut down my laptop. Maya convinced me to squeeze into one of her dresses, a black number that only revealed some leg but was so tight it still showed every curve I had.

I didn't know what was worse: the dress or the fact Taylor was driving to the party.

"Ugh, why couldn't I just wear jeans and a T-shirt?" I strapped myself in and grabbed onto the seat like I was about to go on a roller coaster.

"Cata, please. Don't get me wrong—you're a total knock-out—but jeans and a T-shirt aren't a look that impresses anyone." Taylor drove off the parking spot so abruptly, the car bucked.

To distract her and myself from how close Taylor drove to the curb, I asked her, "Aren't *you* wearing jeans and a T-shirt?"

"Yes. But my jeans are ripped in strategic places, and my T-shirt is cropped. It's a lot more eye-catchy than any combo in your closet."

"Whatever. So, is it true that Malik is coming to this party, or was that just a ploy to get me out of my room?" I asked.

"Both." Maya grabbed the door handle in a vise grip at a particularly sharp turn. "He's tired of his roommates fighting all the time and wanted to do something different. I told him I'd been invited to this party, and he signed the hell up faster than I could give him details about it."

In that case, I should have put on a little more makeup than just mascara and lipstick.

I cleared my throat. "And whose party is it anyway?"

"Amber's," Taylor said, catching my glare through the rearview mirror. "Don't worry about it, we're good. She invited me the other night, and I said no at first because it's not like her current girlfriend likes me that much. But thinking about it afterwards, I figured we should just get over ourselves and move on."

"And your idea of moving on is spending a whole night watching them be lovey-dovey in the same room?"

Maya shrugged. "I asked her the same."

"Yep," Taylor said. "That sounds like exactly what I need to kill off any remaining feelings. Shock therapy."

In other words, this night would be a disaster.

By the time we reached our destination, I felt like dropping on my knees and kissing the ground, except with this dress that would be a bad idea. I pulled it down and followed my two friends to a party I no longer thought would be any fun. I volunteered to be the designated driver because, after tonight, Taylor would likely be nursing a massive hangover.

Amber lived near campus in one of those student housing complexes that looked like a regular residence, except the closer we got, the louder the music became. People stumbled in and out of apartment doors like there were no property boundaries.

The walls vibrated with a popular reggaeton song. A bunch of White kids shook with what they thought were sleek dance moves, and I did my best not to judge them for their lack of sabor. Which was to say, I judged them a heck of a lot for their bad taste, but I just kept it to myself.

Across the floor, someone's expression mirrored my thoughts, and of course it was Gabe. He almost burst out laughing when a girl shook her shoulders as if spiders were crawling on them. We made eye contact, and for a second of truce, we shared a common thought.

Que mal baila esta gente.

I followed my friends into the kitchen. Maya pulled out her cellphone and fired off a rapid series of texts before saying, "Heads up, incoming Malik any second now."

I braced myself against the counter, the minutes stretching forever until finally the most beautiful boy strode in.

Suddenly, there was no more oxygen in the kitchen, and it wasn't because there were about ten people crammed inside looking for drinks or snacks. No, it was because I'd sucked it in with a single gasp.

Malik was gorgeous tonight, in a simple red T-shirt and a cap worn backwards. He hugged Maya, high-fived Taylor, and waved at me. I barely managed to wiggle my fingers at him.

Then, from behind him, Gabe strolled into the kitchen. Maya and Taylor zeroed in on him with the same awareness I had for Malik.

I got it, Gabe was attractive. He was about a head shorter than Malik and was built different. Where Malik was naturally lean like a model, Gabe was fit with muscles and a trim waist that spoke of hours of effort at the gym. Or hours of playing a sport. Either way, he had that little something that had coined the term Latin Lover Bae: the turn of his lips, the five o'clock shadow, and the swagger in his body that made his movements look more like he was dancing through a room rather than walking. He was hot and flashy whereas Malik was more unassuming, and I liked Malik better for it.

"Look who's here," Maya said, smiling with a wicked glint. I hissed a warning at her, but she paid no mind.

"Evening, señoritas," Gabe said, raising his beer bottle. "Anybody want a drink?"

"Please," Malik said, following him to the fridge in search of cold ones.

The joint effort made them automatic friends, and in the next moment, they'd exchanged names and handshakes. Seeing them like this gave me a bad feeling I couldn't explain, as if two worlds were colliding and I was in between, waiting to be crushed. This was what I got for chatting with Cora even for a few minutes—it turned me overdramatic like this.

Taylor accepted a beer from Gabe and asked him, "So, how do you know Amber?"

"Who?" he asked before taking a swig.

"The person who lives here," she said.

"Oh, I don't." Gabe shrugged. "One of my buddies invited me, thought it was a good way to nurse my broken heart."

Both of my friends cooed, and I glared at them. Who were they to feel sorry for the enemy?

"Never a bad idea to distract your heart by using your eyes," Malik said.

I hoped I had successfully masked the surprise on my face and busied myself opening a beer bottle.

Maya turned to her brother. "And are you here to distract your eyes too?"

"Better than looking at my roommates, at least." Malik smiled.

"Well, you're in fine company to do that," Gabe said, giving me a blatant look, as if I were the eye candy of this group. But since he was most likely teasing, I was about to volley back a good jab when suddenly Malik spoke.

"Oh, no. Maya here is my sister," he said as he pointed at her. Then he waved a hand at Taylor and I. "And these girls are her best friends, so they're like my little sisters too. I'm mostly here to take care of them and, sure, sightsee a bit too."

The look on Maya's and Taylor's faces confirmed what I'd just heard. To him, I was a little sister. The sound reverberating in my head wasn't the music in the living room or the many voices shouting over each other, it was the sound of my breaking heart.

And it was all worse when I turned and saw the realization on Gabe's face. In a few seconds he'd connected the dots and now pitied me. Nothing hurt more than that.

But just when I thought the party couldn't possibly get any worse, Gabe's ex walked into the kitchen with a red cup in hand and an unmistakable sway in her step. Her eyes set on Gabe standing next to me.

"I knew it!" she yelled, pointing at us. "You were desperate to be with her!"

All eyes turned to me.

I froze like a deer caught in the headlights. The exit was too far, even though that was my new goal in life. As Liz advanced, I looked around, calculating how many people I would have to elbow out of the way.

Suddenly, an arm draped itself around my waist, pulling me flush against a warm body. The scent of some delicious cologne numbed my brain as I sucked in air. Twisting, I glanced up at Gabe's face. His dark eyes trained on Malik for a second before refocusing on his ex.

Gabe's voice rumbled through my body as he said, "You're right. I was."

CHAPTER NINE

"Qué carajo estás haciendo?" I hissed at Gabe so only he would understand the extent of my outrage.

All he did was hold on tighter and whisper, "Tranquila."

Which was precisely the opposite of how I felt.

Liz stumbled on her high heels but caught herself in time. The same couldn't be said for her drink. It spilled over the rim of her cup and down to the floor. She stared at the puddle at her feet like she'd just lost another major thing aside from her pride.

I felt for her, really. But I also knew that trying to console her could land me in the ER with a scratched-out eye.

"I didn't think—I mean, I thought you'd—" she stammered, looking back up at us with a world of hurt in her eyes. "I thought you'd come back to me, not run to *her*."

Maya gasped and covered her mouth. I thought she might start laughing.

Taylor's jaw hung. She looked at me as though she believed this farce.

Right, I had to catch her up on a few things.

If that weren't enough, Malik added, "Wow, I didn't know you had a boyfriend, Catalina."

At the sound of his voice, all my attention went to him. There was a different type of appraisal, as if previously he hadn't even considered the notion possible. Although that cut me, it also made me wonder if that was why he hadn't seen me as someone with girlfriend potential.

The opportunity to make Malik see me as not-a-sister was right there, so I jumped headfirst.

"Ah, yeah. It's kind of recent." I glanced up at my supposed boyfriend and with a nasally voice said, "Babe, I don't want to make a scene, so I'm just gonna go."

So far Gabe had been getting an A+ in acting, but this change of tack from me caught him off guard. Unfortunately, it also served to amuse him. "You're right, bebé. We should just go."

No. That wasn't what I'd had in mind. I just wanted to leave that place and get some fresh air, not do so *with* Gabe. Then again, as he steered me out of the kitchen, murder was written all over Liz, and I was thankful for the safe escort.

Two possibilities stood in front of me. One, I kept walking out the apartment door. Outside, I could text the girls and suggest relocating to a nearby McDonald's or something, because I was certainly not in the mood to party anymore.

The second option was to head in the opposite direction, down the empty hallway that led to the bedrooms, where thanks to the noise I could tell Gabe off while not straying alone into the night. Once I was done ripping him a new one, I could text my friends and we could leave together.

I pulled Gabe's forearm until we were sequestered in the dark hallway.

"What the hell, *babe*?"

"Two birds with one stone, huh? You're welcome." Gabe rubbed his arm and gave me an annoying grin.

"What are you even talking about?"

For a minute, all he did was lean against the opposite wall. His hair had fallen forward over the side of his face, lending him an air of danger compounded by his lopsided smirk.

"You're not an unfeeling robot after all," he said at last, jerking his chin towards the kitchen. "Te gusta ese muchacho."

My first impulse was to shush him, but we were alone, and music still blasted from the living room. In an effort to recover some dignity, I combed my hair with my fingers and leaned back against my wall.

"So what?"

"So," he continued with a shrug of his wide shoulders, "that certainly spiked his interest in you."

I muttered, "Guys are so weird. Why do they care about a girl only when she's with someone else?"

"We're competitive, and dating is a sport."

That settled like a brick in my stomach. There was something called *love* that had nothing to do with competitions. Yes, Liz wasn't entirely innocent in this mess, but she was just the latest in a string of Gabe's breakups. And now I felt like he'd used me for his latest game.

"You're the worst," I said, pushing off the wall. "And if that's how you treat all your exes, that makes you even lower than dirt, and I hope every girl on campus sees you for the heartless player you are. Leave me out of your games, Gabe."

I ducked my head back into the kitchen but didn't find my people. Instead, Liz had grabbed hold of some random guy, and they were making out with such abandon that soon the scene would turn R-rated.

In the living room, the music had changed to one of the latest pop anthems on the radio, which matched the crowd's dancing abilities a lot better. Or maybe the alcohol had turned their limbs more fluid than before. It didn't matter, since none of my friends were among them. I fired off a few text messages to the girls and figured I could wait outside on the balcony, close enough to the apartment that I wouldn't be risking myself.

Except the most dangerous person found me anyway.

"Don't tell me you thought I was that much of an asshole all this time?" Gabe carried on with our conversation as though I hadn't just stormed away from him.

I folded my arms. "I've seen little proof to think otherwise."

"You wanna know why I treated Liz like that?" Gabe said, catching up with me in a few easy strides. He'd put his beer bottle down somewhere and had his hands stuffed in the pockets of his distressed jeans.

"Not particularly, no."

"Right." He rolled his eyes. "Because your judgment of me is already made, and no one will change it. Watch me try anyway."

I checked my phone again, but the screen remained free of messages. Did I have bad reception? But as I scrolled around, I noted that the texts had indeed sent off.

"I invited Liz home once, and she said Mom's food was disgusting. To my mom's face."

Whatever reason I had imagined he would say, it wasn't this. Recalling the moment of their breakup, Liz had mentioned his mom as a reason why things weren't going well. Based off the few encounters I'd had with her, I could imagine what a Liz versus Gabe's mom scene might have looked like, and I could easily picture Liz botching the entire thing with her selfish tantrums.

Nope, I didn't care. I wouldn't sympathize with him.

But then again, if I ever took a boyfriend home and he complained about Mami's cooking, she would murder him, and I would help her hide the body.

Then I remembered why Gabe wanted me as his fake date, and I narrowed my eyes at him. "I thought you didn't get along with your mom."

"I don't, but it doesn't mean I'm going to let anyone else insult her." He leaned against the railing outside of the apartment, overlooking a dark parking lot that had tipsy people milling about. "I thought dating Liz would finally make Mom happy, but no, it was a disaster."

"Why?" I shook my head, confused.

"Liz is White. But not Catholic." He ran a hand through his hair. "That one thing became the cornerstone of Mom's disapproval. Liz caught one whiff of that and started acting out. I was going to put up with it until the wedding because I figured that drama would take Mom's full attention and prevent a repeat of Magdalena's wedding, when Mom got drunk and said Magdalena was going to . . . empeorar la raza by marrying a Black man."

My jaw dropped.

"Uh, has no one told your mom that's not a very Catholic way to think?"

"Qué va. Tú sabes cómo son las viejas generaciones." Gabe's expression scrunched up like he'd swallowed a lemon. "Yeah, so this isn't some game I'm playing with you. My brother and his fiancé are in on it too. Even my abuela, my sister, and her husband know about it. We're *that* desperate. And I know you're the right woman for the job because if you don't put up with my shit, you also won't let Mom jerk you around."

I steeled myself against the sympathy I'd started to feel by folding my arms. "Is that why you only date White girls, then? Because it'll, um, deflect her racism off you?"

"What? No, she hates White girls too. And I don't just date White girls," Gabe added. "It just so happens that a couple of my most recent exes are, but I have a diverse interest in all girls."

"You're not helping your case, you know?"

"And what's that?" he asked. When it was clear I had no idea what he meant, he clarified. "My case."

I thought about that with much more intent than I'd ever meant to dedicate to him. Tilting my head, taking in the jeans that hugged his shapely calves and thighs, the buttoned shirt with sleeves that molded tight around thick biceps, and the couple of buttons that showed off enough of his neck and chest that he didn't look sleazy but was definitely aware of his own appeal, I finally said, "That you're not just some heartless player."

"And do you want me to be more than that?" His eyes pinned me.

My heart stumbled upon itself to beat harder, and in my mind, I screamed a mantra at it that consisted of a single word.

No.

Which was also what I was about to say when my phone went off. I checked it right away, thankful for the distraction. It was a text from Maya that read SOS.

The second I started typing a question, a familiar voice called from inside the apartment.

"Gabe!"

He and I shared a look of panic upon recognizing Liz's particular wail. When she followed it up with her distinctive, "Babe!" it sounded a lot closer. I turned for the stairs, but they were blocked by a group of people lounging there.

"Shit," I said upon realizing the confrontation was imminent. "She's going to kill me because of you."

"No, she won't." This time Gabe pulled me towards him and settled me against the wall. "Let's give her such a shock she won't be able to react."

I was conscious of how this looked, and I put my hands against his chest to push him away. "Don't you dare do what I think you're about to do."

Gabe's eyebrows went up. "What do you suggest instead? We jump over the rail onto the cars below?"

That almost sounded like a better alternative.

Then we both heard Liz next to us saying, "Babe, let's just—"

She never finished the sentence because, seeing no other way to divert her focus from us, we both took a deep breath and dove in. Or Gabe dove in, and I met him halfway.

A gasp echoed the second our lips met. That was the last thing I was aware of outside the cocoon his arms created.

My hand holding my cellphone remained wedged between us, and not even the incessant vibration of an incoming call could snap me away from the moment. My entire body had become a ball of heat that, far from letting it consume him, Gabe stoked with his own. His lips brushed a caress over mine so intent it coerced my mouth open. When his tongue touched mine, my chassis lost all structural strength and collapsed against the wall.

It momentarily pulled me away from him, but with a growl, Gabe held me up against him again. In the back of my mind, I wondered why a second kiss was necessary if we didn't hear Liz's voice anymore. Except he held the back of my head at an angle that allowed him more access to my mouth, and my brain short-circuited. All I could process was his other hand blazing a path down my back, lower still, until it settled over the curve of my butt. I clutched two fistfuls of his soft hair and pulled him flush against me from head to toe.

The sound of my phone clattering against the floor finally tore me apart from him.

Gabe's eyes were at half-mast, dazed as he looked down at me in a way he never had before. It sent a shiver down my spine, more intense than the feeling of losing his heat. He licked his lips with the same tongue he'd used to stroke mine just a second ago, and I gasped.

Qué carajo acaba de pasar?

With the last of my strength, I pushed him away so I could pick up my phone. The case had saved it from getting cracked. The relief was short-lived as two missed calls from Maya lit up the screen.

"What's going on?" I asked when she picked up, my voice shaking as I looked everywhere but at Gabe. I noticed that Liz was nowhere around.

"Finally," she said, sighing. "After you left the kitchen with your new beau, Taylor saw her ex making out with her current girl, and it didn't cure her one bit. She's in despair."

I cringed, feeling the brunt of the blame. Wasn't that exactly what Gabe and I had just done to Liz?

My stomach tightened at how easy it had been to be an accessory of heartbreak. I glared at him as though this, too, were his fault.

"Shit, okay. Where are you?"

"In the parking lot with Malik, watching Taylor cry her heart out with one eye and watching you make out with Gabe with the other."

Blood rushed in and out of my face, leaving me hot and cold in turns.

"Um, I'll be downstairs in a second."

As I disconnected the call, I contemplated what had been worse: coming to the party thinking it could help Taylor move on from her ex or helping Gabe get rid of his.

While I could definitely help my best friend heal from her broken heart, I couldn't help Liz, and I refused to help Gabe any longer if it left me feeling like trash.

I faced him for the first time since my brain had glitched and I'd agreed to kiss him. Reservation lined his eyes and radiated from his posture. It was almost as though he braced for a physical blow, which told me he knew he deserved it.

Taking a deep breath, I said, "To answer your earlier question, no. I don't want you to be more than what you show you are. You play with girls' feelings like they don't matter, and I don't want you to make me a part of that ever again."

He took a step back like I'd hit him after all. Gabe swallowed with difficulty.

"But I was also helping you get that guy's interest."

I bit my swollen lip and shook my head. "People's feelings aren't a game to me, and maybe you should grow up and learn that lesson too. Figure out a way to break things off cleanly with Liz that doesn't involve me. And just . . . get your mom in therapy."

"What are you trying to say?" he asked, pushing his hair away from his face with both hands. "Are you dropping out of our deal?"

My head throbbed. I wanted that full-time position. If I tore up the contract we'd both signed just yesterday, Gabe would no doubt amp up the intensity of the competition. But deep down I knew if I tangled with him any further, it would be an even worse idea than just agreeing to kiss him.

It was as though a hand squeezed my heart when I raised my chin and said, "Yeah, I—I don't want to do this anymore."

Gabe sucked a deep breath, but the second his lips parted I turned around and left, not wanting to hear what he had to add.

And this time, he didn't follow.

CHAPTER TEN

I took time off work on Monday morning to run around campus, collecting the last documents I needed to renew my OPT. I still had time before the deadline, but other international students recommended getting it done ASAP, since processing times kept getting steadily longer. This spoke directly to the part of me that wanted to be ahead of the curve, which was why I went for it. My academic counsellor engaged in the process, and after a few days of getting the final signatures and approval stamps, I was ready to file the application.

When I made it to the office, I was drenched after catching every single red light on the way. The blast of air-conditioning was welcome, even if I faced an afternoon of putting up with my nemesis. Who I now knew kissed like a rom-com movie star.

Fortunately, he was away from his desk when I barged in. After firing up my work laptop, I set myself as Do Not Disturb in the instant messaging system and set to work.

Emails pinged in my inbox a couple of times, but I ignored them. My full attention remained on the application, double-, triple-, and quadruple-checking every character I typed. Every time I had to do anything with immigration, it felt like there wasn't enough oxygen in the room to keep my brain functioning normally. Instead of being calm and logical, I panicked, thinking about getting a rejection if I made the littlest typo. I was so engrossed in my task I didn't even notice when Gabe arrived at his desk.

At some point, I started to pray that this would go well, that it could lead to buying me all the time I needed to impress Metal Systems into hiring me full-time and also sponsoring me for an H-1B visa. That was my dream, to establish roots and grow and thrive without fearing for my safety.

It wouldn't erase the fear I carried within me over my family's well-being. But maybe if I worked hard enough, if I rose within the company to better paying positions, maybe I could help support my family. And if I achieved the ultimate goal of citizenship, maybe I could bring them here. At least Mami. I highly doubted that Papi or Cora would ever consider it.

Finally, the cursor blinked as it hovered over the button to finish and submit. I went back one more time—perhaps the twentieth—to ensure everything was perfect. I wished I had a second pair of eyes, but there was no one here I trusted with my life like this.

After gathering my nerve, I clicked the button. All the adrenaline coursing through my body rushed out. My entire body drooped from the drain. I allowed myself to lower my hot cheek to the surface of my desk, close my eyes, and breathe until my heart rate slowed to normal.

It was done. Gracias a Dios.

When I opened my eyes again, it was to meet Gabe's directly.

His eyebrows were scrunched up and raised, as though he'd been analyzing a complex equation he couldn't solve. I opened my mouth, ready to fire some choice Spanish words at him, but he just turned back to his screen and ignored me.

Con que es así.

Okay, two could play that game. I straightened and checked my inbox. Sixteen emails had come in the course of the time I'd taken filing the application. Moreover, all of them were between Gabe and Jeff.

I scrolled down to the first one in the thread. Jeff had requested a quick calculation from Gabe and me. The familiar hot flash of instant stress returned. Quickly, I skimmed through the entire thread and found that the request was due for a conference call Jeff was already in with his boss, Marty, and Marty's corporate bosses. And of course, I hadn't even noticed because I was too busy securing my future.

Except this was part of securing my future too.

I tightened my jaw as I opened the attachment Gabe had sent in his response, probably after working on it silently beside me. Of course, I'd known after rescinding our deal he would go on a full frontal attack. I had no right to feel like he'd betrayed me by not telling me we had this urgent request. And yet I still felt like he'd gone behind my back to send the calculation quickly and get all the praise.

In full spite mode, I went over every detail of his calculations. A flare of joy erupted in me when I found a mistake. After combing through everything and confirming it was only the one, but that it caused a five percent deviation in the result, I fired up a very kind and helpful note to both Jeff and Gabe with the correction.

Jeff responded with his gratitude for catching that detail

right away. I wanted to punch the air when Gabe responded, admitting to the error's existence due to the quickness of his response.

"Haven't you heard?" I told him over my shoulder in a sing-song voice. "Quick doesn't always mean better."

He rolled his eyes and still dared to retort with, "That's what she said."

"So that's how it's gonna be now, huh?" I folded my arms, taking pleasure in ignoring his comment. When his attention returned to me, I added, "Cutthroat and backstabbing."

"Wow, you make me sound like some mustache-twirling villain." Gabe snorted and shook his head. "What did you think was gonna happen, Kitty Cat? You should've kept to the deal if what you wanted was to have no competition."

The logic was sound. If our positions were reversed, I would think precisely in those terms. And yet out of principle, I could never agree with someone who called me Kitty Cat.

"Well, if you weren't such a massive jerk, I wouldn't have dropped out." The argument lacked finesse, but it was exactly how I felt. "Hopefully, this serves as a lesson for you that girls aren't toys."

I could tell that lit a fire within him when his nostrils flared and his brow plunged. He wheeled himself closer so he could whisper, "For your information, I took your advice and had a nice little chat with Liz that resulted in this." Then he turned to show the side that faced the opposite way. He had a bandage on his cheek. The thin elastic stripe didn't fully cover the scratch across his skin.

My mouth opened.

"So yeah, I'm not the jerk here," he said with a grunt. "I'm done putting up with her shit."

Too quick to stop myself, out came, "Then maybe you should screen your girlfriends for quality over quantity."

Heavy silence fell over us as the implications of what I'd said sunk in. Maybe tangentially calling him a man-whore after he'd admitted to suffering abuse from his partner wasn't my best move.

It wasn't far-fetched that guys could be victims too, yet I never would have expected such a situation for Gabe, Everyone's Babe. The guy deemed most attractive on campus for two years in a row. There were so many girls who would stop at nothing to make him happy, but he'd landed Liz, who not only had a thick jealous streak but who I knew for a fact also resorted to violence easily.

I thought back to the scene where she'd threatened to hit me just a few weeks ago right outside the office, and how quick Gabe had been to block the upcoming blow to my face with his hand. As if he'd already known his then-girlfriend could react that way. As if he'd had practice. And although we'd done a shitty thing by making out in front of her and breaking her heart, I now wondered if Gabe had done it as last resort to completely remove her from his life. Out of desperation.

I'd been angry he'd made me behave like an unethical fool. But that paled compared to the shame I felt at myself now for blaming him for the failed relationship he might have been a victim in.

I couldn't believe this . . . but I was about to apologize to Gabe Cabrera.

Except Jeff swooped in at that moment and completely changed the atmosphere. "Guys, thank you so much for the save. You know Pierre, Marty's boss. He wouldn't stop screaming at us, and I couldn't do the math myself on the fly while trying to do damage control. You both really saved the day."

"Oh, no problem," Gabe said easily, as though a charged conversation hadn't just been interrupted.

I smiled at Jeff. "Any time."

"Great, I'm so happy you both can perform well under pressure." He glanced at us like a proud father. "Trust me, I'll keep this in mind for the selection process."

My stomach blended every uncomfortable feeling in it until I wanted to puke.

Once Jeff was done with our chat, I excused myself and sequestered myself in a bathroom stall, taking deep breaths to keep the nausea at bay.

Gabe was a jerk, but I was a straight-up asshole. I'd always got it in my head he was the reason why bad things happened to me or the reason for my bad moods, but the shittiness was inside me all along. I just chose to dump it on him because he showed himself as this guy with a perfect life who could stand to be taken down a few pegs. The perfect target for my self-projections.

I fired off a whole-ass essay to Maya and Taylor via text explaining what had just happened, including all the details I'd left out after the party. We'd spent the entire weekend consoling Taylor, which had conveniently allowed me to gloss over my own shenanigans. Nearly half an hour later, I was done with the essay that detailed my culpability, and I signed off with, What should I do?

CHAPTER ELEVEN

My terrible life decision had allowed me the lay of the couch, as Maya took the armchair and Taylor the floor.

"First of all, I want to acknowledge how difficult it is for you to come to us with any problem," Maya started, touching the tips of her fingers together like she was a therapist and I was her patient. "However, you're at fault here."

"So, what you're saying is I should apologize?"

It was the right answer, and I didn't like it. Hopefully, Taylor had a different one.

From below, Taylor said, "Yeah, you should apologize because you just victim-blamed, and that's never cool. But I kinda agree with you as well in the sense that next time, Gabe needs to be more careful who he hooks up with. It's similar with Amber. Now my ex is with a girl who treats her kind of like she treated *me*, and she chose that—she chose mediocre love over the real deal just to not stay alone. And that's a lesson Gabe needs to learn. So anyway, if I'd had my hurt thrown back at me, I'd want an apology too."

Maya reached down to pat Taylor's shoulder. The latter wiped a tear.

I set my laptop aside and threw my power generation textbook on the cushion beside me, groaning. "You know, for years I thought Gabe was the most privileged guy in the room. Everything I have to bust my ass for comes easy to him—relationships, grades, work. But what if he's not so bad?"

"I did tell you so maybe about a million times." Maya shrugged at my glare.

"What if I can't accept that anyway?" I said in a whisper that made them strain closer to hear. I raised my knees and hugged them before continuing. "If it turns out he's been a mostly good guy all this time, does that mean I've been a bad person?"

"You're not a bad person," Maya said, eyebrows crashing with seriousness. "You just sometimes make shitty decisions."

"Who doesn't?" Taylor snorted.

"That's the problem. I'm not perfect, neither is Gabe. But he's obviously the better person. The better student. The better employee." As I tilted my face down, strands of my long, dark hair obscured my face from them. I was glad for it, because my eyes were tearing up. "Doesn't that mean he's going to be the better choice for the full-time position, then? Without this deal, I don't stand a chance."

"Nuh-uh. None of this!" I heard rustling as Maya stood up from the armchair and shifted over to me. "Life isn't a zero-sum game, Cata. You're also smart and capable."

"I bet Gabe can't weld like a badass," Taylor added, her voice also sounding closer.

"That doesn't factor into the selection criteria for a technical project manager," I mumbled.

"So—what? Are you going to give up?"

I snapped my face up. Maya's question rattled me to the bone.

Everything in me rebelled against that notion. Just because I felt like crap for Gabe's situation, it didn't mean I had to lose sight of what was important. Yes, every odd was stacked against me in a way that wasn't true for him. He was smart, a guy, a citizen. He was the easy choice, but that didn't mean I shouldn't even try. I had to be my own champion.

"No." I took a deep breath. "Of course not. I'm going to make that job mine even if it means . . . apologizing and . . . begging to take up our deal again."

"*What?*" The fact the question came from both in unison should've alarmed me.

Wiping the wetness off my face, I said, "It's insurance."

"Do it." Taylor jumped to her feet, her body suddenly electrified by the idea. "He'll accomplish his goal while also being in a pseudo-relationship that won't put him on a pedestal and will teach him to not play with other people's feelings, and you get yours."

"No." Maya dragged the o for a good while. "This is not a good idea. Just apologize to him and don't get involved any further. You'll get the job on your own just fine."

I threw my head back and laughed. "No, I won't. But I'm going to make sure I get it anyway." Shaking my head, I sobered myself. "You don't get it, Maya. I have no other prospects lined up. I have to take any chance I can to stay in this country."

"Besides, he previously agreed to the same terms," Taylor added, clearly on my side. "It's not like she's cheating him out of the position."

Maya stood up from the couch and parked herself back in the armchair, folding her arms. "Yeah, but would the company think it's so simple if they were to find out?"

"They won't. We have a contract. If he leaks this, he'll be just as implicated," I said, maybe more ferally than necessary.

"Yeah, get it, Cata!"

"I hope you won't regret this."

I lifted my chin at Maya, fumbling around until my hand closed around my cellphone. His contact was at the top of my text message list. After the party fiasco, he'd tried to reach out a couple of times, and I'd ignored it. Until now.

Yes, let's talk, I texted back, days after he'd messaged, Can we just talk about this calmly?

Not long passed from the lull of conversation before we went back to our schoolwork. Occasionally, Maya would lift her face from typing up her report to glare at me.

"How are we even friends? I shouldn't hang out with terrible people like y'all."

"You probably want to save our souls, that's why," Taylor responded without even glancing up.

I tried to focus back on the power generation report. This semester was pretty easy, except for the senior design project. Having to work on it with Gabriel Cabrera had been a total demotivator. But now putting up with him everywhere wouldn't be for nothing. That thought gave me renewed energy.

"There's nothing wrong with quitting twice," Maya continued, setting aside her laptop. This had become the universal sign that another lecture was coming, and automatically Taylor and I also put ours to sleep. "In fact, in this particular case it's the right thing to do."

Taylor shrugged. "You know what they say, just because you can doesn't mean you should and all that."

I almost laughed at Taylor's twisted logic, but the way Maya's dark eyes blazed stopped me.

"Pretty sure this isn't the kind of situation that saying applies to." After one last sour glance at Taylor, my roommate's attention fell back on me. "Think about it. If you accept this deal again, you'll have to get close to Gabe. Real close. What happens if someone catches feelings? Is getting the job that way going to feel good?"

My other friend snapped her fingers. "A-ha! So you admit this plan *can* work."

"Well, yeah. She's hot—how can Gabe resist her?" Maya huffed. "The point is, what if Cata can't resist Gabe either, and this gets messy?"

I couldn't contemplate that. Instead, I evaded by asking, "You think I'm hot?"

"Yes," Maya said while waving her hand. "And the sky is blue, and the grass is green. Are you hearing what I'm saying?"

I'd spent the whole afternoon feeling horrible, but the nonsensical turn of this conversation was doing a lot for cheering me up. I leaned into it when I said, "Wow, typically people say Cora is the hot twin."

"You just need a little bit of makeup and some sexy dresses to look like her." Taylor clapped her hands so hard the sound echoed in the living room. "This calls for a makeover!"

"No, this calls for Jesus!" Maya threw her hands up, which ended with them sliding down her face.

At that point, I couldn't help laughing.

Unfortunately, there was a lesson I had to learn too, which was that every time I enjoyed myself, something had to come along to knock me down another peg. My phone buzzed with such abandon that it trekked across the couch cushion and all the way off. The clatter against the floor alerted me to the incoming phone call.

It had to be Mami.

Dread filled me, because even if the conversation was mild, there was always heartbreak in our calls. I still picked up. "Bendición?"

For the first time in my life, Mami didn't respond with her typical "Dios me la bendiga"; instead, a cry greeted me.

"Mami?" I sat ramrod stiff. Even as my eyes focused on nothing, I felt both of my friends' attention. "Mami, háblame por favor."

What she managed to squeeze out in between sobs was something along the lines of *your freaking sister*. My world ceased spinning as the implications sunk in.

Had something happened to Cora?

Was she still alive?

Should I feel something? Wasn't there supposed to be some magical bond between twin sisters that would let us know when the other one was in danger? But there was no tingling sensation at the back of my neck, and though my stomach had sunk, it was because of the state Mami was in. And she could only get like this over something really bad.

Suddenly, I heard Papi shouting in the background. He was too far from the phone for me to make out the words, but the anger was unmistakable. He hadn't even reacted like this when Carlos died. What was happening?

"Qué pasa?" I insisted, repeating it until Mami finally heard me.

Her answer was, "No puedo creer lo que tu hermana ha hecho."

Some relief allowed me to fill my lungs with air again. The fact she'd said *ha hecho* instead of straight-up *hizo* must mean Cora was alive to tell the story.

"Everything okay?" Maya mouthed in front of me, and I shook my head.

After much coercing, Mami finally passed the phone to Cora, and I slumped back on the couch. The confirmation I still had one sibling had me feeling like I'd run a full marathon and had just made it back home.

"Oh, thank goodness. What happened?" I asked her.

Her sigh traveled through the phone and all the way to my alarm center. It was the same one she released when she'd done something terrible but found everyone's reactions to be overboard.

Which was exactly how Maya felt about me right now. I shook my head.

"I'm okay, if that's what you were wondering."

I bit my lips to hold back from telling her exactly what I'd been wondering. Instead, I said, "Tell me what the big deal is."

"I went to a rally," she said. Cool, calm, collected—unlike Mami's crying in the background.

Okay. It wasn't the first time Cora had been to a political rally, especially considering who her boyfriend was. Something made this time special, though.

"Did you get arrested?" I ventured to ask, since she wasn't offering any answers.

"No." I could almost hear her eye roll. "Nothing so bad."

"Then?"

After a long pause, only interrupted by Papi yelling at Mami to pull herself together and at Cora to not make our mother suffer so much, Cora gave another sigh and fessed up. "An opposition group met ours, and things got violent. I got tossed around a bit, I tossed around in turn, we got tear-gassed and water-cannoned, and yeah, my picture's in the newspaper."

"What?" I screeched. "Which newspaper?"

The little shit was proud as she recited which one. I kept her on hold as I searched for the website of our hometown's biggest newspaper, which had my freaking sister's face plastered all over the front page. She appeared with her pro-government T-shirt and a tricolor bandana around her forehead. Her muscles flexed as she threw a live tear gas canister like a pro baseballer.

I stared at the photograph. I hated that T-shirt. But she looked like an Amazon warrior in battle, which explained why the photographer had plastered her image on the front page.

But that was my face too. She'd gone out there and put *my* face in front of the entire country, so anyone who saw me could be confused into thinking I supported the system that had led to my brother's death.

I was so livid, my whole body shook.

And then I zeroed in on one important detail. She'd thrown the can with her bare hands. The same girl who did her mani-pedi routine every week with more dedication than going to church.

"You burned your hand," I said, my voice shaking with the barely contained desire to curse her out.

"It's a small sacrifice for the cause."

"What cause?" Finally giving in to the rage, I screamed my throat raw at her. "The cause that probably is making it impossible for you to find medicines to treat your burns? Because surely it can't be the same cause that killed our brother!"

"Screw you!" she screamed back at me. "You don't get to pin his death on me! I'm not the one who told him to march straight into it."

I couldn't help it. A sob burst out of my throat, and tears followed suit. My friends jumped to their feet, heading over to comfort me, but I didn't want any of it. I got up and stumbled to my bedroom, locking myself inside.

"Tienes razón," I bit out as I slid down to the floor and wrapped my arms around my knees. "But you don't get to throw that at my face when you're risking your life alongside the people who killed him."

"That's not true. I was with my friends, and they're not murderers." Her voice shook. I didn't know if she was crying, but I wanted her to be. I wanted her to suffer just like I was—which would never happen because Cora didn't understand the concept of being wrong. She reinforced this by saying, "What I did isn't wrong. I believe in the revolution. I believe this is the way to pull the country out of its misery. Your friends up there in North America aren't the ones who will help us, it'll be us in the streets."

"No," I whispered. "You're wrong. But I don't care about what lies you've bought into. All I care is that I don't lose you too."

This broke through her shell of pride and patriotism. I heard her shut the door of our bedroom, the knockoff Barbie sign that said BEAUTY SLEEP on one side and BEAUTIFUL DAY on the other clattering against the wood. Finally, she broke down, gasping for air as she cried over the phone with the same distress Mami had started the call with.

"It hurts," she whispered, and my heart broke for her.

"I can try to ship over some first aid stuff."

"Bring them over," she said, sniffling. "Come visit. Stay for a bit. I miss you."

I missed her too, but my heart twisted knowing this wasn't enough to make me return. My hope was to *never* have to, to never again see the bridge over the lake, the palm and mesquite trees that lined the streets, to never again be in a procession for our Virgin Mary, La Chinita. To never taste the sweets the old women made or the hot guayoyo they sold from coolers in the blasting sun of Maracaibo. To never see my friends from school or be there for their weddings, the births of their children.

All of that was to remain a mirage of the timeline I lost after Carlos passed away.

Florida was where I had to stay, where I had to be if I wanted to have a chance at growing old. But at that moment, as we wept together and apart at the same time, I worried that maybe Cora would never grow old like I wanted to. That I'd selfishly saved myself and condemned my family to an uncertain future.

Maybe I could ease their burden from afar? If I tightened my belt, I could save up enough to send them a box of food and medical essentials every couple of months. When I got the full-time position, I could start sending them actual money. I could at least do that much. This was exactly why I had to take that ridiculous deal with Gabe again.

"I can't," I finally said, even as the words hurt me more than her earlier ones had. "But I won't leave you alone. Ever. I promise."

I'd make certain of that.

CHAPTER TWELVE

Saturday morning, a week since the terrible party, I sat in bed scrolling through my phone. I was on a mission, and it was to find a reliable mailing service to get some essentials to my family. I also kept checking my text messages, expecting more from Gabe than the lukewarm okay I'd got after I said we needed to talk.

Sighing, I focused back on the main task. A Facebook group of Venezuelan expats in Miami had recommendations for shipping companies. As I read through the reviews, I jotted down what the pros and cons were for each. Some could do the shopping for the customer and take it directly to the recipient's door, but those tended to be higher priced than the services where I would have to do the shopping. Of those, there were some that picked up the parcel at the sender's home and others that I would have to drive considerably for in order to consign the shipment.

Still no more texts from Gabe. Maybe his okay was meant to put the ball on my court.

I tapped on my phone's calculator, estimating how much I'd be able to spend on the entire operation to restock my family's shelves versus how much I had left from my internship after basic expenses. The resulting number wasn't as high as I wished, but maybe I could collect things over a few months and send them all together by the end of the summer.

What I couldn't wait so long for was to talk with Gabe. His unfairly handsome face kept appearing in my mind, distracting me. Setting aside my notepad on my bed, I grabbed my phone and fessed up. I selected the contact I'd named Not My Babe and called.

"Good morning, Kitty Cat," his smooth voice said after picking up. It made me want to fling the phone away because it was too much.

"Hi."

Nonplussed, he asked, "Is this a booty call?"

"Shut up. We need to talk."

"I can't do both of those things at once, you know." He cleared his throat, which indicated that a nefarious purpose was still afoot anyway.

I forced myself to take a deep breath and remind myself I had two missions today. First, make peace with Gabe and get back in the deal. Second, go buy the stuff for my folks. The second would clearly not happen until I got the first item off my chest.

"Listen, I am trying to be nice here, but you're making it very difficult."

"Okay, sounds like this is the part where I shut up." I could almost hear the smile in his voice, and it calmed me down. At least he wasn't as upset as I'd thought he might be.

"Um. So, about what I said last time I saw you at the office . . ."

I fiddled with the paper I'd been doing math on. "When I sort of victim-blamed you—no, not sort of. I did. Ugh, the point is, I shouldn't have done that. I'm sorry."

Silence on the other end of the line stretched out for what felt like eons.

Finally, Gabe said, "Wow, I wasn't expecting that. Uh, thanks?"

"That said," I continued.

"Hay más?"

"I've been thinking about the deal too."

"Funny, so have I."

"Huh?"

Gabe chuckled. "Why don't we talk about this part in person?"

The irrational part of my mind kicked in. I jumped to my feet as if expecting him to walk through my bedroom door and catch me in my underwear and oversized T-shirt. But seeing Gabe today wasn't part of my plan, so I said, "I have plans today. Can't we just talk over the phone?"

"Nope, I'll pick you up in half an hour."

"What? Didn't you hear what I just—"

"Yeah," he drawled. "I could practically hear you crossing your fingers too. You have nothing going on today, and we both know it."

I spluttered, but I couldn't come up with a defense. Yes, there was something very important I had to do, but it wasn't the kind of thing that would take me all day. At most a couple of hours.

Shifting my phone to my other ear, I said, "Regardless, I'm not going to agree just like that without knowing what I'm getting into."

"Here's precisely what: we're going to talk about the deal. Face-to-face. In detail. So, see you in half an hour, Kitty Cat."

Gabe hung up, and I glared at my phone.

My phone's calculator came back up. As a last-ditch effort, I switched over to texting and told him that I really was busy. He didn't respond. So, I guessed I was about to see Gabe in person. I couldn't believe I was about to *beg* to spend more time with this insufferable guy. Put up with nonsensical nicknames. See his pretty face up close, where it was harder to hate him.

No, I shook my head to myself. I wasn't ready for that.

A couple minutes later, Maya strolled in, looking like a million dollars even in her pajamas. "Why is Gabe Cabrera calling me this early and asking me to make sure you're ready?"

"Hijo de—" I cut myself off and ran to the bathroom to get ready. I called out to her just before shutting the door, "And how the hell does he have your number?"

Her voice drifted from the kitchen. "I'm not a recluse, you know."

Unlike me. The only reason I even had his phone number was because of our internship. I'd survived with only faraway encounters with him for three years up until the point Jeff had put us together, expecting us to collaborate.

I blew out a sigh. But this was good. I might stand a better chance of convincing him to retake the deal in person. Besides, he didn't say where we were going, and since this wasn't a date, I could just coerce him to take us to Walmart so I could do my shopping while we talked. Two birds with one stone.

I managed to make myself presentable with a quick shower and brushing my teeth. However, not wanting him to think I'd made much of an effort, I let my hair air-dry and put on a simple T-shirt with my most comfortable pair of jeans that looked like I'd stolen them from Papi.

Gabe was waiting for me downstairs in a similar ensemble, except with aviator sunglasses and his jaw-length hair free. He leaned against his red Jeep like he was posing for a magazine and I was on the other side of the lens, looking at the magic happening on camera from a different world.

When I approached, I said, "Change of plans, we're doing this my way."

Gabe tilted his face forward to glance at me over the rim of his glasses. "Oh?"

"We're going to Walmart. I have to buy some things, and we can talk at the same time."

His lips arched into a frown, but he shrugged. "Why not? Hop in."

The words were somewhat misleading as he opened the passenger door for me and even offered his hand to help me. I tossed him a glare, not because I didn't appreciate the gesture but because no doubt this was one of his favorite techniques with the ladies. Smooth like butter, he hopped into the driver's seat.

"So, why Walmart?" he asked, turning his car on. It had functional air-conditioning, and his phone could connect to the radio system. I bet I wasn't hiding my jealousy well, but he didn't notice it and added, "Do you want to go to a public place because you're afraid of me?"

"I'm sure that's what your Tinder dates say, but no." I glanced at my nails for emphasis. "You're not much taller than I am, it wouldn't be hard to knee you in the cojones."

I had never heard him laugh as hard as he did then. He was still going even as we parked at the East Colonial Walmart.

I frowned against the bright sun of the late morning. "It wasn't that funny."

"You're right," he agreed, which was a bad sign. "I should feel threatened right now."

The flashback of Liz's raised hand made me cringe. "Sorry."

A corner of his lips tilted. "But I'm not—you're all snarl but no scratch, Kitty Cat."

To prove him wrong, I punched him in the shoulder, which only made him giggle.

We grabbed a cart, and as he cleaned it with wipes, it was hard not to feel like there was something very domestic about the scene. Like this was a tradition rather than an exception. It was also difficult not to notice the glances we attracted. The other patrons of the store probably weren't used to seeing someone as good-looking as Gabe walk among them.

"Where to?" he asked, and I pointed ahead.

He followed me to the pharmacy section, where I pulled out the list I'd been making this morning. I grabbed gauze, antiseptic, bandages, rubbing alcohol—everything typically found in a first aid kit. I motioned him to follow me down the aisle to find some other basic items when he stopped, picked up a box of condoms, and tossed it into the cart.

"Those are for me," he clarified as though I'd asked.

"I don't care."

"What else?" Gabe asked, smiling as though he imagined I did care.

I turned my back on him and headed for the dental care section and picked three toothbrushes. He eyed the items in the cart but had the decency not to comment on them. Instead, he brought the main topic back up.

"So, about the deal." Gabe ran a hand through his locks, then rubbed the back of his neck. After a second, he met my eye. "Would you consider taking it back up?"

I froze, a big pack of toothpaste in one hand and another pack of floss in the other. "Sorry, what?" I couldn't believe I didn't have to beg.

He cringed a bit. "The thing is, my whole family's getting together tomorrow, mi abuela, tíos, primos, mis hermanos, y mi mamá," he said, his Boricua accent slipping through seamlessly between the English, "for a cookout to celebrate Chris and Ellen's engagement. I can't find a convincing new girlfriend in one day."

Huh. So this was how it felt when things aligned in my favor. What a change.

Meanwhile, I sounded very Venezuelan even as I responded in English. "And you think I will be a convincing girlfriend in a day? How is that even possible?"

"First of all, the deal needs to be back on." With his head lowered, Gabe looked at me from under his eyebrows in a way that would disarm a lesser woman. "You canceling was an unexpected curveball, because I had already told everybody I have a new girlfriend and that you're *the one*."

It was so strange to hear those words directed at me. My heart got confused and skipped a beat. I ordered it to settle back down as we strolled through the expanse of the store, closer to the groceries area.

"And they believed it?" I lifted an eyebrow to show him how little I would.

He smiled. "Para nada, which is why you have to act convincing."

I skimmed through the list and looked up at the signs hanging over the aisles to make my way around efficiently. I asked, "What does a convincing girlfriend do?"

"Oh, you know. You have to look at me like you can't believe you're so lucky." From the corner of my eyes, I saw him tick the items with his fingers. "We'll have to hold hands, call each other by cute but very embarrassing names, occasionally kiss—"

"Whoa, whoa," I said, stopping in the middle of the aisle.

Gabe kept going, though, both his mouth and his feet. "And we should probably make up a story about how we fell in love and get to know a few obscure details about each other. What's your favorite color, and what is your biggest fear?"

He had to be off his rocker.

"I'm not kissing you again," I said.

Twisting his upper body to give me a mocking look, he said, "Did you forget? It's in the contract. There isn't a couple in this world that doesn't do PDA."

I folded my arms, dismissing the fact that yes, we'd put *discreet* PDA into the second contract. "I'm sure that's not true. There are plenty of couples out there who don't place the weight of their relationships on the physical aspect. Besides, I haven't agreed to your proposal yet."

"Sure, but I'm not like that, and neither are most people our age." At my dubious look, Gabe pushed the cart into the aisle with the canned food, where a teenage couple was holding hands while shopping for cat food. "See?"

"They're holding hands, bobo," I said, shrugging. "It's not like they're sucking fa—"

I didn't even get to finish the sentence because at that exact moment, the teens dropped their basket to the floor and grabbed each other like someone had just given them the FYI that the world was ending. My face scrunched up, and unfortunately looking away faced me square with Gabe's smug expression.

"Shut up."

"I didn't even have to speak further to prove my point." He kissed his fingers. "Beautiful."

I made a point of marching past the young couple to the cans of food for humans and grabbed sausages and sardines. I would've grabbed tuna too, if it weren't so damn high up on the shelf. Who put one of the most popular products out of reach of short people? I stretched onto my tippy-toes and barely skimmed the bottom of the top shelf.

Suddenly, a wall of heat approached from behind, and a familiar hand grabbed a can. Gabe asked behind me, "How many?"

I wanted to scream that I didn't need his help or his body so close to mine, but a peep came out of my mouth saying, "Six," even followed by, "please." In my defense, the delicious smell of his cologne addled my senses. It was a little spicy and a lot of him, and I knew I'd never forget the scent after this. Gabe kept me trapped between him and the shelf as he grabbed cans one by one, a clear indication he was doing it so slowly to get under my skin.

Worse, it was working.

Even after he'd taken everything I needed, he stayed close and leaned in to my ear to whisper, "You can't be a convincing girlfriend if we don't touch."

A shiver traveled through me, and finally I found enough spine to elbow him out of the way and take the cans from his hands. I put them in the cart and made a show of going through my list again, even though I had the items committed to heart by now.

"Yeah, okay. You've proven your point. What else?"

After a brief pause, he continued, following me as I pushed the cart to the next aisle. "It's going to be pretty informal, but not enough that we can show up in jeans and a T-shirt."

"Fine, I'll wear a dress."

He gasped in such an exaggerated way, all he was missing was the subtitle GASPING IN SPANISH.

"Kitty Cat, does that mean you're in?"

Oh, crap. I'd slipped up.

I tossed my long hair over my shoulder, pretending to think about it. Even though when he used this kind of delaying strategy it rattled my patience, the spark didn't dim from his eyes one bit.

Finally, I sagged and SIGHED IN SPANISH. "I guess. I have no plans tomorrow."

Gabe smirked. "We both know you're not doing this to pass the time."

"No." I turned around, pushing the cart. "I'm doing this to get you out of my way."

"Sure." He dragged the word out far longer than necessary while keeping pace beside me. His hands were in the pockets of his jeans, forearm muscles bunching. A woman down the aisle zeroed in on him with such intent she didn't even notice me. We passed her, and I glanced over my shoulder to catch her eyes still glued on him.

"Doesn't that get tiring?" I grimaced.

"Hmm?"

"Being the apple of every woman's eye," I clarified, glancing back to where the woman was blatantly checking out Gabe's posterior.

"I don't notice anymore." A moment later, he added, "And also, not every woman. You've proven very immune to my charms."

I wasn't, but I was pleased he hadn't noticed. Even so, there was something strange about the phrase.

"What does that even mean? Have you tried your charms on me?"

"Sure." Unlike the previous time he'd said the word, now there was no particular emphasis. "It's not like I can turn my charm up and down like a dial. It's just always there."

"Yeah, like your modesty."

In truth, I was just a little miffed at hearing him admit he'd never made a particular effort on me. But it wasn't like it mattered.

"Which makes you both the best candidate for this con and also the worst, because you'll have to work really hard to make everyone think we're together. But there won't be any risk of feelings, right?"

Geez, what a player.

Gabe grabbed the cart from me after I'd stopped to pick out some canned veggies. "By the way, are you preparing for the apocalypse? What's all this?"

In a way, that was exactly it. "It's for my family who are in the middle of the Venezuelan apocalypse."

"Oh. Shit." Gabe drew to a complete stop and looked at me with wide eyes. "Things are really bad down there, right? Are they okay?"

"As can be. I'm just trying to help a little, which I should've done a long time ago—but back on track. To answer your previous question, I don't have a favorite color and my worst fear already happened."

"And what's that?"

I sighed, realizing I'd turned this entire conversation too somber. I turned to Gabe and caught his attention already on me. "Five years ago, I lost my older brother in protests back home. I guess losing any more of my family is my next biggest fear."

His lips parted, but no words came out. Not a sight I'd seen often.

I kept dumping items in the cart as I spoke. "Let's just say we met in college but weren't close at all until we got stuck doing our internships together. Sometime after your latest breakup, we had to stay late for a project one evening and one thing led to the other. I don't know. Any more than that will be hard to keep track of."

Gabe cleared his throat but followed me in silence for long enough I felt compelled to keep talking—that way, I could put more miles between my sob story and the present.

"You should say your favorite part of me is my legs or something, and I'll say my favorite of yours is your hair, how about that?"

"Your eyes," he said. "Those are my favorite part of you."

I nearly dropped the pack of sugar in my hands, and the traitorous parts he'd complimented turned to him. He was brushing his hand through my fake-favorite part of him.

"So, you like my hair?"

"No," I blurted, hoping the heat in my face wasn't translating into a blush. It was his eyes too. The honey wells that darkened when he had bad thoughts in his head and naughty words in his mouth, that shone under the light like twinkling stars. Of course, what I said instead was, "I don't have a favorite part of you at all."

"Lies." He smiled wide, and suddenly that was a contender with his eyes. That smile. It could be used to produce electricity because suddenly that coursed through my veins. He continued, saying, "Everybody has a favorite part of me. The lady from earlier definitely liked my ass."

I couldn't blame her—he had a really nice one. The kind that was a little bit genetics and a little bit exercise, resulting in a lot of squishable.

No. I had to cut this train of thought off right now.

"Whatever." I waved a hand. "You like my eyes, and I like your hair."

"Does that mean if I go bald you won't like me anymore?" He puckered his lips in a little pout. "My family won't like that."

Since I was done with the shopping, I pushed the cart to the nearest cashier and said, "Fine, your smile. Am I the perfect girlfriend now?"

"This will be a work in progress," he said, gently shouldering me out of the way so he could offload the cart onto the empty conveyor belt.

"I can do that—"

The cashier cut me off by asking, "Is it gonna be cash or card?"

"Card," Gabe responded, and I clawed at his arm with enough strength that he looked back at me.

With wide eyes, I whispered, "Don't you dare."

A slow smile spread across his lips.

"You're still learning, but here's today's lesson—every time I take a girl out on a date, I pay."

"No," I choked out, shaking my head. "Besides, this isn't a date."

And then came the biggest shock of the day. Gabe leaned down and pressed a soft kiss on my forehead before saying, "There, we kissed, therefore it's a date."

He took advantage of my stupefaction to pay for my shopping, like some sort of good Samaritan turned fake boyfriend turned the most confusing person in my life.

CHAPTER THIRTEEN

The makeup tutorial I'd selected on YouTube was going too fast for me. I could follow the most complex engineering calculations with relative ease, even while seeing them for the first time, but this tested me. Concepts like air flow, viscosity, and entropy were much easier for my brain to grasp than how to contour my face. Why it even needed contouring when it naturally had planes and edges, I had no idea.

I donned one of my floral dresses that best complemented my shape, one I'd got at a steep discount at the Outlets, and emerged from my room to show my roommate the look.

From the armchair, Maya peeled back her lips and showed all her teeth in the universal expression of *oh honey, no.*

"What?" I sighed. "Where did I go wrong?"

"I don't like this mess you got yourself into, but as your friend, I can't let you go out looking like It." She waved her hand over to the restroom. "Go wash that gunk off and come back. I'll do your makeup."

"Oh, bless!"

I dashed off to do as the queen bid and later sat patiently while she fluttered all sorts of brushes and sponges about my face, doing magic with my measly makeup kit. At one point, she even used lip stuff for my eyelids or eyelid stuff for my cheeks. I had no idea what she'd done, but at the end, when she put a mirror in front of my face, it wasn't my face staring back at me but Cora's.

My phone pinged with a text from Gabe, who was already downstairs. I grabbed a thin white cardigan and stuffed it in my purse.

"Wish me luck."

Maya's expression caught between a grimace and a smile. "Sure, you'll need it."

Despite the earlier hurry, I took my sweet time to emerge from my building and walk up to him. Gabe was waiting at the same spot as yesterday, ready to hold the car door open for me. Even with the sunglasses, he made a show of sweeping his eyes up and down my frame a couple of times. I made sure to keep my gaze ahead, so I wouldn't do the same. The tan pants he wore clung like a second skin in a way that should be criminal.

I turned the air-conditioning vents towards me when I climbed into his Jeep. To fill the awkward silence between us, I said, "You haven't accepted my Venmo transaction."

"And I won't," he said, setting the Jeep in motion.

"Fine," I said breezily. "I'll just stash the cash in your car in secret next time."

Gabe gave me a quick side glance. "Now I'll know who it came from, so I'll just return it."

Dang it.

"You didn't have to do that." We'd had this exact same

conversation yesterday, and I was hoping repetition would help it sink in. "It's a family thing, and you're not family."

He sighed. "It's called a *good gesture*, maybe we'll have to get you familiarized with those."

I folded my arms, watching the buildings pass as he drove deeper into the city. "I can take care of myself."

"I know you can," Gabe said, looking away to the next lane before shifting to it. "But there's no shame in getting help or asking for it every once in a while."

"Maybe. For others."

I would have to find another way to reimburse him. If I'd thought about it earlier, I could've gone to the ATM to get the cash and given it to his brother or something. Although that would've made an even stranger first meeting than the one we were on track for.

"Changing topic, is it okay if we show up empty-handed to this?"

"Trust me, there's gonna be enough food to feed all of us five times over." After thinking about it further, he said, "Puñeta, debí traer Tupperwares."

That tore a big laugh out of me.

I hadn't been to a family thing with people like me since I'd left Venezuela. Even though I wasn't going to this with any personal stake in the matter, I was still a tad nervous. The only person I'd know there was Gabe—who wasn't precisely my bestie—and if I needed refuge from everybody else, there would be no one for me to commiserate with but myself. And perhaps Taylor on my phone, because Maya would certainly just spit *I told you so* left and right.

"So, we're going to mi abuela's house from my dad's side, which means several things." We were already in a nice neighborhood in South Chickasaw Trail, and the house was probably close. "First, it'll force my mom to behave just a bit because Abuela doesn't like her. Second, my entire family on Dad's side is going to be there, and only a handful from Mom's side. All in all, this is the best setup to introduce you."

Sure, Jan.

I sighed. "Should I turn up the bitchy dial or what? What's the big idea for my character as Gabe's 'The One'?"

"Nothing major," he surprised me by saying. "At this point, Mom will get pissed at meeting another girl she hasn't picked for me, so just be yourself—but with PDA."

I'd managed to forget about that, and the reminder sent my heart into a gallop. I glanced away from him, seeking a way to center myself before the show began. But almost at the same time, he pulled over by the curb. The whole street was packed with cars of all makes and sizes. We walked for a solid two blocks until he finally led me up the path to a midsize house that vibrated with salsa and the voices of a hundred people.

I grabbed his arm in a vise grip that stopped him dead in his tracks. "Are you sure we should do this?"

Gabe took his sunglasses off and hung them from the collar of his white button-up, offering me his arm in an official capacity. "Never been surer. C'mon, let the ruination begin."

How come he was calmer about this than I was? It wasn't my family I was going to cause drama with. Gabe definitely was looking forward to it, and yeah, by the stories he'd told me of his mom, I could see why. Revenge for his siblings would be sweet up until it was his turn to come home with a fiancé. Then his mom would make his life, and Gabe's partner's, a living hell. Unless he didn't care. Or unless by that point he'd be fine with his mom choosing a perfect Puerto Rican wife for him. I couldn't picture him just following the life path someone else had laid out for him, so it definitely had to be the former.

When he opened the door, the avalanche of people was instantaneous. Three older ladies threw themselves at him and alternated giving him choking hugs and covering him in kisses that left lipstick all over his face.

Then he was passed on to a bunch of uncles, and a swarm of little cousins rushed him like football players. He barely managed to sidestep the more zealous ones before squeezing me against his side and announcing in a booming voice, "Everyone, this is my girlfriend, Catalina."

Every eye in the living room settled on me. Gabe held me tighter as I froze up.

I cleared my throat and barely squeaked out, "Hola."

Someone gasped and dashed out of the living room and into the open backyard, no doubt to share the news. Meanwhile, one of the aunts asked point-blank, "Eres Boricua o no?"

"Este, no. Soy venezolana."

She clicked her tongue and said to Gabe, "When are we going to see you with one of our own?"

"Ignore her," a different voice said. I turned to an older lady approaching us while fanning herself. "She's Gabe's aunt on his mother's side. From *my* side of the family, we're just happy if you make our Gabriel happy."

"This is my abuela." Gabe squeezed the woman in such a tight hug, her feet lifted from the ground. After he put her back down and amidst their giggles, he whispered to me. "And she knows about our plan."

His abuela winked at me. "Go take my awful daughter-in-law down a peg."

"Um, okay." I offered an uncertain smile.

"C'mon, let's find Mom and rip off the Band-Aid." Gabe guided me through the maze of the house. The backyard was packed with people of all ages, kids running from one end to the other, teens congregating around the lone DJ trying to liven up the place. The sunset shone in shades of orange and purple behind the back fence, where a bunch of chairs had been set up for the older folks. That was where we were headed.

"Nervous?" Gabe asked.

"Yeah. It feels like I'm meeting the in-laws for real."

His chest vibrated with a chuckle.

"Yo, Gabe!"

The shout drew our attention to the side. A guy who looked only a couple of years older walked towards us, holding hands with an East Asian girl. They had to be Chris and Ellen, the groom and bride. Chris looked enough like Gabe that it was clear they were relatives, but he was slightly shorter and had a buzzcut and eyes so green they looked like emeralds against the brown of his skin. Meanwhile, his fiancé was almost a head shorter than him and was decked in the most adorable dress I'd seen in my life, yellow with white cartoon daisies all over. Even with the enormous glasses she wore, she was stunning.

Gabe let go of me to embrace his brother in a way that had to hurt. The girl turned her attention to me. "Hi, I'm Ellen! And you are?"

"Catalina." I stuck my hand out. "Cata for short."

She shook my hand and glanced at her soon-to-be brother-in-law, a question written over her face. He grinned at her and said, "This is 'The One.'"

"Oooh." A smile that had nothing of sweet and a lot of evil bloomed on her face. "Nice to meet you, 'The One.'"

Chris also offered his hand, and I shook it. "Thank you so

much for your service." Chris glanced over the top of my head and added, "Oops, speaking of. Incoming."

We all turned.

A middle-aged woman marched towards us with purpose. The gold earrings hanging from her ears swung this way and that to the tune of her angry steps. Collectively, we braced for impact, and that alone, if not her features, told me this was Gabe's mom.

"Gabriel Cabrera." Her mouth was set in a harsh hot-pink line as a clear sign of displeasure. "Llegas tarde."

Gabe didn't offer her the same kind of attention he'd given to the people in the living room—hugs, kisses, and questions on their well-being. They just stood there, staring down each other as though it were a face-off.

"Mamá," he said.

"Who's this?" She cut a glare in my direction as though she knew the answer already.

"This is Catalina, my girlfriend."

"What happened to the blond? Al fin te cansaste de gringas?"

"Sí," Gabe responded, shrugging. "You were right all along. My heart is for Latinas."

The song in the background shifted to one of Daddy Yankee's club bangers, which right now sounded like the soundtrack of a horror movie as she slowly gave me a once-over. "De dónde eres?"

"Venezuela," I responded. It was almost funny how she dismissed that with an eye roll.

"More foreigners, when are you going to learn?"

Gabe's expression turned into that of a little kid about to do mischief. It was all the warning I got before he tucked me under his arm. "What can I say, the heart wants what it wants." He proceeded to plant a kiss on my lips.

It was quick and chaste in comparison to our, uh, first one, but the fact we had a wide audience for this one turned me into a stiff plank. In contrast, Gabe smiled placidly like nothing was amiss.

The rage that built up in his mom had her quaking in her shoes. She had Gabe's eyes, a very light brown that turned dark when emotions were high. They set on me like hot stones that scalded my face.

"Let's see how long you last with this green-card-digger and then we'll talk."

With that, she whirled and stomped over to where the older folks sat. A few of them directed curious stares at me that felt tame in comparison. I wheezed out a breath and put my hand on my heart, willing it to trot slower.

"Well, that wasn't so bad," Ellen said. "When I met her, she straight-up cursed at me."

It was hard to imagine there could be something worse than that woman accusing me of being with her son for papers.

"This is only the beginning," Gabe said, smirking at me as though I shared the joke. "You know how we can horrify her even more?"

I shook my head to get rid of the sting. "I don't think there's anything I can do that won't. I just stood here breathing, and she already hates me."

Chris shrugged. "That's just the remaining backlash from the endless parade of Gabe's girlfriends."

I tossed the subject of our conversation a look before asking, "How many?"

"Since middle school or just in college?" his brother asked, eyebrows raised as he started doing the math with his fingers.

Gabe chimed in. "Anyway, Mom can't stand 'immoral music,' so we should dance to it."

"Excellent idea!" Ellen's eyes lit up, and she grabbed her fiancé's hands.

They headed over to the middle of the yard and started dancing to "Dura" with different levels of proficiency. Although Chris guided her, Ellen still did her own thing to her own tune, which caused much merriment to the two of them and secondhand embarrassment to Chris's relatives. A few other people joined them, and I felt Gabe's body angle us towards them.

"I don't love dancing."

"But can you?" he asked, throwing a deliberate challenge.

I sighed. Nothing would spare me from this mess I'd got myself into, and as Americans said, go big or go home, right?

So, I responded with, "Guess you'll find out."

It turned out *I* was the one about to have a life-changing epiphany, which was that when you put together a Boricua boy with a Venezuelan girl on a dance floor, sparks could fly.

Gabe put a hand on my lower back and pulled me scandalously close to him. Not wanting to let him see my surprise, I pretended his hand had been there all along and wrapped my arms around his neck, bringing him even closer.

His eyes flashed with something, which was disarming enough when I considered I'd never been this close to him. We found a single rhythm, and suddenly I had the impression this wasn't dancing anymore. His hand sat at the curve of my back, firm but gentle, guiding me closer until his thigh settled between mine.

The song changed to a famous Romeo Santos bachata, and Gabe's hips moved slower and somehow more intensely. A little gasp escaped from my lips. I wished I had the strength to look away from Gabe's eyes, but I was trapped by the challenge in them. I knew he was pushing the PDA button, but we had an audience, and . . .

Who was I kidding? My heart was dancing a jig in my chest. Goosebumps rose all over my skin. As I ran my hands up the muscles of his shoulders, I knew I hadn't felt this alive in years.

We danced a couple more songs like that until every one of my muscles ached and we were drenched in sweat. Gabe left to find a couple Fantas for us in the kitchen, which was great because I didn't want to talk about what had just happened. I sat in a corner with Ellen, gasping for air.

"Phew, girl. Watching you both made me blush."

I cleared my throat. "Bet his mom now hates me as much as the gringas, huh?"

"More, because you do stand a chance at taking her last baby away." The look of incredulity I gave Ellen sent her into a fit of laughter. "Look, Chris and I know that this thing between you both is supposed to be fake, but there's nothing fake about the way you look at each other. There are sparks there."

"No. No sparks," I said, looking away at the people still dancing in the middle of the lawn. "I don't even like him."

"I've heard that before, and it never seems to be true." She slapped her thighs and stood up. "Oh well, looking forward to seeing if you just lied to me or to yourself."

Ellen left me gaping after her. I couldn't even think of a clever quip. The last thing I could do was forget that this was all pretend, that there was nothing real about the way he'd gripped me tight against him or that I'd clung to him as though I wanted more.

All that was a mirage of what being with him could be like, which wasn't something I needed. I didn't want to join him at family functions and be compared to his myriad girlfriends, or to feel like the span of his attention on me had an expiration date when a prettier, more fun girl came along.

Gabe came back with the unopened soda cans, and I struggled to make conversation. A lump had parked itself in my throat that wasn't there before. I had to remind myself this was a task I'd agreed to and nothing more. The so-called sparks Ellen believed she saw were only acting. There was no doubt in my mind that Gabe thought the same.

Maya was right: this was dangerous. I had to fulfill my end of the bargain with minimum effort or involvement with him and his people.

Which was why, hours later and in the comfort of my bed, I wondered why I'd agreed to take part in every freaking event leading up to the wedding.

CHAPTER FOURTEEN

I bit my thumbnail softly as I waited for the streetlight to turn green. Beside me, Taylor positively bounced with energy. I was her opposite, just wondering what had gone to my head. Had it been the dance that had set every one of my nerve endings aflame? The way the soon-to-be-bride and groom had made me feel like I'd known them my whole life? Or had it been the arroz con gandules y pernil that Gabe's abuela had made? Which of those had clouded my judgment as I'd navigated the rest of the night in the happiest food coma I'd had in years?

Bottom line was, Ellen had invited me to join her and her friends dress shopping, and I'd said yes—but only after hesitating a bit and causing her to suggest that bringing a friend would make *me* feel more comfortable, as though this weren't a major life event for her.

"This is going to be amazing," Taylor said. "I've never tried on a wedding dress before."

"Pretty sure that's not what we're going there for."

She twisted on her seat to smirk with abandon. "You really

got them all thinking this thing between you both is for real, huh?"

"No, Ellen and Chris know what's up." I pulled into the parking lot of a strip mall. Apparently, the idea was that as Ellen tried on possible wedding gowns, the rest of us would also try bridesmaid dresses, because—surprise—I'd just become one last weekend.

"What?" Taylor's question came out higher pitched than normal. "Well, that's no fun."

My face scrunched up. "I actually have the impression they're finding great fun in this."

I sought the closest free spot to the shop, the better to make a quick retreat. At the same time, I filled Taylor in on the new details of this bizarre situation.

From what I'd seen, Gabe's mom was a walking rift in her own family, caused by her harsh words, her judging eyes, and her lack of tolerance for anything outside her comfort zone. I'd seen her cross herself as people danced to reggaeton and merengue, spit Bible verses for spite in a show of exactly what a Catholic shouldn't do, and turn her nose away from wherever Ellen was.

That latter had been the most infuriating part to me. Ellen was *adorable*, in all senses of the word, and here was this woman refusing to recognize that her son had found a wonderful partner, simply because his fiancé didn't fit her preconceived idea. She was the kind of mother who probably thought no woman was good enough for her sons, not unless she was the one to come up with the match.

At some point, Chris had caught my horror, and he'd said, "Just wait till you see the way she acts around Magdalena and her husband, Jason." And in case Gabe hadn't clued me in, he'd leaned closer and whispered, "He's Black."

The woman was horrible. No wonder Gabe had all the women issues he had. He burned through one after the other like cigarettes, looking for one that didn't have the slightest whiff of his mom.

Based on all that, it made sense that if Chris and Ellen wanted their special day to be not as catastrophic as it could be, they needed some help—a new recipient to the outrage of Mrs. Cabrera. Cue Gabe, the unruliest child of the trio. And cue his nefarious plan to turn the whole wedding experience upside down. As in, cause enough drama that attention got pulled away from his brother and the bride.

"Huh, maybe you guys are doing a good deed after all," my best friend said as we walked up to the shop.

"It's a stretch." Taking a deep breath, I grabbed the door handle and added, "But at least I understand now what he's trying to do."

Stepping inside was an out-of-body experience. Taylor and I had spent the whole morning smacking hunks of metal into shape at school, making progress on the vehicle before the boys subbed in for us in the afternoon. We'd barely had time to stop by my place, take quick showers, and change into clean clothes: denim overalls and a graphic T-shirt for her, and for me my dad-jeans and a pink T-shirt I'd thrown on in an attempt to look girly.

Child's play compared to what greeted us. Not only were the mannequins shaped in a way impossible for living women, but they were decked in confections of fabric and shimmer that, as I squinted against the sunlight cascading through the windows, made me think they were made of frosting. Some were so sleek and tight I didn't think it was possible to walk in them. Others were so long and sprawling, the clerks had to arrange the trains in coils because there wasn't enough real estate in the store to display their full glory. What surprised me was that not all of them were the stark white I'd imagined. There were champagne dresses, off-pink, and many colorful ones.

An attendant jumped from between a couple of massive dresses like a soldier about to ambush the enemy. "Hi! Welcome to Sugar Weddings, what can we do for you?"

"Huh, what a fitting name," I blurted out.

Nonplussed, she said, "Thank you!"

"We're looking for Ellen Young's party."

"Oh, absolutely! We're waiting on a couple of people, but the group is in the back." She whirled around, and her long ponytail slapped her in the back. "Follow me."

Taylor and I walked through the maze of dresses in a haze. A particularly flamboyant one had a price tag of ten grand, and I choked on air.

The whole group was out back, indeed. Ellen and an older woman I guessed was her mom were chatting with a different clerk. A redhead with a backwards cap stood off to the side, chewing gum as she scrolled through her phone. Then there were a couple of girls sitting on a love seat, heads over a catalogue I assumed contained even more fabric monstrosities. Finally, an older lady snoozed in an armchair slightly removed from the main group, the loud chatter unable to snap her awake.

I envied her. I also did not belong here.

What if I just turned around and left? No one would notice.

"There you are!" Ellen's eyes shone as she spotted us. She pushed everyone aside and skipped over to hold my hands. Probably to shackle me in place. "So glad you made it. This must be your best friend."

Even Taylor was a bit nervous about our intrusion. "Yeah, hi. I'm Taylor Schneider, nice to meet you."

"Likewise." Ellen shook her hand before pointing at everybody. "That's my mom, you can call her Mrs. Young because she doesn't like anyone mispronouncing her name. Then my best friend, Peyton, in the baseball cap I'll burn after this. Behind her is my *halmeoni*, she responds to 'Grandma' when she's awake. And those are my cousins Jenn and Hannah. Girls, say hi."

They looked up, and sure enough, the resemblance was there. They gave us wan greetings before going back to gushing about what I figured were their favorite bridesmaid choices.

Basically, this was a family and close friends affair . . . and here we were.

"Are you sure it's okay for us to be here?" I asked the bride-to-be. "We literally met just a week ago, and this is such a private moment."

She smacked me with surprising strength. "Nonsense, you're here because I want you here. Now, let's wait for the last two before we begin."

We got a round of mimosas as we waited until finally, two more girls joined us, so beautiful and stylish they looked like they belonged in the cousins' catalogue. They wore designer clothes from head to toe, manes of hair so perfect they must have come straight from the salon, a cloud of expensive perfume hovering around them.

The most stunning of them said for a greeting, "Okay, the stars are here. Let's get this party started, bitches."

Mrs. Young's face pinched, but the redhead started laughing. "Good to see you, Jess."

Jess responded with, "I imagine it is."

"No love for me?" the other newcomer asked.

Peyton grinned. "Actually, all of it is for you, Gigi. Jess can suck it."

The banter made the bride squeal. She collected all her, uh, bitches into a big group hug before everybody was ushered to different fitting rooms. Taylor and I sat on the now vacant love seat beside the snoozing granny, but next thing I knew I was also pulled by a clerk to try on some dresses.

I hadn't shaved my legs for this and had a second of panic, but when I noticed all the gowns were long, I calmed down.

"The bride's idea," the girl helping me out said, "is that every bridesmaid wears the same shade of burgundy but different styles. We just need to find you the right one."

As I stripped to my skivvies and put on the first dress, I vowed I wouldn't give Sugar Weddings any of my sugar. I'd have to find a nice burgundy dress at a thrift store or some online discount retailer because I couldn't afford anything with so many digits.

Still, I went with the flow. The dress was *pretty*, all right. The kind of thing Cora would wear if she could. The bodice was tight, but the skirt flared around me. I felt like I was missing a tiara.

Taylor agreed. As she snapped pics to send to Maya, she said, "You look hot but also not you."

"Yeah, I look like my sister."

I tried a different one after that. Drapes of silk wrapped around me as though I'd got tangled in bedsheets. Moreover, it was too revealing. Just a glance at the mirror, and I knew the temperature couldn't be any colder than this or I'd be giving everyone something to stare at. And the back plunged down to my waist and made it impossible to wear a bra. I requested a different one and was busy shimmying into it when I heard a commotion outside.

When I finally waded out of the dressing room in a mermaid cut that made me skip more than walk, Ellen was standing on a tall podium in a dress that was perfect for her. The top was tight and lacy, turning transparent around her shoulders, the top of her chest, her back, and down her arms. Below her waist, the dress flared with yards and yards of fabric. One clerk put a matching veil on her hair, and everyone in the room gasped.

"Stunning!"

"Perfection. This is the one."

Mrs. Young fired off some quick words in rapid Korean before bursting into tears. Meanwhile, Ellen's best friend went full photographer despite her dress barely letting her move as well. One of the cousins gaped, and the other one teared up. The two fancy girls were too busy fixing each other's dresses to notice the emotions dancing around the room. They both wore the awful silky dress in a way I'd never feel comfortable with, and I imagined it would be their choice.

"Oh my goodness," Ellen said, bringing trembling hands to her mouth. "This is real."

The Peyton girl got in her face as she recorded a video. "What does it feel like having your dream of marrying your high school sweetheart come true?"

Ellen giggled. "You'll find out soon enough."

"You guys are so cute. I can't stand you." Gigi, one of the fashionable girls, grinned.

I shook my head. This wasn't a scene I was meant to be a part of—maybe not even to experience in my lifetime. My big brother would never get himself a bride. If Cora married, I wouldn't be close enough to join her on the day she tried on wedding dresses. I'd miss the emotions flashing through her face, the happy tears for a love finally being fulfilled in its highest form.

"I have an idea," Ellen said, breaking through my thoughts. "Why don't you all try some wedding dresses? I'm curious to see what your styles are."

Taylor jumped to her feet before anyone else. "I want to get married in a white tuxedo."

"We have a couple you might be interested in," a clerk said, rushing my best friend to a dressing room.

Soon enough, all of us were modeling various shades of white, and even I started to have fun. Taylor and I posed together as though we were a couple, and I found the second super fashionable girl, Jess, giving us an intrigued look.

"I liked the mermaid dress from earlier on you," my friend said. "You should try that style in a cream color."

I shrugged and decided to play along. But as I slipped on a fancy number in my size, I knew if I were to ever marry, it'd be in a dress like this. My heart pinged as I stared at myself in the mirror, flushed from the exertion of trying on clothes as much as from the epiphany I was having. I looked like a bride. All that was missing was the smiling groom next to me.

Suddenly, my mind filled in the blank with the last boy I'd want to imagine in that role, one who had luscious jaw-length hair and a disarming smile.

My breath shook while I stared at myself in the mirror. "What am I thinking? This isn't me." The loud chatter outside drowned out my voice.

I knew I wouldn't experience this for real. Deep in my bones, I knew myself to not be marriage material. I'd never been one of those girls who knew, at age ten, exactly what their wedding gown would look like or what song they'd dance to for their first dance with their husband. I'd never been interested in romance, and what I'd seen of it around me left a lot to be desired. My parents had loved each other once, but it hadn't been enough to fix the chasm politics had carved between them. And my sister and her boyfriend weren't the kind of couple I'd ever look up to. She clung too much to him, and he hurt her feelings too often.

The only love that had stirred my heartstrings had been from movies, and no man on this wide earth cared for acting a fool that way. Therefore, I wasn't interested in acting a fool for a man who made no effort for me.

It was why Malik was a faraway fantasy I could enjoy up close. Gorgeous enough to make certain parts of me quiver, but safe, because he'd never shown any interest in me—so I could continue to pine for him without doing anything about it, and so prolong my comfortable forever-alone existence.

In contrast, Gabe was terrifying. It was easier to imagine something with him when he looked at me like I was made of sugar. Like when we'd danced together.

Suddenly, I needed to get the silky concoction off my body. I twisted and jerked in bursts, trying to undress as fast as possible. I shouldn't have come. I didn't need to see this glimpse of other people's happiness. I didn't need these silly daydreams. Feelings, dating, marriage . . . none of that was part of the plan. Those things were, in fact, distractions from the plan. Those goals people made for their lives went up in smoke the second I became an immigrant and had to start over, relying only on myself.

I wasn't a normal American girl who worried about the same things other American girls did. No, I had those worries too, on top of my own, but I couldn't turn my attention away from the heavy ones for a single second. Not even for a happy second. Or the whole plan could collapse.

And yet when the dress lay pooled at my feet, I glanced at my reflection once more and found tears running down my cheeks. My chest rose and fell with violent gasps, and my whole frame shook.

No, I couldn't afford this dress, just like I couldn't afford love.

CHAPTER FIFTEEN

I was still rattled while driving with Taylor back home, enough to miss the signs of my car acting up until it was too late. "No, no, no," I said as the car started stalling.

"What's happening?" Taylor looked up from her phone.

I noticed the blinking light in the dashboard, right beside my brother's picture. I didn't recognize the symbol, so it had to be bad. Even worse, the car suddenly fully powered off in the middle lane of Alafaya Trail, not far from our college. Someone honked aggressively at us, and soon, every car zooming by joined in.

"Mierda." I groaned, but that did nothing to stop the honking. "This can't be happening."

"Holy shit." Taylor glanced all around, grabbing the handles the way I would if the roles were reversed and she were driving as usual. "What are we gonna do?"

There wasn't enough energy in my tank to respond. All I could do was turn on the emergency lights, but since the honking didn't stop, I wasn't sure they even worked anymore.

I rested my forehead on the steering wheel, quietly sending a prayer to the heavens. Alafaya was one of the main roads in town, and this particular section was busy every day, even early on a Saturday evening. Even without a car stalled in the middle of the road, it was also one of the most dangerous roads thanks to old-fashioned accidents or road rage. The latter explained the continuous, aggressive honking. I had no idea how we were getting out of here unscathed.

Crying was my first impulse, but it was the worst possible moment for it. Cars didn't stop zooming by; walking out to the sidewalk would be impossible. I took the key out of the ignition and put it back in again, wishing I could trick the car into starting. Of course, it didn't work. Then I stepped hard on the gas, since the stick was still on Drive.

Nada.

"Does your insurance cover this?" Taylor asked, expert in car issues of this degree. I shook my head. Unfortunately, I didn't have enough money for good coverage. She deflated. "Do you have a mechanic you trust? I'd recommend mine, but he's been price gouging lately."

Immediately, I thought of Manny, but I hadn't got his number last time. I'd hoped there wouldn't be a second time soon. After all, he'd said my car was definitely worse for wear but probably had a couple more years in it—with more technical words that flew over my head. I was about to be a mechanical engineer, but it didn't mean I spoke *cars*.

If Manny wasn't too busy, maybe he could help, except it meant calling Gabe and putting him in the knight in shining armor position. Not a prospect I looked forward to.

Then a car swerved so close, Taylor and I screamed. Next second, I swallowed my pride and dialed Gabe. It took two tries before he noticed I was calling, probably because he was hard at work at the metal shop with the other guys from the group project.

He picked up, sounding out of breath. "To what do I owe the pleasure of this call, Kitty Cat?"

"I need help."

The extra note of panic in my voice must have been apparent because he dropped the teasing tone right away. "What's wrong?"

I filled him in as best I could. Taylor had to help with exactly where we were so I could convey the information.

"Deep breaths, Cata." Gabe coached me through them for a moment. Then he said, "I'll figure this out, hang in there." The line disconnected.

I wished I had asked him how long we'd have to hang in there. Manny's shop could be anywhere in town, and traffic was getting busier the later it got. I restarted the breathing exercises.

"What if we call the police?" Taylor asked.

"No! I absolutely cannot have a single blip in my record. It could affect my status!" The last word came out in a wail. Oh, Lord. I hadn't thought about that until this second. If the police arrived to the scene on their own and wrote me a ticket that I wouldn't be able to afford—or worse, if this caused an accident that brought the police, and they decided it was all my fault—my prospects of getting a visa could be shot to hell.

"Okay, okay. I'm sorry." Taylor patted my back as I sobbed. "Um, let's talk about something silly to distract us."

"Like what?" I glanced at her through tears that blurred her face, and even then, I could see the deep crease between her eyebrows.

"So, uh. Have you changed your mind about Gabe now?"

Sniffing, I lied. "No."

"Are you sure?" she asked after a pause. "Because Gabe's dropping everything to come get us out of this."

My chin trembled. "Yeah, but he's still a player." I hadn't forgotten how Chris had teased Gabe for the constant parade of girlfriends.

"Is that the only thing that stops you from liking him?"

Yes.

But I wasn't about to open that can of worms in the middle of this mess.

As a saving grace, I added, "Not just that. He's bent on showing me up in school."

"Yeah, but a little competition never hurt anyone." This topic was giving her too much food for thought, going by the way her eyes got lost in the distance. "Besides, wouldn't you downright hate him if he let you win? At least he's not condescending that way and sees you as a worthy rival."

That landed like a bucket of cold water. I'd never thought about it in those terms, since I was focused solely on winning. While he had a better overall GPA than I did, there were a few classes where I'd done better or some exams I'd aced where he'd struggled. I'd always been irritated by the fact he didn't put anywhere near the effort I did but still did better, just coasting on his smarts. But if he were perfect, he would always be on top, and that wasn't the case.

Maybe I'd been wrong all along. Maybe he was naturally better at engineering, but I still gave him a run for his money. I was his worthy rival. The only. Because the third best in our class was quite a few decimals removed.

Understanding this made me both proud and aggravated. I wanted to go back to just resenting him from the shadows, but that wasn't an option now that I'd got so entwined with his life.

As I wiped my face with a tissue I got from my purse, I decided to change the topic. "What are you going to do with this whole Amber situation?" As much as I preferred thinking about my entanglement with Gabe over my stalled car, I didn't want to compound my anxiety. Better to focus on Taylor for a bit.

"Avoid her," she replied with a sigh that blew away her bangs before combing them back into their rightful place. "I think I need to just be by myself for some time to find out what I truly want."

"Sounds good. I support you." I squeezed her hand, and she returned the gesture. "Singlehood never hurt anybody."

"Wait a second." She squinted at the rearview mirror. "Isn't that Gabe's Jeep?"

I shifted around, and sure enough, it was. He drove up slowly in the middle lane, hazard lights flashing, and stopped at a distance behind us, enough that a long-haul truck could fit in. Then he called me.

Fumbling for my cellphone, I noted that fifteen minutes had passed since we'd talked. When I picked up the call, I asked, "Qué carajo estás haciendo?"

"I'm going to come and get you both," was his response. He continued speaking over me. "Stay on the line so I can tell you when."

"No!" I looked all around. Cars kept coming every few seconds. "It's too busy. We're gonna get killed."

"I'll wait until the light's red before cars start to turn onto the road. Unbuckle yourselves and open the doors just a bit."

This was reckless. There had to be a better option. I couldn't think of one, though. It was either run to the sidewalk and abandon my car, wait for the police to arrive, or wait until a distracted driver crashed into us from behind. Or into Gabe, who now shielded us from oncoming traffic.

"Okay," I finally said. "But wait, we need to get to the back seat."

Taylor got the hint and started to contort her way to the back seat. I tossed my purse, keys, and phone back to her before grabbing Carlos's picture from the dashboard. I stuck it in my pocket, and although it would wrinkle, I preferred that to leaving him alone in my junk of a car. In my haste to make it to the back, I slammed my rib cage against the middle console in a way I knew would bruise, but I made it.

We told Gabe we were ready and waited, looking back. His door popped open just a tad, not enough to be a major danger. Any second now, he would jump out, and so would my heart out of my chest.

"Now," he commanded, calmer than I felt.

He jumped out of his car, and so did Taylor and I. We ran back to him as he extended his arms out to us. We didn't even think of disconnecting the call. I slammed against him from one side, and he pulled Taylor against him from the other, peeking to see if cars were coming. There was a lone one just turning at the light, so we dashed to the sidewalk.

I panted, and my legs shook.

"Holy shit," Taylor drew a big gasp. "That was a trip!"

"Are you both okay?" Gabe asked.

He sounded worried, but I couldn't see. My entire weight was propped up by my hands on my knees, and all I saw were droplets falling on the concrete, leaving dark spots that faded quickly under the relentless heat. I didn't know if it was sweat or tears or both. I was afraid of what I looked like right now, so I stayed in that position.

"Catalina?" His voice drifted closer, and suddenly, a warm hand rubbed circles on my back. "It's okay, Manny's on his way with a tow truck. We'll fix this."

"Will we?" I cried, and almost as an out-of-body experience, I saw myself from a distance crouch on the sidewalk and start sobbing like a child. "Really? Because we could've died. And I can't afford to fix it. I can't even afford dying, for that matter!"

Taylor made a tentative sound.

"It's going to be okay," Gabe said beside me, lowering to the hot concrete to sit next to me and pull me into a side hug. "At least you're not alone, right?"

"Yeah." My best friend crouched on my other side and squeezed my shoulder. "We'll stay here with you and get this all sorted out."

As we waited for Manny, every car rushing beside ours shaved years off my life. With a patience I never imagined, Gabe rocked me gently. I was too eaten by worry to snarl at him like I normally would. I might have, in fact, burrowed closer to him.

Taylor preferred the ache of standing still to scalding her ass on the concrete like Gabe and I did, which also made her the first to jump in excitement when a tow truck appeared in the distance.

"Is that it?" she asked, shielding her face with her hand.

"Does it say Martinez on the side?" Gabe pulled me to my feet with not a grunt of effort.

"I think so."

Sure enough, the white truck pulled up from the slow lane, right besides us. Across its cabin, a massive sign saying "Martinez Auto Service" greeted us.

From the driver's seat, Manny's voice called out, "Ay bendito, pero si se están cocinando. Hop in!"

That last command was clear enough to Taylor, and she was the first to get into the back seat. Gabe held the door open for me, as though there was any risk it would close by itself, and I climbed in with the elegance of a boulder.

Meanwhile, as Gabe climbed into the passenger seat, Manny fired off quick instructions for his cousin to help him. Everything went over my head as I sagged against the seat, glad this was finally coming to an end without tragedy.

Manny maneuvered the truck in front of my car, and both boys got out to work, as though there was no risk of a wild Florida driver running them over. I watched them from the back seat the entire time—not because I particularly cared how they treated my car—I just prayed they were safe and quick.

Finally, Manny gave Gabe the thumbs-up, and the latter headed over to his Jeep. My heart twisted with the same feeling I got when I didn't get away with what I wanted. I sat forward when Manny got into the cabin and strapped on his seatbelt, trying to understand what I could possibly not want about Gabe getting in his own car. The empty passenger seat was answer enough.

"So," Manny said, "I'd ask how you're doing, but it's pretty clear."

My face soured.

"Thanks for coming to the rescue. I'm Taylor, Cata's friend from college." She stretched forward to offer her hand, and Manny twisted over to comply. Even in my grey mood, I counted a long moment before they let go.

We were underway, and before I asked anything, Manny explained, "The shop is really close. I'm just gonna drive there and take a look at your car. Sound okay?"

"Yes," I mumbled before clearing my shaky throat. "Absolutely. Thank you so much."

"No hay problema." He flashed me a smile from the rearview mirror. "Hopefully I can help you fix it, or Gaby will kill me."

"Gaby?" I asked, perking up just a tad for the first time.

"He's too pretty for a Gabe."

I almost giggled.

Seeing this, Taylor smirked at me before saying, "Since he's not here, wanna know the nicknames Gabe has at school?"

"Oh, absolutely." Manny's entire being lit up at the prospect.

Taylor scooted closer to the center. "Here's a particularly cringy one—Gabe Everyone's Babe."

Manny made a gagging sound. I couldn't help laughing.

"There's more," she said in an exaggeratedly dark tone. "The other engineering girls call him Grind My Gears Gabe."

I groaned. "Oh my word. I totally forgot about that one." It became popular after the whole module on machine elements, where Gabe had come out with the top grade. "It was followed by the variant Grease My Gears Gabe and hits such as Hot Nerd Gabe and Gabe the Campus Boyfriend." Just saying these made me want to wash my mouth with bleach.

"I've also heard Latin Lover Bae, but really, the one that stuck the most is Gabe the Campus Babe," Taylor finished.

"Don't you have, like, football players to pine over?" Manny asked in a guffaw as he pulled into what unmistakably was the car shop.

Taylor wheezed. "But they're not as pretty as Gaby!"

We got out of the truck in stitches, struggling to get a breath of fresh air in between laughter. That was how the Boricua Bae found us. He parked his Jeep in a spot by the shop's office and walked over, his body taut with the apprehension anyone would feel at the prospect of facing three feral raccoons.

Gabe ran a hand through his hair, slightly damp around his face with the sweat that trickled down his skin. It glinted against the light, and the image struck me. He was a shining knight without armor, coming to the sweaty damsel in distress's help so fast he must have broken the speed limit.

That sobered me. He'd risked himself for me more than once today. It changed everything, and at the same time it didn't. I'd already known he was actually a great guy, but now I could no longer deny it.

Gabe did that funny handshake with his cousin that boys did before turning to us. "C'mon, ladies. The expert's gotta work on his diagnosis, so I'll take you home."

"Wait, I need to give you my number." Despite saying this to me, Manny glanced at Taylor a couple of times as he dictated the digits to me. My friend pretended not to notice, instead combing her bangs away from her damp forehead.

I caught Gabe's look, eyebrows raised. It was clear we'd both seen the same. We shared a smile.

It was at that moment, not while he'd cradled me in his comforting embrace, not while he'd kissed me with reckless abandon against a wall, not as he'd held my hand in front of his entire family, but when we had a reason to smile together, that I knew I was done for.

The instinct I'd had for over three years of steering clear of Gabe Cabrera had been right. He was dangerous. He could easily grab hold of my heart if I let him. And I worried it was already too late to keep myself safe from him.

CHAPTER SIXTEEN

Today I was on my own. Me and my legs.

Maya had left in the early morning for one of the most important practices in her public health career. I didn't want to add to her stress by breaking her routine, especially if I could get a ride from Taylor. The problem was the latter had a doctor's appointment and wouldn't make it to class today.

I'd paced in my room last night until I'd made a trench in the floor. One downside of having focused entirely on the academics portion of college was that I didn't have anyone else to ask a favor like this. Aside from working on a few group projects together, I wasn't close with Adrian and Jasper. At least I did know neither of them lived in my building, so asking them for a ride would be a definite imposition. Stalking Tom and Brandon—the other two guys in my senior design project—online resulted in learning that one of them got around by bike and the other was too hungover from a party to even go to class.

Which left Gabe as my only option. And I'd rather not use that wild card again.

My bank account wasn't healthy enough for a back-and-forth Uber ride. Even a single trip would put me in financial hardship for the rest of the week until my internship check came on Friday. But the off-campus shuttle could get me most of the way, right?

Wrong, because today it was down for unscheduled maintenance.

In the end, I figured walking was the best course of action. With just three miles between the apartment and school, I could at least walk one way and Uber the other. I'd eat cereal for three meals a day the rest of the week. Since the office was about halfway between my apartment and campus, I'd just get a lot of steps in the rest of the week.

It would take me about an hour to walk, considering the streetlights and stop signs on the way, so I got up early and slathered on a thick layer of sunblock. I considered wearing a cardigan to protect my arms from the sun but decided against baking myself. The day was pretty hot, but we weren't in the thick of summer, so it should be no big deal. Class would end near noon, and returning in a car with air-conditioning was a better idea than using that option in the morning. I could put up with a little morning heat.

I put on a baseball cap, shouldered my backpack, and set off.

To say I'd underestimated the weather was an understatement. I'd only made it one block and was debating whether to call in sick to class and go back home. Except if I didn't push through, I would truly end up depending on other people, and that was the entire opposite of who I was.

Putting one foot after the other, I fixated on getting to campus with the same type of determination as an athlete at a triathlon. Sure, I was nowhere near as in shape, but I made up for it with gumption.

As I walked across a zebra path at an intersection, a car nearly ran me over even though I had the green light. I hurried my step, but the man still threw the car forward like it was a bull and I was the poor torero. I took pleasure in flipping him the double bird and carried on.

Safe on the opposite sidewalk, I checked the GPS on my phone and cursed in some colorful Spanish. I still had so much left to go, and I regretted not bringing a water bottle. My throat was parched, my T-shirt was soaked in Cata juice, my skin itched under the heat, and my calves throbbed. I told myself I was being silly. I was from Maracaibo, the City Loved by the Sun. Orlando heat was nothing in comparison to the temperatures of my hometown, which I'd seen reach 120 degrees Fahrenheit and 80 percent humidity.

With that reminder, I pushed on, occasionally checking my phone for progress. I wasn't doing that good on time, and my lack of athleticism slowed me down. If it had been Coralina taking on this challenge, she'd have trotted all the way and made it to school with a healthy glow.

Huffing and puffing, I celebrated the midway point by stopping under the shade of a tree for a breather. My clothes couldn't possibly absorb any more sweat, so I tried to wipe my face with my hands. Up ahead was a Starbucks, but right now I couldn't afford either the expense or the delay. If I didn't hurry, I'd be late for class, and all this suffering would be for nothing.

I picked up the pace, and my vision swam. Maybe this hadn't been my brightest idea.

There was a funny little ache in my chest I attributed to the fact that breathing had become the biggest task of the moment. The UCF Knights monument grew bigger on the horizon. Checking my phone evaporated the hope the monument had given me that I was almost there. A couple of geckos scampered out of my way as I stomped with heavy feet across the sidewalk, an endless string of curses running rampant in my mind.

No doubt this was all because of my abysmal physical condition. Could I even do this again tomorrow? But I had to. I needed to save money to repair my car. Or buy a bicycle.

At last, I set foot on campus with ten minutes to spare. Normally, that would be plenty of time to get to the lecture hall, but at this point I was running on empty. Anyone who paid attention to me would think I was a zombie and another had eaten my brains. I earnestly wished for a golf cart to drive by so I could hail a ride the rest of the way.

Alas.

A few people I vaguely knew walked by, but I couldn't even muster the energy to say hi. I zeroed in on the shade of the building I was headed for, imagining the air-conditioning washing over me. For that alone I had to make it. Plus, my perfect attendance record.

And then I pitched forward. With a jolt, I straightened myself, my heart hammering in my throat at how close I'd seen the pavement. I halted in the middle of the path, wondering what the hell that had been. I was tired, but I didn't think it was to the point of passing out. Or was I?

I shuffled to the shade and almost slammed against the nearest wall. I propped myself up against it and glued my forehead to its coolness. Okay, I was really tired. The kind that seeped into my bones and made them weigh twice as much. But it had only been three miles, and we were technically in spring. My hand fumbled getting my phone out of my pocket. It was all soggy, and I lit up the screen to see the temperature. It read "101F," which meant it had climbed a lot of degrees in the past hour or so.

I slowly slid down to sit on the pavement. Whatever the reason—whether the sun, the heat, or my lack of physical condition—the fact was that my head pulsed to the rhythm of my heart, which was galloping, and I wanted to puke up my breakfast. This felt a lot worse than just the regular exhaustion someone got from exercise.

"Kitty Cat?"

My ears buzzed, and it took me a while to recognize the words. I lifted my head towards the voice. Gabe, Tom, and Brandon approached, looking cool as cucumbers even though Brandon was nursing a hangover and Tom had cycled over.

Gabe broke off from them and joined me. I couldn't stifle a groan.

"You look awful," he said, crouching next to me.

I attempted to say, "Is that how you treat girls?" but it came out more like an inarticulate collection of sounds.

His forehead creased with worry. "What the hell happened?" he asked, daring to touch my clammy forehead.

I lifted a hand to bat it away but failed. Instead, I rolled my head away and grunted, "Walked."

"In this heat?" Gabe recoiled as though he'd been hit, blinking his wide eyes for a moment. "Serás pendeja."

Next thing I knew, he snaked his arms around and under me and lifted me up. I gargled a high-pitched noise, but at that point I was a rag doll.

"No." The word came out as a gurgle.

Gabe ignored that and carried me down the side of the building, in plain sight of anyone walking towards the lecture hall I'd been trying to get to. My cap hit his cheek when I tossed my head over his shoulder, and he grunted.

"Stop squirming."

By that point, I'd gathered enough strength to bite back with, "If you put me down."

Finally, he did, by sitting me on the walkway at the back of the building, conveniently tucked out of sight behind a vending machine. I glued myself to the cool wall with a groan. Meanwhile, he tapped on the machine's panel for a while, and a minute later, bangs went off in the silence as one bottle after another slammed against the bottom of the machine.

"I've seen this before playing baseball, and I think you have heat exhaustion." Gabe crouched before me again with a bunch of water bottles tucked between his arms and chest. He let them drop where they may, catching only one to uncap it. "Here, start drinking slowly."

Heat exhaustion. Holy shit.

"That sounds serious," I rasped out as I accepted the bottle and drank. The cool water felt like knives digging into my sore throat, and yet I couldn't stop. Gabe grabbed hold of it when I was going too fast.

"It can be, when fools like you push themselves for no good reason." I glared at him, and he surprised me by giving me an even angrier look. "Take off your shirt."

"What?"

His brow plunged until he looked truly fearsome. "Not like that. It's so soaked it won't help you cool down anymore."

"No." I lifted shaky arms to hide, I didn't know, I guessed the T-shirt.

Lowering his voice, Gabe said, "I will tear it off if it means I don't have to take you to the hospital, you stubborn woman."

Well, yikes. A hospital bill was not what I needed right now. I jabbed his chest with a weak finger. "Fine, but don't look."

He batted it away. "Stop stalling."

In the end, he had to help me peel it off. My T-shirt fell with a heavy plop to the concrete floor. Gabe sprinkled some water on me, and I shivered as the cool drops hit my skin. A storm still raged in his face while he leaned back to take off his shirt as well, but he didn't leave me enough room to freak out when he started to fan me with it.

I was moved. And also confused.

"You know," I said low and slow, "you could've used a note-book for this."

He grunted. "Less efficient."

The repetitive swoosh of air was soothing. Even though I was a little freaked out that we were half naked in the middle of school, my breathing began to even, and my heart rate slowed. I closed my eyes, not even caring if that gave him ample opportunity to ogle my pink bra from my favorite store, Target. It wasn't like what he saw would interest him anyway, going by his previous girls. They were all so hot—not like heat exhaustion hot.

Those thoughts ground to a halt when I opened my eyes. Gabe crouched in front of me, still fanning me with his clothes. He was built like a dream. Sharp angles and ridges that played with the light while his muscles worked the T-shirt back and forth in the air. His shoulders were wide, and his narrow waist tapered to the hint of a nice V. Moreover, his skin looked softer than mine, except for the fuzz of hair on his chest and down his belly.

My stomach flip-flopped as the image imprinted itself on the back of my eyelids. I didn't think I could dare to open my eyes to face him again without giving away the new direction of my thoughts.

"Never thought I'd see you half naked in these circumstances,"

Gabe said, completely doing away with all our hard work of cooling me down.

I choked on air. "W-what? You thought you'd see me half naked in different circumstances?"

They soaked in the way his shrug made the muscles of his shoulders and arms flex so deliciously.

"I'd hoped so, yeah."

I gaped. Long enough his face shifted into a smile.

My arms tried to cover my chest with not much success. If anything, I brought his attention to it. "Well, don't hope for a repeat."

"Too late; it's not like I'll forget this view anytime soon." I was strong enough now to give him a convincing smack. Except when the palm of my hand connected with his shoulder, a spark traveled through my skin as though there'd been static. Gabe tossed the T-shirt at my face. "Put this on, and I'll take you home."

His cologne became everything I could inhale even as I plucked the fabric away from my face. "No! We have class and—"

"And?" Gabe folded his arms. "Are you planning on attending it in just your bra?" I glanced down at his chest, and he caught on. "Yeah, I'm not going to class shirtless either."

"Won't you thrive in the attention?" I asked in a weak attempt at a joke.

His mouth turned up at one side. "I'm thriving in yours, but I don't look forward to anyone else's right now, especially the lecturer's."

"Stop!" I scrambled to put on his T-shirt because he was right, not only was I not wearing my gross shirt again, I also wasn't showing off my wares to anyone else. The fact he'd caught me ogling him was mortifying enough. "Stop talking, please."

"Fine, I'll stop if you let me freaking help you," he said, his irritation returning. "This is all because your car broke down, right? You could've just asked for a ride."

I shocked myself by replying with a small voice, "Everyone was busy—"

He ran a hand through his hair, messing it. He looked even better that way. "Not me." His eyes bored into mine with intensity. "I'm not too busy for you. Didn't I prove that this weekend?"

He had. And more. He'd shown a willingness to drop things for me that scared me. Or more like, the possible meanings behind it freaked me out. I was much more comfortable considering myself his nemesis than I was with this—this sort of intimacy with him.

Without me noticing, we'd become this close already. I hugged my arms around me, bringing the softness of his T-shirt against my skin.

"Stick those against your skin and follow me." Gabe handed me the two remaining water bottles, let out a heavy sigh, and grabbed our backpacks.

I had no other choice at this point. We attracted eyes wherever we went. Him, unabashedly shirtless, which fortunately for us didn't bring the cops like it would have if the roles were reversed. Me, holding cool bottles against my neck and forehead, a soppy shirt hanging from the loop of my belt.

In his car, Gabe turned the air-conditioning vents towards me and cranked it on. I was about to strap in when he reached over me, which made his shoulder brush against my cheek and lips, and put on my seatbelt.

We rode in silence—away from my perfect attendance. Gabe only spoke again when he dropped me off at home, and only in commands. Drink a lot of water, take a cool shower, sleep, call him if I took a turn for the worse, and he'd drop by in the morning to give me a ride to work. He'd let Jeff know I was sick today, and I didn't need to worry about a thing.

I saved all my energy for after he was gone. Then I burst into tears.

CHAPTER SEVENTEEN

I paid the consequences of my actions for days. A full one flat on my bed with something that felt like a persistent hangover, and the next one suffering the insults fired by my friends at me. Mostly, they were offended I hadn't thought of asking them for help. Maya mentioned, almost casually, that my pride would kill me one day. Taylor cried on the phone as she imagined that very scenario coming to pass.

Chastised enough, I asked them for help.

Maya carted me around for anything related to groceries and essentials, Taylor took me to school, and Gabe made good on his promise of driving me back and forth to work. There was a whole lot of silence going on in those drives with him, a contrast to Taylor as she took me to the car shop for the final verdict on my hunk of junk.

"Tell me the truth." I swallowed and grabbed on tight when she took a particularly violent turn. "Are you being a good friend right now, or is this all for the eye candy?"

"What eye candy?" she asked in a pitch so high the windows didn't shatter only by miracle. And that was answer enough to my question. She grunted. "Oh, stop giving me that look, will you?"

"What happened to being by yourself and learning what you really want in life and all that?"

"Who said I'm not doing that?"

But she combed her hair with her fingers and pinched her cheeks once we parked in the lot of the shop.

I made a sound from my throat and let it go. For now.

Did I want to tell her that she was moving too quick? Yes. But at the same time, I thought of Amber, who'd moved on to her next partner maybe just a couple of weeks after breaking things off with Taylor. And that had been a long while ago. What hung me up was that Taylor was using the logic of "un clavo saca otro clavo," a.k.a. replace old feelings with new feelings, a road that often led to rebounds rather than relationships. But what did I know? I'd never gone through something like this. In fact, I could never even pursue the only serious crush I'd ever had. Maybe I shouldn't judge, and that was why I figured I'd best stay quiet.

Taylor and I walked into the reception area. A girl not much older than us sat at the front desk, her back to the front door while she cleaned up an empty toy cradle. The almost cooing sound from Taylor's throat gave us away, and the girl turned to us with a smile.

"Oops, sorry. I keep getting distracted with my daughter's things. What can I help you with today?"

I cleared my throat. "Yes, Manny recommended I drop by today to talk about my car. He towed it for me last weekend."

"Oh, yeah! He mentioned that." She fiddled around with the documents on the desk like she wasn't used to them. "Sorry, I'm helping my dad out, and he's not exactly the most orderly person. A-ha! Please fill in this form while I go get Manny for you."

I stepped back after grabbing the sheet pinned to a binder and sat in a corner to fill it in with my info. Meanwhile, Taylor and the receptionist were busy becoming the best of friends—to the point where the girl, Toni, as she'd introduced herself, had difficulty tearing herself away to get Manny. My friend looked at the door Toni had disappeared through, not with interest in her but with obvious expectation.

"You're really into him, huh?" I asked in a whisper.

Taylor glanced back quickly, but I didn't miss the blush on her cheeks. "That obvious?"

Before I responded, Toni came back with Manny in tow. I did a double take at the small girl around five years old hanging out on his shoulders like she did this every day. Taylor froze, watching as Manny lifted the little girl up and handed her to her mama. I looked from one to the other.

"Hey, girls." He greeted us with a friendly wave. There was no mistaking the way his eyes returned to Taylor. "Good to see you again."

"Likewise," I said, standing up and handing him the paper.

"Wait," Taylor asked. "Are you guys . . ."

Manny's eyes went wide as saucers. "No, no." He shook his head before he started to laugh. "Toni's my boss's daughter."

"Mama." The little girl tugged at her mom's pants. "I hungry."

"*I'm* hungry," she enunciated. "Y acabas de comer, mi amor."

Her accent perked me up. Distinctively Venezuelan, but a little different from my own. I was debating whether to remark on it when the door leading to the shop opened again and a gorgeous blond guy came in, leaning on a cane as he limped. The little girl pitched herself at him, and he caught her before she made him crash. Must be the father. Except they looked nothing alike.

He made eye contact with me as the kid climbed over his back. It looked like she enjoyed perching on her favorite people. "Oh, this is the owner of the Acura?"

"Yep, that's me," I said, and the fact that he winced could either be because of the situation with my car or because of the kid's nails digging into his neck.

"My friend Sawyer here helped me take a look," Manny said, stuffing his hands in the pockets of his overalls. "At no extra charge. I just wanted to make sure about what I'm going to tell you."

"It's dead," the Sawyer guy said, shrugging.

Manny smacked him. "Dude!"

I sighed, losing some of the tension on my shoulders. I'd come expecting terrible news but hoping for the best. Now that I knew for sure, I could let go of the worry that had been gnawing at my insides.

"Well." Sawyer shifted his weight onto his other leg. "It's not *dead* dead. It's just going to be more expensive to repair than what you probably paid for it. You might as well sell it for scrap and buy a new car."

His friend gaped. "I was going to break it to her gently."

"No, that's okay." I sighed. "Sometimes you just need the Band-Aid ripped off."

Just like I'd been ripped off when I'd bought the car in the first place.

There were a couple restaurants on campus that were hiring.

If I could work at one of them for the rest of the semester, plus the internship and another gig, I could maybe afford another shitty car. But even if I could sustain that pace, would my visa even allow it?

"Well, thank you for helping me out, everyone. How much do I owe you?" I asked.

"Nothing," Manny said.

I looked at the other guy for confirmation, but he was too busy playing with the little girl. She was using one of his very sturdy arms as a swing. Then I looked at Toni. She smiled at me with the same serene kindness she gave to her little gymnast of a toddler.

"This isn't really free, right?" I asked, flustered and stumbling upon my words.

"Um." Manny looked around for help, but none came. With a big sigh, he motioned me to a door opposite the shop's. "Would it be okay if we speak in private for a moment?"

Like a rusty robot, I followed him into a small break room and took a seat at a corner table. He joined me opposite.

"Te voy a ser sincero," he started saying. I braced for something terrible, but instead he said, "Normally it does cost money, but my cousin threatened me with castration if I dared charge you a cent. And after I told you the other time that your car was good for a bit longer and ended up being wrong, he said my professional reputation was on the line. Which, I hate to admit, but he's not wrong. That's why I asked Sawyer to take a look this time too."

My jaw hung. "Gabe did what?"

Manny cringed. "Don't tell him I just spilled the beans. When he says he's going to do something, nothing in this world can stop him."

"He did not!" I accentuated the last word by banging on the table and shooting to my feet. There was a fire starting in my heart in a way Adele would be proud of. "I have told him I don't want charity—"

"Why's that a bad thing, though?" Manny leaned back in his chair to look up at me. "He's doing a good thing for you."

More than a good thing.

Just a few days ago, he was willing to take the clothes off his back to help me. He missed class, subbed in for me at work, and volunteered to drive me around. Almost like a real boyfriend would. And now this?

It was messing with my head. And my heart. And the latter was scarier.

"Yes," I admitted, flopping back on the chair. "Because he's doing too much. I can't depend on him for everything."

"Not *everything*. But you definitely should depend on this and save yourself the money."

We shared a grin over that. I liked Manny. He was practical and had proven as helpful as his annoying cousin. Moreover, he was even more down-to-earth than Gabe. I wished I'd met him instead of Gabe so I could have developed another harmless crush like the one I'd had on Malik, rather than getting tangled in a mess of conflicting feelings for a complicated guy who was bent on proving himself better than my estimations.

"Let me ask you something," I said, folding my arms. "Are you single?"

His eyes bulged. "I—yo, qué?"

I smiled. "Are you single *and* attracted to women? I should clarify because while I don't judge, there's a reason I'm being specific."

"I, no. I mean yes, but Gabe would kill me—" He clammed

up at the look I gave him. I felt as though ice had trickled down
my back and left fire in its wake.

"What does that mean?"

He evaded by asking, "Why do you ask?"

We leveled hard stares on each other, but ultimately, I
decided that tangent wasn't worth pursuing if I wanted to leave
this place with a restful mind.

"Fine, be that way. The reason I ask is because I kinda have
the impression you're interested in my friend Taylor."

Manny's skin was several shades darker than mine, but he still
blushed to the tips of his ears. "Puñeta. Am I that transparent?"

I laughed. "No, that's a good thing. She seems interested too.
So I would like to repay you by giving you her phone number."

"For real?" He leaned forward.

Normally, I would never do this, especially without con-
sulting my friend first. But this was the exact reason Taylor had
made the effort of bringing me here in the first place. If Manny
turned out to be an asshole, I wouldn't need Gabe's help to chop
off his 'nads. After he accepted the payment, we walked out of
the office with smiles on our faces.

"Thank you guys so much for the help," I said like a brand-
new person. "I honestly can't thank you enough."

"You already did." Manny grinned towards Taylor. "And, um,
in any case, it's not me you have to thank."

I'd have to think about that, though. At the rate I was going,
I would owe Gabe my firstborn or something.

We said goodbye to Toni and her daughter, who was now
fast asleep on the blond guy's shoulders. He just nodded at us
for farewell.

As soon as Taylor and I got in her car, she asked what Manny
and I had spoken about. I revealed nothing the entire way back

to my place, though I did make sure to tease her a bit. The crowning moment of this achievement was when, upon safely reaching the parking lot of my apartment complex, she pulled out her cellphone and found a text message from an unknown number that read, Hi, your friend gave me your number. I hope that's okay? It's Manny.

Taylor's face split into a smile so bright that it nearly blinded me. Her fingers moved in a flurry as she typed back, trailing behind me as we walked into the apartment complex.

While she was busy, I stopped by the mailboxes and found a small envelope addressed to me. Frowning, I opened it right away.

To Catalina Diaz,

You are cordially invited to Shenanigans with Ellen's Girls. The events will range from girls-only brunches to spa days, culminating in the bachelorette party two months before the wedding because I have a boring business trip in between. As part of the bridesmaids, you are strongly encouraged to partake of all the free food and booze to be had in said shenanigans.

Please RSVP by texting me

Yours truly,
The Bride

P.S. This isn't just because you're Gabe's fake girl. I truly think you're cool, so I hope you say yes!

Now I also sported a grin to rival Taylor's.

This was a much better way to fulfill my end of the bargain with Gabe. I could easily pretend to be his girlfriend if he wasn't around. And at the end of all of this, I'd have a full-time position. All I had to do was hang in there until the wedding and until graduation, and once I started making my own money, I could buy a car and officially bid him adieu from my mind forever.

With that happy ending now in sight, I texted Ellen saying, Absolutely, I would love to join in the girls' shenanigans.

Let the wedding games begin.

CHAPTER EIGHTEEN

A few days later, we were at a red light on the way to the office when suddenly Gabe cranked up the radio.

"Oh, no. You didn't." I laughed as the familiar rap verse of "Gasolina" started playing, the classic reggaeton song that had launched Daddy Yankee's career ages ago.

Gabe's eyes glinted. Soon, his lips started to form the words, and they spilled out with enough confidence, anyone would think *he was* Daddy Yankee. The people in the car parked beside Gabe's Jeep glanced over, either because they could hear some of the noise or because Gabe's entire body was electrified with the song. I wanted to hide, except I was still laughing.

"C'mon!" He motioned at me to join in for the chorus, where the woman's nasally voice expressed her love for gasoline.

"No way," I said amid guffaws.

"Vamo'!" And then he lowered the windows. The music spilled out onto the street, and then the people in the other car started jamming too.

The light turned green before I could gather the nerve to join in. "You're wild, Gabriel Cabrera."

He grinned. "You need a little fun in your life, Kitty Cat." While he kept his eyes on the road, he missed how that statement made me deflate. "Speaking of, I have an idea."

"Don't tell me you're gonna play 'La Factoría' next."

Gabe gasped. "Should I? But no, this idea is even better."

I didn't even have to ask. We were close to the office, and we were supposed to take a right—right here. Instead, he drove past and took the next turn into a McDonald's.

"Gabe . . ."

"What? I'm feeling peckish. All the singing, you know." After joining the drive-through line, he fished around for his wallet in the back pocket of his pants. "Are you a chocolate or a vanilla person? Or both?"

"Oh, I'm okay. I'm not hungry." I folded my arms. It wasn't so much that I was or wasn't hungry, more like I couldn't afford to waste a penny.

His eyes widened in an exaggerated way. "Wait, I never said I'd buy you anything. It was just a question to get to know you better. Fake dating and all that."

I gave him a skeptical look, but he prodded me with his elbow. To distract myself from the remains of his warmth against my skin, I said, "Fine, I'm a chocolate person."

"Me too!" Right at that second, we made it to the ordering area, and Gabe lowered the window. "Two chocolate ice cream cones, please."

"Gabe!"

"What? They're both for me." He laughed.

My heart fluttered, and I had to use all my willpower to

appear serious and unaffected. "Yeah, right. I'm sure you're gonna double-fist while driving."

"Ah, I've been caught." Sparks danced in his eyes. "I've been called talented, but I'm not *that* talented."

I smacked his arm. "Anyway, I'll Venmo you for it when we get paid." I had to, because even though my financial situation was pretty dire right now, I couldn't continue accruing debt to Gabe.

He waved a hand. "Just buy me another one next time."

Those last two words echoed in my mind. He sounded blasé about it, but I couldn't allow him—or myself—to think that such things were for granted. Nothing good lay down that road.

A few minutes later, we were exiting the parking lot, twin ice cream cones in our hands. As I took a big bite out of it and chewed in the least feminine way possible, I said, "This is still a fake relationship, you know? I'm not gonna fall for you just because you feed me ice cream."

He choked. With tears trickling out of his eyes, he managed to say, "Wouldn't dream of it."

As soon as we got to our desks, I dumped all my belongings and sequestered myself in the women's restroom. It was the most legitimate place to hide. I was still shaky from the sugar rush from the ice cream. And from the look on Gabe's face when I'd reminded him what our relationship really was.

He'd wanted to say something else. It was obvious with the way he glanced at me every few seconds, opening and closing his mouth around air and not around his cone. I'd played oblivious the entire time, too afraid to hear whatever had him in knots.

Pff, forget it. You and I could never happen, came to mind.

Another option was, *And what if I don't want this to be fake anymore?* Which was a lot more nonsensical, and yet this was the option that had tingles running up and down my body.

I slammed my hands on my cheeks and spoke to my reflection in the mirror. "Acuérdate de por qué estás haciendo esto." I was doing this for the full-time position and the visa that came associated with it. Everything else was just a side quest.

With that reminder, Maya's words from weeks ago returned to me. Did I really want to achieve my goals dependent on Gabe's whims? I wasn't like that. I was a go-getter. Someone who carved her own path and didn't let others define her. If I wanted this job, I had to make it mine on my own terms.

She'd been right all along. Why did I need to put myself through this emotional roller coaster for something that was completely unrelated? I had to take matters into my own hands somehow.

I rushed back to my desk and pulled up Jeff's Outlook calendar. I booked him in for a meeting towards the end of the business day to talk about my prospects. In minutes, he had accepted the invite, and my knee started bouncing. It didn't stop for hours.

Close to the time of my meeting with Jeff, Gabe picked up his laptop and disappeared from his desk. This had the curious effect of making me breathe easier. Out of sight, out of mind, they said, and that meant the guilt I felt around him also lessened. Thanks to this, I was cool as a cucumber when I met Jeff at a conference room.

"I appreciate you taking the time to meet me on such short notice," I said, settling a notepad and pen before me in case there was anything noteworthy.

"Oh, no problem! We actually haven't had a one-on-one in

a while—my bad." He clasped his hands on top of the desk and asked, "So, what did you want to discuss?"

I drew a blank for a second. I wished someone had given me lessons on how to address situations like this. Just wanting to talk about my career with someone who had a lot of say about it, in a way that was assertive but not aggressive—or worse, desperate, which was exactly how I felt. The conversation hadn't even started, and my heart rate was already through the roof.

"So," I started, drawing out the word for longer than was natural while I tried to give myself time to think, "I know that you guys are considering one of us for the full-time position after the internship, and, well, I wanted to know how I stack up and how I can improve to be the best candidate."

Was that too blunt? Did I show my cards too early? I wasn't digging at Gabe that way, was I? Because I didn't want to come across as a cutthroat individualist who couldn't be a team player. At the same time, I wanted to sound modest but not downplay my accomplishments so far. Had I even had accomplishments so far? I couldn't think of a single highlight I could brag about.

Suddenly, I felt like I was getting too ahead of myself, especially as Jeff sat there, blinking as though his CPU had a hard time processing my question.

"Oh." He cleared his throat, but his voice was still high as he continued. "You're great, excellent performance! I'll be absolutely honest, though. The reason it's so hard to choose for Marty and I is because you both are the best interns we've had in years—don't tell anyone I said that. We definitely want to keep you both, but we only have one placement."

"Right." I nodded, prompting him to give me more intel.

"To be honest, there isn't much you can possibly improve that you aren't already doing well." I would glow at the praise, except I sensed a *but* in that sentence. Sure enough, Jeff said, "But the decision is Marty's. I've already given him a full report on you both that he'll use to draw his conclusions."

Marty. He who barely showed his face to the interns, since he considered us far below his station.

My knee started to bounce again when a terrible thought occurred to me. Assuming Gabe and I were pretty much tied in performance and potential, there were two distinct things that differentiated us. One, he had a penis. Two, he had an American passport.

Addressing the first point in a department full of men, half of whom were around Papi's age, was a surefire way to be labelled as hysterical and not the right fit for an engineering company. STEM wasn't exactly a field renowned for its excellent inclusion of women and minorities, both of which I was.

The second aspect, I could ask about. I *had* to ask, in fact.

"Jeff," I started, taking a moment to find the right words. How I asked him would have an impact on his willingness to help me. "Um, does the fact I need a work permit sponsorship affect my odds of being selected?"

He shook his head even before I finished the question. "Absolutely not. The legal team has given us the okay for that possibility."

Okay, great. That had to be a sign there was interest in keeping me in the company. The sigh of relief that came out of me deflated me.

"You don't know how much this means to me," I admitted, pressing my lips tight to hide the sudden quiver.

"I understand." Jeff gave the kind of small smile that softened his face and almost made him look like a young Santa Claus, with his bald head and extremely blond beard.

We chatted about other things, somewhat skirting around what we had just discussed as though we were both equally uncomfortable. But I'd got some good information, and we both left the meeting room with smiles on our faces.

I felt better about everything. If I could just focus on doing a stellar job and making it clear to Jeff and his boss that I was the best choice, then I wouldn't feel so guilty about whatever happened with Gabe. Success would be achieved by the right means. And meanwhile, I could continue with our silly fake-dating plan as insurance.

Besides, Gabe would be fine. With his dangly bits and American citizenship, the world was his oyster. Odds were high that he knew it.

Speaking of, as soon as I headed back to our desks, I heard Gabe's laughter drift towards me. When I cleared the rows of cubicles, I noted the reason for the hilarity wasn't the accounting interns this time, but Marty.

The older man patted Gabe's shoulder like they were buddies, shooting the shit in the middle of the office. They saw me staring, which made me feel like I'd been the one caught doing something out of the ordinary during office hours.

"Hi," I squeaked out.

Marty's face sobered up, although it wasn't like he seemed hostile upon my appearance either. "How are you, Catalina?" he asked.

I'd never felt quite as comfortable around him as I was around Jeff, which was too bad because this was the guy to impress. I tried to give a calm, friendly smile and responded with, "Very good, and you?"

"Good, good. Talking with Gabriel here about how much you guys like ice cream."

I shot the boy a look that probably spoke volumes. In return, Gabe gave me a bright, childlike smile.

Marty patted him once more. "Anyway, I'll let you guys go home. It's getting late."

We sent him off with polite farewells, and I waited until he was out of sight to round on Gabe. "What did you say to him?"

"Nothing." Gabe lifted his palms up in the air. "He's the one who brought up wanting to have something cool to deal with the changing weather, and I recommended ice cream."

Narrowing my eyes didn't get any other information out of him, so I started packing up my things. "Fine, be all chummy-chummy with the big boss behind my back and laugh at my expense."

Gabe had the nerve to chuckle. "Is that what you think happened?"

"Sure." I zipped my backpack up with such strength it was a wonder I didn't rip it out. "Forgive me for drawing obvious conclusions."

Gabe shook his head but hastened to grab his things and join me at the door. He used an ominous tone of voice to say, "One day you'll learn to trust me."

"That day won't be today," I said as we headed to his red Jeep, which sounded silly coming from someone who was bumming rides off him every day.

I walked around his car to the passenger side and stopped in my tracks. The car parked next to it had a massive red bow on top. Who would even drive with something like that on the roof of their car?

Two people jumped out from behind the car. I screamed and bumped into Gabe, who was right behind me. He grabbed my shoulders and held me firm as the two people attacked me with . . . confetti?

That was when I looked at them properly. It was Taylor and Maya.

"What the . . ."

No further words came out as both my friends embraced me, and since Gabe hadn't let go, in a way he was hugging me too. Which was all too much because I didn't understand what was going on.

"We got you a gift," Maya said, pulling back to point at the massive bow.

"What am I supposed to do with a bow?"

All three of them laughed. And laughed. My brain began to kick into gear, and I finally understood it wasn't the bow they were giving me but the whole-ass car beneath it.

"No!" I shouted, trying to back away.

Gabe whispered in my ear, "Yes."

"I—I . . ." I was still sputtering as Taylor put the keys in my hand.

Gabe pushed me gently towards the car. It was a Corolla that had seen better days, and not just because the grey paint was peeling off and revealing some rust in places. I didn't care about that, though. If it turned on and freed me from being a burden on all these people, it'd work out just fine.

"Don't get too excited," she said. "Manny helped us recoup some money from parts of your old car and found this one. It's kinda shitty and will probably kaput soon, but we hope it can tide you over for a bit."

"Until you're able to buy yourself a Cadillac," Maya said with a grin.

Picking up on that, Taylor said, "Or a Bentley."

"Or marry a guy with a fancy ride," Gabe said. All three of us glared at him. "Okay, okay. I get it. Feminism."

Turning back to the girls, I whispered, "Thank you. You didn't have to do this."

"We wanted to," Taylor said, chucking a light punch at my shoulder.

"How much do I owe you all?" I glanced among them.

To my surprise, Maya turned to Gabe. "If you hold her down, I can kill her."

"It's a gift, you daft woman." Taylor pointed at the car. "That's why we put this massive bow on it."

"No takebacksies," said Gabe. "Unless you really enjoy my company. I'm fine if you want to keep being my copilot."

I tested the remote button, and the locks opened with a satisfying click. Even better, the doors actually opened. Giving him a grin, I said, "Nah, I'm good with this development."

Later, I learned that the three of them had pitched in a little extra beyond the scrap money. They didn't want to reveal how much they'd raised to purchase it, but when I was working on the documentation to circulate with the car, I saw it had cost slightly more than I'd chucked out on the old Acura. Even though now I was free to roam around town by myself, there was no doubt in my mind that without these people in my life, things would have been much harder. And unexpectedly, that included Gabe.

CHAPTER NINETEEN

Shenanigans One was communicated via text message in the middle of the week. The bride informed her collective of women that the weekend weather would be perfect for a pool party, and thus she invited everyone to the pool at the Cabrera household.

Better yet, there would be no men in sight.

The catch? The groom's mom would be in attendance.

In Gabe's opinion, it was the perfect opportunity to start pissing Mrs. Cabrera off and drive her attention away from Ellen. For once, I agreed with him. Ellen had been so nice to me, and if I could repay her kindness with this, I was all for it. It was dangerously fun to brainstorm with Gabe about ways to become the villain at this pool party. Mostly his ideas came from his past girlfriends' attempts at impressing the mother-in-law and blundering it beyond redemption.

The afternoon before the party, we were at the office grabbing coffee as he reminisced. "This one time, one of them brought homemade mac 'n' cheese for a Puerto Rican Thanksgiving."

"That's not terrible," I said, blowing steam off my cup. Work had been a chore today, and we both needed the pick-me-up of caffeine to make it until clock-out.

"I guess not, but Mom was making a whole roast pig with naranja agria, and she felt like American cuisine was an insult to her efforts." His eyes got lost in the horizon. "Then there was another one who kept trying to talk me up to Mom and mistook her silence for interest, which for some reason made her think it was okay to say I had good moves in bed."

I choked on a sip of the hot brew, and I was definitely awake now. "No!"

Gabe cringed. "I wish it were a lie. Oh, and there was another one who told Mom she wanted to give me twenty children."

"There's a worrying pattern here." I put a hand up to stop him in his tracks. "If by chance you're suggesting I brag about sexual exploits to piss your mom off, while yes, it's the easy way to do it, I won't."

The way he smiled made me nervous. "Okay, fine. I guess you can just insult her cooking. That riles her up real bad."

"Is it bad? Because if it is, I'll be more willing to use this alternative."

"No, she's excellent." Gabe shrugged as we started heading back to our seats. "Honestly, you don't need help from me to get on her bad side."

"The hell is that supposed to mean?"

Was he implying I was insufferable? Because if so, I would have to pull out a mirror and place it in front of his ridiculously handsome but irritating face.

My outrage made him laugh. "No, she's just that eager to hate anyone I could possibly choose. You'll be fine."

—

Famous last words, I thought then and now, as I drove my brand-new old car to Gabe's house. Or technically his mom's. It wasn't far from Gabe's grandmother's—where the now infamous cookout had happened—in the south suburbs of the city. During the days when he'd been chauffeuring me here and there, he'd been traversing town, passing the school and heading farther north to where I lived to pick me up and make a U-turn back to the school or the office. It had been a lot of effort. Knowing that, plus everything else he'd done, had given me a new determination to be the worst possible girlfriend his mom could ask for.

Taylor had had far too much fun the night before helping me brainstorm my girlfriend persona. Her first suggestion had been to be a high-maintenance kind of girl, all bling-bling and air in my head. From the background, Maya had suggested I had too much stuffing in my cranium to pretend having none. I'd thanked her for the praise, though by the look on her face she hadn't meant it that way. In the end, I decided to be an augmented version of myself. Finicky. Picky. A stick-in-the-mud.

I parked by the curb near the house and hauled up a massive duffel bag with everything anyone could possibly need for a pool party. Sunblock, lotion, three towels, two changes of clothes and two pairs of chancletas, my own snacks and drinks, and a whole selection of books.

The front door was open like there was no crime in the neighborhood. I guessed that was a good thing, but these reminders of how different things were back home always jarred me. I glanced this way and that, as if asking for permission to enter, but the house was empty. Rather than overstepping, I walked around the outside, following the sounds of voices coming from the backyard. I didn't know what Gabe's parents did for a living, but their house was huge and well kept. It even looked like it'd been repainted recently. The landscaping had nothing to envy from the mansions in Winter Park, and when I finally made it to the back, the pool made my jaw drop.

It could be used for training for swim competitions with how long it was. A dozen lounge chairs circled it. They'd placed a bunch of large shades in between, so if people didn't want to toast under the sun they could still partake of the heat. Off to the side, there was a wooden gazebo with a grill, which was where the groom's mom stood, tossing meat over the fire. There was a table next to her, overflowing with buns, sauces, and every sort of stuffing one could imagine. It almost felt like I was back in my hometown, watching the street sellers of burgers and hot dogs stack them sky-high with anything the customer requested.

There were only women, all right. While I recognized some faces from the wedding gown fitting were hanging out in a big group in the middle of the yard, there were also about ten more I didn't know. The attendees ranged from girls as young as ten all the way to Chris's and Ellen's grandmas.

"There you are!" Ellen waved me over. She'd been talking with a thirty-something woman who was just a couple inches taller than Ellen. Which was to say, not very tall either. "Let me introduce you to Magdalena, Chris and Gabe's older sister."

"Oh." I wiped my clammy hand on my T-shirt and extended it to her. "Nice to meet you, I'm Catalina. You can call me Cata."

It was eerie seeing a woman with Gabe's exact eyes. They twinkled as she shook my hand. "I've heard all about you. Kitty Cat, right?"

I wrinkled my nose.

She grabbed my arm in that way only Latinas could, as if

she was never letting me go because we'd already become best friends. It wasn't a hardship to sit with her by the pool after slathering on enough sunblock to look like a ghost, showing off my black one-piece swimsuit in the fashion of a little girl in swim lessons, and just talk about nothing with someone who found as much enjoyment in making fun of Gabe as I did.

An hour later, while I lined up for burgers, Ellen's fashionable friend Jess stood behind me. Boldly, she said, "Please let me take you shopping. You're too hot to wear this hideous thing."

That made the other girl, whose name I recalled was Gigi, start laughing to the point of choking. "You're getting so much better at compliments these days."

"Too bad Peyton's not here to agree," the bride said.

"Where's she at?" I asked her. The redhead had seemed the most level-headed of the bunch to me.

Ellen was just about at the front of the line for her mother-in-law to toss a patty at her plate, but she still answered. "Her boyfriend has an important game tonight, and she wanted to be there for him."

I was going to ask for more details when Gabe's mom barked the word, "Next," and it was Ellen's turn. When it was mine, and I approached the grill up close, the grease dripping down from the meat made my stomach churn. It wasn't even acting when I asked her, "Is the meat low-fat?"

The woman's brow plunged until her eyes looked like thunder. "If you're going to be necia like that, go eat a salad."

"Maybe you're right."

Feathers successfully ruffled, I pulled my plate towards me and left my spot in the line. I put together a burger stuffed with anything but the greasy patties that looked like they'd been cooked in motor oil. An hour or so after lunch, when Mrs. Cabrera offered to get drinks for everybody, I asked her if she had alcohol-free beer. Later, I complained that the pool water was too chilly for me, and after that, that the sun was too hot.

It was, but what burned me wasn't the sun's rays but the power of Gabe's mom's glare.

After a while, Magdalena and I headed into the house to drink some water, like the only two responsible people in the house who didn't want nasty hangovers tomorrow. I asked her for the restroom, and she directed me to the one upstairs, which was likely cleaner than the one on the ground floor. I had this bizarre feeling of invading Gabe's private space as I headed upstairs, even though he wasn't the only one living there. In the past few hours of shenanigans, I'd learned that Chris still lived at home per his mom's command. The whole thing about couples living together before marriage was grounds for dismembering, in very Latin American fashion.

No one made any mention of Gabe's father, though. The wall by the stairs was adorned with framed pictures testifying to their family history. I caught sight of a handsome man who showed up here and there in pictures where the three siblings were still children, and he disappeared as they grew older. My heart pinched. There was probably a painful story there, and I was familiar with those.

Only when I walked out of the restroom did I notice the door right across from it had a sign that read GABRIEL. Off to the right, another door read CHRISTOPHER. There was also a door with Magdalena's name emblazoned on it.

Bouncing on my tippy-toes, I checked that there was no one nearby and pushed Gabe's door open. Now I was intruding for real, but I couldn't stop myself.

Gabe's bed was full-size with navy-blue bedding that looked soft and plush to the touch. I didn't know what I'd been expecting the rest of his room to be, though, because I was surprised at the clutter. He presented himself so competently and efficiently at school and at work. But his walls were covered in posters of cars and motorbikes, with pictures in frames that didn't match next to each other.

I hovered over his desk to get closer. There was a whole section of pictures from a baseball team, and it took me a minute to make out the face of middle-school Gabriel among them. He had the same cheeky smile of someone who ate the world on a daily basis.

"Qué haces aquí?" a voice accused.

I screamed in alarm. Whirling around, I found Gabe leaning against the doorframe, arms folded as he made no effort to hide the fact he'd been checking me out. That was when I remembered I'd gone on this entire quest in my one-piece swimsuit and nothing else.

"Not that I'm complaining." Gabe picked himself up and strolled into the room. His eyes swept over the front of my body from head to toe, like he'd no doubt done when I'd been turned around. "This is better than any of my fantasies."

I smacked his arm, but it wasn't enough to pull him out of the gutter. All it caused was a smirk.

"You don't need to act like a pervert."

"Hard not to when you're standing half naked in my bedroom."

I crossed my arms over my chest in an attempt at modesty. "Wasn't this party supposed to be girls only?"

"It was. Until the drinks started to run low and the bride-to-be called for reinforcements." His smile touched his eyes, even as he struggled with keeping them at the level of mine. "So, what brought you to my room?"

I pursed my lips but fessed up. "Curiosity."

His eyebrows went up. "And? What did you find?"

"You played baseball?" It was the first thing that came to mind.

Gabe took a step closer. "I did, up till middle school."

When I realized we'd suddenly got too close, I took a step back that took me right up against his desk. It was so cool against the skin of my thighs that I jumped forward and fell right into his arms. I tried to pull away, but he embraced me like he'd wanted me there all along.

I glanced up at his face. Amusement played there, as though this were a game. But there was something else. Something that made heat pool in my belly and shivers raise goosebumps all across my skin.

One of his hands traveled up and down my bare back, slow and steady, as though he was trying to ignite a fire in me to chase the cold away. The sensation was intoxicating. Scary. Wonderful. I leaned into it even as a part of my mind screamed at me to run from the intimacy.

"Why?" I whispered, just to keep my mouth busy instead of doing what it suddenly wanted to do.

There was no way I was going to kiss Gabriel Cabrera in his bedroom while he was fully clothed and I was almost not.

"Because Chris got injured playing ball." Those sparkling eyes of his were trained on my lips as he spoke. "He's the one who loved the game. Wanted to have a future in it. Losing that was hard on him. I didn't think it was worth committing to something so risky, especially when I wasn't so into it."

I tried to pour a cold bucket of water on him by asking, "Is that why you can't commit to relationships, then? You're afraid of getting hurt?"

His eyes came up to meet mine, and for a long moment he said nothing. His body had grown tense, but he still didn't release me. Instead, he lifted a hand to brush away a damp strand of hair from my face.

"Who isn't?" he asked, tilting his head lower. "Aren't you?"

Deathly.

I was so afraid of getting hurt that I'd never tried to get close to a guy. And now I was far too close to the most dangerous of all—and it felt good. The way I fit against him, how his arms held me tight, the way the baritone of his voice washed over me like a mantle of warmth. The way his eyes raised my pulse and set aflame my nerve endings. He could crush me if I let him. He could crush my heart if I let him.

"Very," I admitted.

"Of me?" When I didn't respond, the shadow of a smile twitched his lips. "But why? This is all pretend, isn't it?"

It was. It wasn't. I wasn't sure anymore. The challenge in the depths of his eyes was the last thing I wanted to face. It was much safer to distract him from this conversation, and I let instinct lead the way.

I breached the remaining gap between us like I knew what I was doing and pulled him in for a kiss that felt illicit. Gabe molded me against him with surprising ease. Without breaking the kiss, he lifted me up from the back of my thighs so I sat on his desk. Nestling himself in between my thighs, he wrapped my legs around his waist until I could feel the evidence of his interest. He curved his torso against mine to better access my mouth, and it was so perfect we both groaned. He fisted my hair, pulling my head back with gentleness that his lips didn't show.

His tongue made a bold sweep against mine that tore a sound from my throat I didn't recognize as mine.

When the need for air overtook us, Gabe's lips traveled down my neck. His hands cupped my sides, dangerously close to my breasts. He pushed me back to lap at the skin at the base of my throat, sucking in a way I felt all the way to my toes. Vaguely, I wondered if losing my mind should feel so mind-bogglingly good.

And then a scream tore us apart. Before I could react, a chancla flew our way.

Gabe intercepted that one with his head, but he caught the second chancla in the air.

His mom stood at the door, her face red-hot with rage. "Te dije que no trajeras putas a esta casa!"

I froze.

Gabe shielded me from his mom. "Cata no es una puta! She's my girlfriend."

"With you that's one and the same!" she spat out. "You're going to end up worse than your siblings if you keep this up with one tramp after the next! What if you get her pregnant, huh? *Outside of wedlock!*"

The way his body tensed told me something nasty was about to spill out of his mouth. Something he was going to regret. Trembling, I grabbed a fistful of his T-shirt and said, "It's okay."

His eyes blazed as he looked back at me. "It's not."

"I want her out of this house right this second!" The woman screamed the words until her throat gave out.

It wasn't okay. I wasn't okay. My eyes welled up. We'd both set out to do this, to piss off his mom so much she exploded, and we'd sure accomplished it with a bang.

Gabe surprised me by holding my hand, even as his mom shouted all sorts of epithets at me. He held it even as we made it downstairs and I picked up my things. And even as I bid farewell to the bride, and even as he walked me to my car.

Neither of us knew what to say. Suddenly, what we'd done felt too real.

CHAPTER TWENTY

The bone-deep embarrassment over the incident with the flying chanclas took about a week and a half to abate. Fortunately for me, I didn't have to be in close quarters with Gabe as frequently as when I'd still depended on him to get to places. At school, we sat at opposite ends of the classroom. During the times our project group worked together, we made sure to occupy different workbenches to let all our feelings out on helpless metal pieces.

Things were trickier at work. Jeff paired us for a lot of projects where we had no choice but to keep it professional. There was a lot of eye contact avoidance, especially on the first few days after that weekend. I decided to book a meeting room for the day whenever there was any availability to avoid sitting in close quarters with him, wrapped up in the most uncomfortable silence of the century.

A conversation neither of us wanted to have was looming. My portion of it went something along the lines of, *Dear Gabriel, stop invading my waking thoughts and my dreams with your decadent kisses. Let's keep this strictly professional, please and thank you.*

The predominant part of me, which since high school had stayed focused on school as my sister and friends got together with boys, was now being replaced by the desire Gabe had awakened in me. It made it hard for me to focus in class and at work. I'd been missing out on something transcendent, the connection you could have with someone else while being so vulnerable in their arms. And more. More that I now was curious about.

But curiosity killed the cat, and Gabe himself made sure to remind me every so often that I was one such Kitty Cat.

It was much easier to avoid him completely than to deal with what might be happening between us. I didn't know which possibility was more terrifying, one where he said that yes, he felt it too, or one where he apologized for having momentarily lost his marbles and said that he wanted to take everything back.

Two weeks after the incident, after I'd finished working on a PowerPoint presentation the team urgently needed for an afternoon meeting, I dashed out of my meeting room hideout and almost smacked right into Gabe. We only managed to avoid squashing our laptops between us by a miracle, and our eyes found each other's for the first time in days.

I was happy to not be the only one feeling out of sorts. He uttered, "Uh."

"Ah, sorry. Gotta go." I ducked away and headed towards Jeff's cubicle. My heart hammered in my throat. "Jeff," I said in between pants. "Presentation's done, want to look it over?"

He tore himself away from his work and motioned me over. We were sitting together, going over the finer details, when Marty showed up to ask about precisely this project. His own manager was bugging him about it, and for the first time in the almost a year I'd been a part of the team, he sat with us to evaluate what I'd done. We bounced ideas off each other, incorporating even my feedback in a way that made me feel like I finally belonged.

Marty looked at me like he was taking in my features for the first time. "Great job here, Catalina. Are you busy after this? I think it would be a good idea if you joined the meeting."

My chest puffed up, and of course I joined in. They made sure to inform everyone during the meeting that I was the one who'd put the analysis together, and it even got me some praise from partners across the ocean. I was pretty sure I blushed a little as I thanked them all for the feedback.

This was how it had to be done. If I wanted to work here, it had to be earned through efforts like this. I returned to my desk feeling completely energized. Jeff had said this could turn into an interesting project for me. I couldn't wait to tackle the challenge.

I was torn between bragging to Gabe and just wanting to share the news. He was in a conference call, though. I set my laptop back in the docking station and noticed an envelope lying over my keyboard. It was a thin, simple one, but some words in the sender's field caught my attention. I opened it and pulled out the letter.

I skimmed through the top until I got to the main message. *Your visa extension has been denied.*

For a second, I wondered what this was about. I hadn't applied for any visas. I'd applied to renew my current OPT, and that wasn't the same.

My eyes flew across the page again. And again. There was a case number listed on the sheet. With trembling hands, I fired up my laptop and clicked through until I found the folder with the documentation for my application. I put the letter right up next to the screen so both case numbers lined up perfectly, and . . .

They matched.

I developed tunnel vision as I went over each digit again. And again. And time and again they matched.

A weird, gargled sound came out of my throat. A sob? In the middle of the office? There was the unmistakable sensation of hot pressure against my eyes. My lungs seized with the desire to scream. All I could see was the number on the screen. All I could feel was the letter crumpled in my fist. A voice vaguely penetrated through the fog in my brain, but I pushed against it. I was breaking down right there and then.

Instinct made my feet move. One after the other, until I made it out of the building and into the parking lot. I weaved through the cars until I crouched behind a tree. Tucking my face between my legs, I finally screamed.

It was a single shout that came from the deepest part of me, the part full of fear. The one that drove me to never be alone at night. To not trust anybody. The one that woke me up drenched in sweat with nightmares about my brother, about what could happen to my family. The same part that knew, for a fact, that if I had to go back to my home country, I would not be able to grapple with what it had become. The same part that craved safety and stability, all the possibilities I had just lost with this letter.

Everything blurred around me, and I drew hasty gasps, tears streaming down my face and dripping from my chin onto my clothes. I hugged myself because I was all I had, and somehow, I'd let myself down. Everything I'd worked on for four years crumbled around me right there. It was a wonder the debris of my dreams didn't flatten me against the earth.

"Cata."

The single word speared through the haze in my brain, but I wasn't able to cling to it. Maybe I had imagined it. It was a struggle to breathe; I couldn't fathom any other part of my body working properly, let alone my ears.

And then I felt somebody hug me. It wasn't just my own arms around me anymore. I fought the embrace off, but in the end, I needed to focus on breathing more than that. Eventually, my eyes were able to focus on the grass I sat on. On the damned letter that lay crumpled beside my thigh, where I'd dropped it. On the white shirt encasing the arm of whoever held me. My other senses began to open up then, my nose registering the familiar scent enveloping me, the warmth around me.

"Gabe," I sobbed.

He hushed me, running a hand up and down my back. "I'm here. You're not alone."

He repeated that last sentence again and again, as though he knew that was exactly what I needed to hear. He didn't even balk as I unraveled in his arms. I hit his chest as though everything had been his fault, crying, screaming with much more violence than I had when my car broke down and the prospect of financial ruin was so close.

This was so much worse. This was *everything* falling apart.

It got progressively darker around us. Cars started and drove away as the day wound down for the employees and they returned home. Today, for the first time, I'd felt so close to becoming one of them. Now it would be impossible.

"What happened?" Gabe finally dared to ask, after the panic attack had ebbed away and I slumped against the trunk of the tree. I felt like I had on the day I'd got heat exhaustion, just barely able to lift my arm to give him the letter. In the waning afternoon light, he read the contents, scanning them twice for good measure. "What does this mean?"

My voice was raspy as I responded. "In two months, my

student visa expires. I'll barely be able to graduate before being kicked out of the country."

The beam of a car in the parking lot illuminated the frown on his face. Gabe shook his head. "But how?"

"No sé," I said, stuttering through the words. "I did every-thing right, and yet . . ." And yet I'd been denied. The letter didn't say why, but there was no sugarcoating the facts.

"Can you appeal?"

I rubbed the ache that had settled in the middle of my fore-head. "There . . . there's no appeal process. I checked."

"And Jeff?" he asked, grasping at straws. "Can't they do something here?"

I looked up at him, unable to feel anything but grief. "They'd have to hire me right now, and even then, getting a work permit would take months. I'd have to leave the country for sure and . . . and . . ." I swallowed with difficulty. "I'd have to go back to Venezuela to follow through with the process."

"Then what?" He sounded almost angry. "Are you just going to have to leave?"

I didn't answer. There was no need. The facts were that, even in the best case scenario where Jeff and Marty decided to start the hiring process right now—which might not even be possible before I had my degree—it would still take months before we knew if the work permit application had been successful. And from what I understood, that was even more of a lottery than this student work permit extension typically was.

I should've been a shoo-in. My grades were stellar, my resume was top-notch. I'd come with a wealth of recommenda-tions from teachers and the people at Metal Systems. I'd pored over my application, making sure every minutia was perfect. I'd learned English better than native speakers. I'd adapted to the culture and lifestyle until I was almost like the average Floridian. I'd immersed myself to the point where my Venezuelan identity had started to become a thing of the past, only brought back to the surface when I chatted with my family.

All of that had gone to waste. I would have to erase who I'd become in the past few years living here and start again. I'd have to go back to my home country, scared but hoping I could make it. That I could endure the scarcity with aplomb. That I could evade the crime every day I stepped out my door. That I could live with the guilt of Carlos's absence and hope I didn't join him too soon. Life here had been so easy. I'd been able to detach from the reality of my people far too well.

"There's another way," Gabe suddenly said. In the dark, he fumbled for my hand until he held it. His skin felt scorching on mine. "Marry me."

The only sounds for a long moment came from the night, as cars drove off in the distance, as the breeze ruffled the leaves in the trees and frogs croaked in the nearby water retention pond.

Finally, his words clicked.

"*What?*"

As though what he'd said wasn't absolutely out of this world, Gabe repeated, "Marry me."

"No." I tried to tear my hand away from his, but he wasn't having it. "That's insane and illegal and—"

"Pretty sure marriage is legal," he said coolly, as though we were discussing the weather. "And it's not like there's no chemistry between us."

"That's not the same as being in love and marrying! It's not like we're Chris and Ellen."

"No, we're not. But no one needs to know that." Gabe inhaled a deep breath and let it go before saying, "And Cata, I think it's the only chance you have left. Let me help you. I can keep you safe."

CHAPTER TWENTY-ONE

I didn't know how I'd got home, but one second, I was in the parking lot with Gabe, talking about impossible things, and the next I was under the blankets in my bed. The only lucky thing was that Maya had class until late, and when she got home, she probably saw no light coming from my bedroom and figured I was asleep.

But my eyes were wide open as I stared up at the ceiling. Lights from outside leaked through the blinds, reflecting on the surfaces in dull beams that faded into nothing. I willed them to twist into either a yes or a no. I wanted them to tell me if I should accept Gabe's outrageous proposal that would allow me to stay and pursue the future I'd worked for. Or if I should accept my fate and return to my family.

Papi would kill me if I showed up at the door, if the trip to my hometown didn't kill me first. Getting plane tickets to Venezuela was two, often three times more expensive than traveling from the US to any other Latin American country. And that wasn't considering the lack of flight availability to Caracas, or from the capital to my hometown, Maracaibo. Perhaps I'd have to travel by bus—a whole nine hours or more—risking an accident on the broken-down roads or being mugged by gangs on the way.

All the help Mami had given me to leave the country would go to waste the moment I returned and Papi said his, "Te lo dije." Cora wouldn't gloat, but she would probably use this as an example of why we shouldn't depend on foreign powers. Parroting her boyfriend, based on his party indoctrination.

A tear streaked down the side of my face and disappeared into my hair. My battery was fully drained, my stomach felt like it was full of acid, and my limbs were heavy like lead. I wanted someone to comfort me as much as I needed someone to scream at me and jolt me back into action. At the same time, I didn't want to explain again that all my fears were coming true, the way I'd spilled everything to Gabe this afternoon. I was exhausted. I didn't want to put that burden on Maya and Taylor too.

Only one person could understand with little explanation and offer the dichotomy of reactions I needed right now. It was late in the night already, but maybe it was for the better. I dialed, and sure enough, Cora picked up right away.

"This is weird," was the first thing that came out of her mouth in her familiar accent. "You, calling me at this time."

"Are they asleep?" I didn't even have to clarify whom I meant for her to confirm that indeed, they were. "And can you talk?"

"You're scaring me. Is everything okay?"

"No," I admitted, balling up my bedsheets and blotting my tears with them. "I'm in trouble."

She could tell it wasn't the fun kind of trouble, the one she enjoyed getting into. Cora stayed silent as I gave her the gist of things, including the closer.

When I was done with the tale, all she said was, "Vergación."

The word was so extremely Maracaibo. I choked upon the sob and the laugh that wanted to come out at the same time.

"Mija," she continued, "like the gringos say, what the heck?"

"My thoughts exactly."

There was a rustle on the other side, like she was burrowing deeper into the cocoon of bedsheets in her bed. "And what are you going to do?"

"I don't know. What should I do?"

Without missing a beat, she said, "Cásate con él."

"What?" I bolted upright, tossed the bedsheets away, and jumped to pace around my room. "I never expected you to say that."

"So you'd rather come back? Because that'd be great, we can hang out again." I could almost hear her eye roll. "But I know you don't want that. You hate it here."

"I don't hate it," I said softly, stopping to rest my forehead on the door of my room. "I'm just afraid of *everything* there."

"Which you aren't about being in a foreign country."

"Isn't it wrong, though?" I renewed the pacing as I spoke. "Marriage, for goodness' sake."

"Since when are you a romantic?" Cora asked, wheezing out a short laugh. "You, who wouldn't even give boys the time of the day."

It was true. I'd never been—and would never be—a romantic. That had been hammered home while trying on wedding gowns. Getting married had simply never been an aspiration of mine. Now that the possibility presented itself in such unorthodox circumstances, I wondered about what it would be like if things were right.

"It sounds perfect to me. You have an American boy willing to marry you so you can stay there. What more can you ask for?"

"I'm not quite happy about the moral implications." I pinched the bridge of my nose.

"You're not bribing him. As far as I understand, he proposed to you on his own accord. For all intents and purposes, it's not wrong."

"But it is." Sliding down, I sat on the floor and hugged my knees. "There are no real feelings."

"Are you sure about that?" Her question stumped me, and as the silence stretched, she added, "Maybe not from your side, but he must have *some*. Otherwise, he wouldn't even contemplate that option, right? There would be no personal stake for him to keep you there."

I blew a raspberry. "Impossible. He was probably trying to help. I mean, I was freaking out. Still am."

"Marriage goes a little beyond just wanting to help, if you ask me."

"Ugh." My head was reeling; I put it back between my knees. "That can't be right. He's never shown any interest in me until . . ."

The events of the past couple of months bubbled up. A montage of scenes that started out with a scorching glance after I'd welded some pipes and culminated in that earth-shattering kiss that had earned us his mom's chancletazos.

"Oh." I stared into nothing as, slowly, I started to pull my head out of my ass. After a moment, I shook my head to clear it. "I thought you'd be pulling all the stops to convince me to come back."

"No," she admitted. "If you were ready to come back, we wouldn't be having this conversation. You had your answer all along. What you wanted was validation."

Brushing away the sudden dampness on my cheeks, I said, "I don't feel good about any of this."

"Then again," she whispered, "you've never felt good about anything since losing Carlos."

She was right. Every plan I'd ever made had been derailed since then. Nothing could ever compare to that feeling of absolute loss and uncertainty, to having love and hope ripped out of my heart in a single day. I didn't think I'd ever feel good again, the way I had when I was a teenager with everyone I cared for safe and sound around me.

After saying goodnight to Cora, I turned on my laptop and started researching online. I read page upon page about US immigration law, forum threads where people talked about their experiences with marriage licenses and the paperwork required after that. I looked up visa types from countries in Europe and Latin America. Most of the requirements for entry were either studies or a work offer. Only a couple of Latin American countries allowed Venezuelans entrance without either, but the employment opportunities weren't guaranteed. If I wanted to apply to master's programs abroad, I needed more time to apply than I had left to stay in the US. Most programs had already announced their next intakes.

In all the options I looked up, I would have to go back to my home country for an undetermined period. I would have to go through the increasingly painful process of acquiring the necessary paperwork to go abroad again, through bureaucratic institutions that had collapsed years ago.

When morning came, I hadn't slept a wink. It was Saturday, and I'd been planning on going out to brunch with the girls. I sent them a quick text canceling, citing stomach issues. That part wasn't a lie—there was so much bitterness in my digestive tract I couldn't fathom the thought of food. I jumped in the shower and scrubbed my face with special emphasis, hoping to erase the effects of a sleepless night full of tears.

After I was presentable, I texted Gabe. Where are you?

His response came almost instantaneously. Going to play ball with Chris and friends. What's up?

Where can I meet you? I asked. The three dots appeared as he typed up his answer, and a few minutes later, I was driving to the location he'd given me. I was surprisingly calm as I made my way through town, maybe because I'd shed the worst of my emotions last night.

Traffic was still scarce this early, and I made quick work of driving from the northeast side of town to near downtown. I veered right northbound for less than a mile before the GPS pinged with the notice that I'd arrived, somewhere south of Baldwin Park.

Dozens of cars were parked on the lot overlooking a baseball field. People were huddled at one end, but a few others were spread across the field. I squinted from the driver's seat, trying to make out which one was Gabe.

I spotted him among the group of people. His cap had a little man bun coming out the back of it. As I got out of the car and walked over to him, I still wasn't sure what to say—or how. I wondered if I could ever repay him for what he might agree to do. This was a bigger debt than anything else he'd done for me. Ruining his brother's wedding would be child's play in comparison.

Speaking of, Chris was there beside Gabe. They were both under the shadow of a taller guy whose shoulders looked like they could carry an entire building, and it wasn't like the Cabrera brothers were small. It was this guy who spotted me first, and his attention pulled the others out of the conversation. When Gabe's eyes met mine, my steps momentarily faltered.

"Guys," Gabe started, extending a hand towards me, "this is Catalina, my girlfriend."

I took a deep breath before smiling and shaking everyone's hands as if what Gabe had said was a fact. The big guy was called Santiago, and I learned he was Peyton's boyfriend and played in the MLB.

Chris smiled as he said, "He's also Venezuelan, by the way."

"No way!"

I asked for his autograph because why not.

Another of the guys introduced himself as Anthony, a budding actor. He offered his own signature unprompted.

After the round of introductions, Gabe excused himself and pulled me away, my hand in his like that was where it belonged.

"How are you?" he asked, as though this were any other Saturday morning and I really was his girlfriend coming to cheer him on in a game against a professional baseball player.

"I feel like I'm going to vomit," I confessed, and that drew a smile out of him.

"Then let me walk you off the field." We sat on some wooden picnic benches, opposite each other as though this were a meeting room. We were removed enough from the others that we could drop the act. "So, what can I do for you?"

"Marry me," I blurted out in much the same fashion he had just the night before. "That's what. I guess."

Seconds trickled by with no reaction from him until he leaned back, folding his arms. For a second, I thought he'd take the offer back, but instead he asked, "What made you decide?"

With a shaky breath, I said, "I spent all night looking for options and . . . I'm fresh out of them."

"Glad to learn I'm your last resort." I couldn't believe he had the nerve to smile. "Even gladder to see you're getting some spunk back."

"It's all coming back to me as I'm trying not to punch you

right now." Still, I gave out such a big sigh I physically deflated. "This isn't going to be as easy as going to the civil registry and getting it done. It's big and scary. Are you sure you really want to do this?"

Gabe looked away, fiddling with the bill of his cap as though he were torn between taking it off and pulling it lower. Even with the shade it offered, his eyes twinkled with the morning light when he looked back towards the field where the others were.

"I don't like the idea of being able to help and looking away, you know? Even if there could be consequences."

I surprised us both by reaching for the hand he had rested atop the table. As though it wasn't an extraordinary action. I squeezed it between mine, seeking his eyes until they met mine.

"The consequences could be catastrophic for both of us."

A slow breath rushed between his parted lips. "Not if I can help it."

"How?" I shook my head, just wondering how his mind even functioned when mine was full of terrible scenarios. "If we're caught by Immigration, I'll get deported and banned from the US for ten years—or more. But you could go to jail."

His other hand fell over mine. "None of that will happen if we make this real. And quick."

Birds chirped around us. The grass was still green. Fluffy clouds still made a slow trek across the blue sky, carried by the wind. Everything else was normal, even as my world completely shifted in its axis.

"I asked you to help me ruin Chris's wedding because you were the perfect candidate, the only girl I knew who would never fall for me." Gabe paused, running the tip of his tongue over his lips, lightly biting the lower one as he finished his train of thought. "And that may still be the case—but joke's on me." He paused, and so did my heartbeat. "You see, I'm not doing this for entirely altruistic reasons. I like being with you, Catalina. I just want to keep you here. With me. Because while we fake-dated, I may have caught real feelings. If we're interviewed by the authorities, that won't be a lie."

CHAPTER TWENTY-TWO

Insanity wasn't a sudden event. It was a gradual process to which the victim succumbed as normalcy receded in increments. To my comfort and horror, I wasn't alone in this decline. Gabe was there, every step of the way. First as the symptom, then as the cure. Also, as I suspected, as a fellow victim.

We'd been barely polite acquaintances before all this had started. Rivals at school and work. Casually tossing challenging glances at each other across the classroom or our desks. Until we made the ridiculous deal of giving me what I most wanted in exchange for causing a family faux pas at his brother's wedding. Yet I'd jumped into it with a lot less hesitation than now.

The truth was that my morals had been skewed from the beginning. To please my favorite sibling, I'd gone behind our parents' backs to sneak him out of the house, leading to his death. To escape living with the consequences, I'd left it all behind and moved to a different country. To get my dream job, I'd agreed to snatch it from the main contender rather than put in the actual effort myself.

It was hard not to feel this was a similar situation. Like I was running away from struggles again. Like in doing so I could be making someone else's life harder by default.

For days after my conversation at the park with Gabe, my nerves were so frayed that Maya and Taylor took notice. My roommate went as far as asking her brother to drop by for a visit, but even seeing Malik's gorgeous self did nothing for me. When he showed up, I couldn't muster the butterflies in my stomach I used to feel. Instead, I kept seeing Gabe's face, stuck in the moment he'd blown out a sigh and said he was doing all of this because he had feelings for me.

The improbability of someone liking me for who I was had always felt sky-high. I was too curt, intense, and competitive, uninterested in socializing or dolling up. And yet this silly guy seriously planned on marrying me. So he could keep me here. Because he liked me.

"Are you sure you don't want to come?" Maya asked from the doorway, purse hanging from her shoulder, about to leave for her family's cookout. "You look like you could really use a distraction, you know?"

I lay curled up on the couch under a fluffy blanket. She hovered over me, and I said, "Yes, sorry. I'm still not feeling well."

It wasn't a lie. In my best moments, I felt like I could puke. She hugged me before leaving, which wasn't too common between us but was exactly what I needed. I clung to her with more strength than she expected. When she pulled away, her brows were furrowed.

"Are you sure you'll be okay?"

I nodded. Swallowed. Attempted a smile. "Yeah, I'll just watch some Netflix and go to sleep. Don't worry."

A half hour later, after she'd got to her mama's, she called to check in and found me deep in a Queer Eye marathon, which was the perfect excuse for me to weep all the feelings thanks to the beautiful stories in the show. She must have alerted Taylor because a few minutes later she was also texting me. I assured her I was fine, and then later, a different text bubble showed up on my phone. It was Gabe.

How's my girlfriend holding up?

Who? I asked him, just to be contrary.

The three dots showed up for much longer than it must have taken him to write up a reply. Looks like I worried for nothing, huh.

Before I could even reply, he called me instead. "We should go on a date," he said when I answered.

The hairstylist in the show was frozen in an expression of utter shock after I'd hit pause on the TV, mirroring exactly how I felt.

"You're wild."

"Not really." I could practically see the smile in his voice. "That's how it usually works. Dating turns into being an official couple, living together if you're not the son of my mother, and then marrying. In our case, the only criterion we need to fulfill before marrying is dating."

I was about to say we needed to become an official couple too when I realized we'd actually skipped to that as our first step. Except it had been fake, and now it was . . . I didn't know what it was. According to Gabe, he wanted to make it real, but how could I possibly believe that?

"Uh." After a few seconds of nothing smarter coming out, I managed to ask, "What kind of date?"

"Whatever you want." As an afterthought he added, "But the sooner the better."

I looked down at myself, wearing black leggings and an

oversized UCF Knights sweatshirt. My hair was wet from a shower, dripping on my shoulders and down my back. The desire to get out of this outfit was zero. But it was Friday night, and this was a typical date night for couples.

Sighing, I resigned myself to my fate. "I was really hoping to stay in my pajamas tonight."

"Sounds fantastic, Netflix and chill it is." The sound of a clap came from the receiver. "Stay put, and I'll bring snacks. See you in half an hour."

He hung up, just like that. And of course, he wouldn't pick up when I called him back.

One look around our apartment revealed a lot of little domestic messes that Maya and I didn't mind, but I wasn't entirely comfortable sharing with outsiders. The bathroom was especially dangerous. I wouldn't put it past him to peep in the drawers just to see what kind of person I was. I became a tornado through the apartment, picking up embarrassing items and stuffing them in my closet. Last was the kitchen. I was in the middle of straightening it up when the doorbell rang. A glance at the microwave's clock revealed that yes, a half hour had already passed. On the dot.

Opening the door, I said, "I don't know any other Latinos who are on time."

Gabe was wearing sweatpants with a threadbare T-shirt under an unzipped hoodie and was carrying a bag of groceries, none of which looked the least healthy. His smile was as though he'd put on a designer suit for a gala: confident, manly, and too sexy for my comfort.

"I debated if you'd kill me if I were late and figured it'd be just as bad if I arrived early." He shrugged. "But I suppose you'd also kill me if I arrived on time, just maybe a little less dead."

I pursed my lips to hold back from smiling, but it still came out anyway. Stepping aside and inviting him in, I said, "Guess you live to see another day."

He'd brought popcorn, ice cream, a frozen pizza, soda, and Doritos. We wouldn't die from my temper but from stomachaches. It was perfect. Gabe put everything on the counter, and I busied myself sorting everything out.

"Mom complained for days that you didn't like her burger patties, so I brought a veggie pizza, está bien?"

"Excellent," I said, turning on the oven before taking out plates to serve heaps of chips and popcorn. "Am I supposed to kiss you in gratitude now?"

He was as surprised by the question as I was. Immediately, I wanted to duck out of sight, but my pride wouldn't let me.

Gabe started laughing, though. "I mean, I won't complain if you do."

"It was a joke," I mumbled.

"Was it, though?" He scrunched up his face, and this time I was the one laughing. "Good," he said, smiling. "If you didn't have a sense of humor, you wouldn't survive a day living with me."

My laughter choked up and disappeared. "Sorry, did I just hear . . . No. I'm not moving into your *bedroom*."

"Of course not. I'm just planning ahead." Gabe rolled his eyes, though none of his own amusement had faded.

The sound of the oven pinging made me jump. I scrambled to put the pizza in. He'd been planning ahead for a future I couldn't even imagine while I sat in my room, moping for the one I'd wanted and lost.

Tingles ran up and down my body as I imagined a domestic scene where Gabe and I hung out in our living room, watching

TV together like we were about do now. Except the image in my head morphed into the less reputable part of the Netflix and chill combo, and I nearly burned myself while I shut the oven door.

"Why is your face so red?" Gabe narrowed his eyes at me, a lethal combo along with the smirk curving his full lips.

"The oven." Tossing my hair over my shoulder, I steered the conversation to other, more productive areas. "Anyway, I can't just leave Maya to carry rent by herself, and we still have four months of it."

He leaned over the counter across from me, holding his chin. "What if we move Maya to my mom's?" The glare I shot him just made him grin. "Hey, just trying to be helpful here."

"Wasn't the whole point of dating to follow the steps in the right order?"

"You're right." Gabe picked up the snack bowls and took them to the coffee table. "We date, we marry, and we move in together. How long do we have to do all that?"

I'd been going over that detail so obsessively the past few days, I didn't even have to think before replying. "One month until graduation, which is when my student visa and my work permit expire, but then I have a 60-day grace period to figure out my life."

"Sounds like plenty of time to make you fall for me." He plopped onto the couch and draped an arm all across the back-rest, patting it as if to say that was my place.

I took my sweet time pouring ice in a couple of glasses and topping up them with soda before heading over. I placed them on the coffee table with the snacks and sat on the carpet instead.

Naturally, he joined me there. "I like girls who play hard to get the most."

"Really?" I peeked at him from the corners of my eyes. "I've only ever seen you with girls who worship the ground you walk on."

He shrugged, which made his hair obscure his face until he pushed it behind his ear. "That's what I thought I wanted."

"Past tense?"

Gabe turned to face me, serious for once. It was the look he had on his face when he was in the middle of work, synthesizing complex abstract information into something that could be applied to practical use. When directed at me, it was as though I was the puzzle his mind was trying to crack.

"Definitely past tense," he murmured. Goosebumps rose on my arms even though I was quite cozy in my sweatshirt. "I like it better when you challenge me or make fun of me, because I know for sure you're seeing me for who I am and not for the dream of me some other girls imagined in their heads."

Heat rushed up my neck. I picked up the remote control and hit Play. "That's because you're not a dream."

"No." Even though his voice was lower than the TV, I heard him loud and clear. "That's because I'm real."

It was hard to watch the show with his body heat so close to mine, but that wasn't why I'd begun to sweat. My heart rate had gone up the second he sat next to me, despite not touching. The memory of his body against mine, his lips coaxing mine open, was too fresh to pretend it hadn't happened. Because that had definitely not been a dream. Not the first time and not the second. I pulled up my knees and hugged them, trying to put as much space between us without making my intentions obvious. It didn't work, though, because when he caught on, Gabe deliberately scooted closer. Just enough so I knew he was there.

The oven pinged, and I thanked the heavens for pre-cooked

pizza. When I returned with full plates, I sat on the couch. This time he didn't join me. We ate in silence, watching the makeover show like we were each alone in the room.

"My favorite is Bobby," Gabe declared. "He's the one who works the hardest, despite not being on screen as much as the others."

I barked a laugh. "I'd have thought you were a Jonathan guy, at least by virtue of sharing similar hair."

Gabe flashed a boyish grin that disarmed me even more than I already was. "Di la verdad, you like him the best because of the hair." Then he tossed his mane like this was a Pantene ad and not my living room.

I couldn't help but smack him. "Just so you know, I'm a Tan girl."

"I see it." He nodded, facing forward again. "Closed off but still so full of goodness to give."

The bite of pizza I'd been chewing went down the wrong pipe. He casually handed me my glass of soda as though he hadn't thrown yet another bombshell.

"I'm not that nice," I said while I continued to choke for a few seconds.

"That's what you say." After a pause he asked, "When's your birthday?"

I stayed silent so long that he paused the show, climbed back on the couch, and motioned for me to answer. "Uh, June fourth. Why?"

"Mine's November eighteenth," he said. "We should know these things about each other from now on, you know?"

"Wait." I raised the palm of my hand. "For real?"

He shot me a look. "Yeah, in case we get interviewed—"

I waved my hand. "That part makes sense. I meant your

birthday. That's the day of my hometown's fair in honor of Virgin Mary."

"See? It was fated." A slow grin appeared on his face in response to my deadpan expression. "What else should I definitely know about you?"

There were so many things, but sitting this close, with thoughts of him kissing me setting butterflies free in my tummy, I wanted to tell him nothing. I wanted to just keep watching TV in silence as though there was no heat between us.

But he had a good point: if we were going to do this, we had to prepare. I cleared my throat. "Okay, um. My hometown is called Maracaibo, it's as hot as an oven. Papi has a metalwork company that supplies goods and services to what's left of the oil business. Mami is a stay-at-home mom, even though the only kid she has left is my twin sister."

"You have a twin sister?" His eyes were wide. "Pictures or it never happened."

I sighed. It was inevitable. The moment I showed him a picture of Cora, he'd be disappointed at getting stuck with the dull twin. I grabbed my phone from the coffee table and scrolled through until I found an old picture with all of us. "There," I said, pointing. "That's me and that's Coralina, Cora for short."

"I see," he said, and I felt like my heart stopped. "Catalina and Coralina. Cute names."

"That's it?" I zoomed in to the picture. "No *she's prettier than you* or *what happened to you*? That's what people usually say when they look at us."

Gabe's face scrunched up. "Que se jodan, me gustas más tú. My only question is who is the oldest?"

"Me," I answered, as though this were an accomplishment. "By a whole seven minutes."

Gabe grabbed my hand to angle the screen towards him. "So this must be your brother, right?"

The question sent a stab of pain through my chest. I zoomed the picture in so his face was front and center. "Yes, that was my older brother, Carlos."

"You said he passed five years ago. Is it still raw for you?"

Gabe looked at me, catching every sign that I was struggling to hold it in. He grabbed my hand, and I welcomed the touch.

With a deep breath, I said, "I sneaked him out that morning. If I hadn't, he'd be alive."

His thumb rubbed arcs across the back of my hand. "Even without knowing details, I'm pretty sure you're not who killed him."

I hadn't shared this with anyone outside of my family. Not even Maya and Taylor knew the guilt I carried. I wiped at the first tears that fell from my face with fury.

"No, but can you blame me for thinking that way? I was the last one who saw him, and I could've stopped him. I could've told him to not go risk himself. Instead, I told him he was doing the right thing and sent him off to fight as though I were some princess in a tower and he were my champion." I shook my head to myself. "I can't go back to where all those memories are. Where something like this can just happen again."

Sighing, Gabe leaned forward and, with surprising ease, lifted me until I sat on his lap. When I tensed, he rubbed my back until I molded against his chest and tucked my forehead against the crook of his neck.

"I was also the last one to see my dad," he said, voice rumbling in his chest against me. "We had breakfast together while Mom was doing the laundry in the back. I didn't even pay attention when he left."

"Oh no," I whispered, fearing the way this would turn out.

"He had a stroke while driving to work. I hadn't even said goodbye, and he was already gone." His arms were around me, holding me, and for a moment I wondered if he needed someone to hold *him*. "So, I guess I kinda know how you feel. For years, I wondered if I'd stalled him, if I'd talked more to him, maybe the stroke would've hit him at home, and we'd have had time to get an ambulance. Instead, he veered off the road; his car ran into a ditch and was out of sight until a landscaper found it hours later. He'd already been dead for a while."

"I'm so sorry." I pulled away so I could look at him. The sadness in his eyes was the same no doubt reflected in mine.

"When it's time, it's time. Which is why I think we should make the best of the time we have in this world." He tilted his head. "Don't you think?"

It explained why he was impulsive, carefree, and confident. Not because he'd been born under a lucky star but because he'd decided to squeeze whatever he could out of anything life was willing to give him.

"Is that why you're doing this?" I wondered, propping myself against his sturdy shoulders. "Because life is too short?"

A small smile drew his lips up. "That and because my patience is even shorter. Me vas a besar o no?"

I wanted to laugh and also to scream and cry. Instead, I said, "Gabe, this isn't about a kiss, we're talking marriage here—and for a few years, at least, until my paperwork is approved. This isn't some small whim like deciding to go on a date with someone or not."

"I know." He caressed a hand up my back, slowly, leaving a trail of warmth until it settled at my nape. His eyes were dark and intense, fixed on my lips as he said, "But life can be over in the blink of an eye, and I don't want to spend whatever I have left of it wondering what it would've been like to be with you."

Air rushed in through my teeth. Gabe leaned forward, and I kissed him.

Too easily, he maneuvered me so I straddled him, which brought us far closer than I'd anticipated tonight, and also not as close as I truly wanted us to be. I sneaked my fingers into his hair, pulling his head back so I was the one setting the pace for the kiss, slow and almost chaste at first as I ran my tongue across his lips, and deeper the next second.

Unfortunately, that let his hands roam. He caressed his way up my thighs, my hips, and sneaked them under my sweatshirt. The touch of his hands on my skin made me break away in surprise. Gabe's face was wrinkled like a kid whose candy had just been taken away.

"Come back," his voice rasped out.

At that moment, all I could do was obey, even though his hands kept moving up, setting me ablaze at the same time. I wasn't the only one who was getting affected by this, and as I squirmed to get better access to his mouth, the friction between our lower bodies tore guttural moans out of us.

"We should do more Netflix than chill," I whispered, my voice breaking when he found the strap of my bra.

Gabe blinked his eyes as though he was having trouble focusing them. "But I like the chill part better."

I rolled my eyes. "I'm sure you do."

The last word died in a squeal as he flipped us over. Now he hovered over me while I lay flat on the couch. "Later," he rasped out. "We do more Netflix later."

Maybe I pulled him to me, or maybe he just dove in for another kiss. The fact was his hands were now pinned beneath me, allowing mine to roam free over him. I was much clumsier in lifting his T-shirt so I could touch his sides, but he must have liked it. His body burrowed deeper against mine, and the first stroke of his hips against mine almost made me scream.

That was when the front door opened, and Maya announced, "I'm back, and I brought Malik."

The gasp that came out of my throat made Gabe pull away. I hid beneath him, but there was no disguising the situation. No doubt Maya and Malik had a great view of the couch, with it being right by the door. The exaggeratedly loud gasp could only have come from Maya.

"Oh, sorry for interrupting." That was Malik's voice, all right.

"No problem," replied Gabe, his voice clipped. He looked down at me, and I was surprised to see the same mortification in his face that had to be on mine.

"We have to stop getting caught like this," I whispered, but it made him laugh.

Trágame tierra.

CHAPTER TWENTY-THREE

The earth did not open up and swallow me whole after my old crush caught me making out with the new one.

After the guys had left, Maya point-blank asked me, "I thought this was all supposed to be fake, no strings attached."

For a wild moment, I thought about telling her the truth about my shifting feelings—about the marriage, even. That this had gone beyond a silly agreement made by two bored and petty kids who'd suddenly decided to start playing at adults. But I feared what revealing the truth could do, and what it might say about Gabe and me too. I wasn't ready for that conversation.

So I replied with, "Strings are getting attached."

She smacked me in much the same way I typically did to everyone else. "Weren't you the one who said we should all steer clear of that player? This is going to come back to bite you in the ass."

"Probably." But not for the reasons she thought.

Meanwhile, Taylor wanted all the details and not the watered-down version from Maya's texts. We agreed to get to school a bit earlier on Saturday morning before meeting the guys at the shop. Today would be an exciting day. We planned to put together the full chassis and start fitting the major components inside.

Taylor didn't care about that, though. Where normally it would've excited her as much as it did me, she was now all about the gossip. There was a text she kept sending every so often that read, AND I MISSED THE DRAMA!!! Which, at the rate we were going, wouldn't be the last of it. Too bad for her I couldn't just kiss and tell. I'd have to find a way to give her enough to keep her satisfied without spilling all the beans.

As I got ready to drive to school that morning, dodging Maya's disapproving looks while she had breakfast by herself, I got a text from the second subject of her contempt. It read, Your chauffeur is downstairs.

Without waiting a beat, I called him. "I have a previous appointment with Taylor."

"I can take you to your appointment, though."

A compelling argument that I wanted to reject but couldn't think of how. "Fine, but I need girl time afterwards."

"You got it."

I had a strong sense of déjà vu when I made it downstairs and found him in the same pose he waited with every time. Leaning against the side of his red Jeep, one foot propped up against the tire, arms loosely folded. His hair waved softly in the wind, and the aviator sunglasses looked like they were designed specifically for his bone structure. His ripped jeans showed a hint of defined muscle, and the sleeves of his white T-shirt caught around the curve of his biceps.

All of which compelled me to tell him, "Is this your signature move to look cool?"

His eyebrows shot up from behind the shades. "So you think I look cool."

I'd walked into that one. I hopped into the passenger seat and strapped in.

Once he'd joined me in the driver's seat, he said, "First of all, buenos días. Second, did Maya give you a lot of crap after I left?"

"Heaps." I sighed. "And buenos días."

He shot me a grin. "Where's my good morning kiss?"

Every fiber of my being crinkled into a ball of embarrassment. "Leave the cheese for your pizza."

"Just so you know," Gabe said while driving us to school, "before this day is over, you'll willingly give me another kiss."

Considering the aftermath of our latest kiss, I didn't think it would be a good idea to embark on such an adventure on campus today. Not to mention I wasn't entirely looking forward to seeing the reactions people might have at seeing me so close to the student body's Ultimate Babe.

"Are you aware of the series of ridiculous nicknames people have for you?"

"One or two might have been made up by me." Gabe flashed a sudden grin.

"No!"

He shrugged. "Being the most popular guy on campus seemed important before."

"Did it get you any perks aside from a lot of booty?"

The question made him choke, and since we were stopped at a red light, he turned to confirm whether I was serious. I absolutely was. Even through the years I'd resented him, I'd been curious to understand if the power he held was just in my head.

"Well, aside from that," he said, not denying all the booty

he'd got thanks to that infamous award, "I got a lot of guys giving me shit about it."

"Really?" I tilted my head, trying to remember any instances of guys dissing him. "But you have a ton of friends."

"Acquaintances. My best friends are Chris and Manny. Some of the guys in the amateur baseball league too." A hum vibrated out of his throat. "Is that boring?"

"No. I'd like you even less if you were popular with everybody."

"If it makes you like me more, cats hate me." His grin was threatening to become contagious, so I looked away. Was that why he called me Kitty Cat, because he thought I'd hated him all along?

We got to school, and as soon as we were out of the car, he grabbed my hand. I pretended it had no major effect on me, but last night had left its mark. Just the touch of his hand against mine or the casual way our bare forearms brushed against each other made my body react as if we were still spilling over the couch, feeling each other up like we were on the clock to get as many handfuls of each other as possible.

While I had a mini breakdown on the inside, Gabe tossed easy greetings to anybody who recognized us. A few people did double takes to make sure their eyes didn't deceive them. That indeed Gabe was showing off a new girl, and it was none other than his biggest nemesis.

Just like that, I became exactly what I'd never thought I'd be: his arm accessory. But he'd also become what he'd never thought he'd be: *my* arm accessory.

A cluster of girls I recognized from a previous class headed in our direction. My first impulse was to snatch my hand away. Sensing it, Gabe draped his arm around me and lowered his face towards mine. Was he going to kiss me?

"Relax," he whispered over me. "I'm not going to kiss you without your permission. That's going to be all on you."

I groaned. "You're killing me, Smalls."

"A girl who knows her baseball references?" Gabe put a hand over his heart. "I'm a goner."

"Oh my gosh, Gabe. It's been so long!" one of them said, and we turned to her.

Her friend squinted at me, as if she couldn't quite place me. Then she zeroed in on Gabe's arm around me. "Wait, is this a new girlfriend?"

"Yeah," he said, writing the fact in the hard stone of school gossip. "And this one's for keeps."

A couple of them groaned as though it didn't matter that I was standing there to see them pine over the guy who supposedly was mine. Even worse, I was actually offended.

After we moved on, Gabe said, "That wasn't so bad."

"Are you kidding? Am I going to need an official credential to prove to anyone who asks that yes, I'm in fact your girlfriend?"

Gabe snapped his fingers and pulled out his cellphone. "Great idea, say cheese."

With a squeak, I tucked myself against his side, which was the worst thing I could've done because I now wanted to stay there forever. Not only did he feel like a dream against me, but the spice of his soap, mixed with the scent of his skin, nearly weakened my knees.

"C'mon, first couple picture." Gabe brushed his hand up and down my back, making everything worse. And by that I meant better. "We have to make it convincing."

He was right. I had to put an effort into becoming a sort of actual girlfriend now. My fate was in his hands.

Sighing, I let him go, fixed my hair, and stood next to him.

"Whiskey," I said, smiling to the front camera of his phone and noting we actually didn't look bad together. I fit well against his side, since I was short and he wasn't exactly the tallest guy. More importantly, the mirth in his face was so genuine, anyone who saw us might think that he was actually smitten.

To make more of an effort, I stood on my tippy-toes and smacked a kiss on his cheek. I heard the shutter of the camera click in tune with his gasp. As though nothing was amiss, I grabbed his phone to check out the result. "Okay, kinda cute."

"Ha!" Gabe barked, which was the start of a fit of laughter from him. "See? I told you sooner or later you'd kiss me all on your own. I was just hoping for it to be a bit more like here." He puckered his lips and tapped them with his index finger.

The invitation was clear and tempting. But I turned and continued walking towards the cafeteria, where Taylor was waiting for me. Naturally, Gabe followed and captured my hand once more. From the corner of my eye, I caught the biggest shit-eating grin I'd ever seen on his face, like he'd won something better than the award for most popular guy on campus or a full scholarship based on his academic merits.

That was how Taylor found us, walking into one of the most crowded places on campus together as a couple. It wasn't just her who zeroed in on that fact.

"Holy shit," she said, attracting further attention in our direction. "This is for real. I needed to see with my own eyes to believe."

I rolled mine. "Happy?"

"Heck no, I need all the details."

"I'd be more than happy to oblige," Gabe said, and I physically pushed him away.

"Off you go." I shooed him. "It's girl time now."

"But you're going to talk about me." He literally pouted. "I wanna hear you talk about me."

This made Taylor lose her mind. She laughed even harder when he finally left—not before blowing an exaggerated kiss my way. I didn't know if he was doing this for my sake, putting on a show so it was clear what was what, but any more of this and I would actually wither away from embarrassment.

As I joined my best friend at a table, coffees in hand, I said, "Can we talk about literally anything but him?"

"You sound like such a girlfriend already." At my look, she said, "Okay, but what if we talk about a different guy then?"

"First of all, if we were in a movie or book, we wouldn't be passing the Bechdel test." After taking a giant sip of my brew, I asked, "Also, what other guy?"

Taylor stared at me unblinkingly, as though somehow that would help me guess.

"Malik?" I asked.

She rolled her eyes. "No. Manny." I returned her look, and this time it worked. "We went on a date last night, that's why I didn't jump to hang out with you."

"Oh, shit." I smacked my hand on the table. "No way! How'd it go?"

It had been a good while since I'd last seen her face morph into a Disney princess's, staring out the window to her flock of adoring birds. "He is honestly the sweetest guy I've met in my life. I should've been dating Latinos earlier."

"Not all Latinos," I said, which should probably be on a T-shirt. "*Manny*. If only you'd met him earlier."

"If only your car would've broken down earlier." She grinned at me. "Hey, maybe after all this is said and done, we'll end up becoming cousins by marriage."

I choked on my sip of coffee. The liquid went up the wrong pipe, and I expelled it through my nose with a powerful snort.

The first thing that came out after that was, "It burns!"

"Oh shit, are you okay?" she shrieked, running for napkins and patting them on my face. She gave me a handful more for my T-shirt. "It was kinda funny, though."

"Shut up," I said, but I was such a mess that I wanted to laugh too. "I'm going to the restroom."

"Want help?"

"Nah." I stood up, balling the napkins against my chest. "I'm okay. I'll meet you at the shop."

She walked with me out of the cafeteria, and before we went opposite ways she said over her shoulder, "Fine, but you still owe me all the sordid details."

I rolled my eyes and went into the women's bathroom. It was empty, thankfully. After washing my face, I took off my T-shirt and gave it a quick wash with hand soap. While holding it under the hand dryer, I wondered what the deal was with me and coffee. At least I'd learned from the first spill—thanks to Gabe—that if I let it linger in the fabric too long, it could ruin it.

Then the door opened, and I came face-to-face with Liz.

I took a quick glance around and confirmed that yes, we were alone. And this didn't bode well for me.

"Uh," I said. "Hi."

She took stock of my appearance and lifted her nose. Without replying, she went into a stall to do her business. I willed the hand dryer to work faster, but the wet splotch was still there. I could wear it like that, but I risked a lot of attention to my chest area that way. Especially from my so-called boyfriend.

Next thing I knew, Liz was done and began washing her hands in the sink farthest from me. The silence between us was heavy. Worst case, I could use the wet shirt as a whip to try to keep her at bay.

None of that was necessary, though. Her hands dripped as she turned to me and said, "I saw you guys being all lovey-dovey earlier." I didn't know what to say, and she felt it pertinent to continue. "Anyway, I just wanted to say congratulations. You got the man."

I flinched like she'd hit me.

"But it wasn't like he ever loved me, actually." Oh, there was more. She shook her hands in the air, apparently more interested in talking than drowning the sound of her voice by using the other dryer for her hands. "I'm going to therapy, by the way. Working on my controlling issues."

Well . . . That was unexpected. At her pause, I said, "Oh. Um, that's great. I'm glad for you."

"It's helped me see that he wasn't for me, and I was clinging. Gabe was yours even before we started dating."

I wanted to laugh, but I also didn't want her to think I was mocking her. Because that wasn't it.

"That's impossible," I said. "We weren't into each other. We just had class and work together, that's all."

"Maybe for you it was like that." Liz shrugged, giving me a once-over as if she were measuring me for size. "But his eyes were always on you. So you best treat him with more care than I did."

She spun and walked out of the bathroom with more dignity than I'd have mustered if the roles were reversed, leaving me drowning in confusion.

CHAPTER TWENTY-FOUR

"Do you actually like him?"

The question caught me off guard, especially as I was sitting on a chair in my room, trying my best to imitate a mannequin. Maya had lent me some of her fashion sense in the form of a gorgeous, figure-hugging emerald gown I'd barely squeezed into, and she was exercising her makeup skills on my face.

"Because if so, I'll start nagging," she said. I couldn't give her an answer fast enough, and it made her sigh. "And here I was playing you up to Malik."

"What?" I jerked up to look at her, and a stroke of luck was the only reason the mascara brush didn't stab me in the eye.

Maya smiled and kept working. "I was trying to be subtle about it, but yeah, he's single, and you were pining for him. But maybe I should've been more forceful about it?"

For a wild second, I allowed myself to imagine how this whole mess would've panned out if it had been her brother instead of Gabe. I still thought Malik was the most gorgeous guy I'd ever seen in real life. However, the fact I'd never been able to have a solid conversation with him should've been a sign. It wasn't just because I got nervous and tongue-tied; I'd just been happier in the role of admirer than that of equal. Secretly, I knew that if I showed my true self to him, it would've earned me the same stupefied expression he used on Maya when she was being *Maya* on him.

Then what he'd said what felt like ages ago clicked. I truly was like a sister to him.

It wasn't like that with Gabe. At all.

As the realizations hit me one after the other, I slumped in my seat. "To answer your question, I don't know."

It took Maya a second, but her eyebrows rose to the roof. "You don't know if you like your boyfriend and yet you're dating him?"

She didn't even know the half of it.

My *boyfriend*—I still wasn't used to the term—saved me by giving me a call, letting me know he was downstairs. I was still unused to him being the kind of person who'd rather talk than read a text and not have to engage directly with someone, the way I was, but here we were.

"I promise I'll explain everything," I told Maya without adding *one day*. I didn't know when I'd be able to, but that day would be my last because she would kill me.

When she was done with my face, Maya made me walk through a cloud of perfume twice. I'd straightened my hair so not a strand defied gravity and put some imitation gold hoops in my ears and around my wrists. Holding a borrowed clutch bedazzled with golden sequins and wearing the only semi-comfortable pair of heels I owned, I half walked and half hobbled downstairs until I emerged from the building with all the grace I didn't possess.

When we caught sight of each other, Gabe and I both froze.

He'd been in his usual pose, but his arms and leg fell as he stared at me, and damn it, I was doing the same. He wore a stark white shirt, ironed to perfection, under a black blazer paired with black slacks. He wore a handkerchief in his pocket in the exact same shade as my dress, as I'd advised. His hair was slicked back into a low bun, and his five o'clock shadow was groomed to perfection.

Gabe looked like a model straight out of a magazine—not the wiry kind, but one that you turned the page for, hoping to see him in less and less clothing with every picture.

Hooking a finger to pull at the collar of his shirt, Gabe said, "Wow, estás dura."

"Gracias." It was a struggle not to let the very Boricua compliment settle like a neon sign on my cheeks. "You're not too bad yourself."

Grinning, he offered me his arm, and since I was in heels, I gladly accepted his help to climb into the Jeep. We'd already been underway for a few silent minutes when, at a stop sign, he glanced at me again and stretched his hand over. The motion made me freeze, expecting anything but him pulling the fabric of my dress around the leg opening to cover my skin.

I cleared my throat and rearranged it myself. "Thank you."

"So," he started in an effort to defuse the moment, "today's the big day we ruin this wedding."

I frowned. "Isn't this just Chris's birthday?"

"His last one as a bachelor and under our mom's eagle eye." He shrugged. "We'll cause a big scene today that will carry over for the rest of the festivities. If we play it right, we might not even have to screw up the wedding itself."

It made sense, just a big cloud of drama hanging over

everybody after one big event. What could possibly cause such a rift, though?

"What's the big idea, then?"

Gabe glanced at me quickly. "I'm going to propose to you."

I just stared at him, waiting for him to start laughing and say, "Gotcha." He didn't.

"Think about it," he continued. "I propose to you in the middle of the fancy dinner Mom has catered. Both mothers will hate me because I'll force everyone's attention away from the main couple, turning you into the recipient of the proposal with the unluckiest timing—in fact, you can even act embarrassed if you want. And this way, we set the foundation for our actual wedding. Two birds with one stone."

My nose wrinkled as an automatic reaction. "It's brilliant, and I hate it."

"Here's what you'll hate even more." Even in the relative dark inside the car, I could tell his eyes twinkled like fairy lights. "After you say yes, you're gonna have to smack me a big one in front of everybody."

"I refuse. It'll ruin my makeup."

What the whole thing did was ruin my appetite. I'd been looking forward to the open buffet with the free food Gabe had promised from the beginning.

Instead, I sat and watched the party as if I were out of my body. Considering that all of Chris's relatives were there, and even some of Ellen's, they'd had to rent a massive event hall to accommodate everyone. I sat at a table with Gabe, our hands always clasped together despite the dampness growing in our skins. I'd never had a boyfriend before and didn't know how to tell him that my hand needed air-conditioning.

That wasn't the biggest drama, though. I was in prime position to catch the murderous looks both mothers occasionally shot at each other across the dance floor. Once the wedding happened, this would be such an interesting family to be a part of.

Not that I'd be in it for real.

I glanced at Gabe and found him already looking at me, his expression intense like his own thoughts had followed mine. There was nowhere else for me to run except into his eyes, and I felt my heart skip. Nerves exploded in my belly like the seeds of a dandelion in the wind. I had to look away before my real feelings also scattered all around for everyone to see.

Gabe leaned towards me and whispered, "Ready?"

"Now?"

"No, but soon. I just wanted to check that you're still up for this."

Had that been the reason for the look on his face earlier? Was he worrying that he was pushing me into this mess, when I was the one who'd made it even worse?

I looked around. Half the people were tearing up the dance floor to the tune of an old salsa. A few sat scattered around the tables, like Gabe and I were. The rest were in line for the buffet my rioting stomach hadn't allowed me to tackle. Chris and Ellen danced by us, and she threw me a wink so exaggerated it caught the attention of two more couples.

There was actually no time better than now, while enough people were close by to witness the proposal without having absolutely all eyes on us.

With a shaky breath, I said, "Ready if you are."

"Okay. A armar el rebulú." Gabe offered me his hand. I took it and stood up. "Let's go find our stage."

He steered me with an arm around my waist, his hand on my hip like it was born to settle there. We joined Magdalena and Jason in the queue for the buffet, which was an excellent distraction from what was going to happen anytime now. She'd also caught sight of the mothers-in-law having a Western movie type duel across the aisles, which had us wondering which mother disliked their child's soulmate the most.

"Definitely your mom," I said before realizing she could take offense.

"You're right." Magdalena nodded as we approached the table full of plates and snatched one for herself and one for me. "When Mom's not in the picture, Mrs. Young seems quite supportive of the whole thing."

We both glanced at Ellen's mom and found her chatting up a storm with Manny a few feet down the line.

"Yup," Magdalena and I said at the same time. We shared a grin over it.

She and Jason were so fun and easygoing that the conversation absorbed me. I didn't even notice Gabe had been silent throughout most of it until we were back at the table and well into dessert.

Which was when he chose to stand up, push the chair aside, and give me a heart attack as he bent his knee next to me, looking up with honey in his eyes.

Our whole table gasped. Magdalena's fork hit her plate with a clang, and Jason choked on the sip of water he'd been taking. The collective shock at the scene traveled in ripples across every other table up and down the hall, until everyone had sucked the oxygen out of the room and left me without any air.

I glanced around, hoping someone would put a stop to this. Instead, I made eye contact with Mrs. Cabrera. While she looked ready to commit murder, the fact she was frozen in her seat across the dance floor told me she wasn't willing to act in front of so many witnesses.

Then I felt Gabe's hand gently hold mine, forcing my attention back to him.

"Cata, my Kitty Cat," Gabe started. His voice was soft and tender, as though meant only for us. Even though this was just a show. Right now, I wasn't so sure of what was right or wrong, or what was real or fake. "You might not have noticed, but I have only had eyes for you since the moment I met you."

Fake or not, I couldn't help the scoff that slipped out.

He grinned. "No, for real. Even when I was with someone else, I kept picking you out in a crowd easier than I could recognize my own mother."

That earned him a smack from me and a few chuckles from around our table. People stopped dancing and moved closer to watch the show. From the corner of my eye, I caught a few phones turned our way. I barely stopped myself from cringing.

Liz's words resonated in my mind, though. She'd said something similar. Goosebumps rose all over my skin.

This isn't real, Cata. Don't forget.

"Imagine my delight when you agreed to date me," Gabe continued, the same cheeky grin I'd always seen on his face in full force, only for me. "By anyone else's standards this may be hasty, after dating for just a couple months. But sometimes you just know that if you don't make a bold leap, you can miss out on the best things in life. And I don't want to miss out on a single second with you."

I sucked in air. Gabe had said that before. If *that* had been real, why was he saying this *now*?

The whole place erupted in cooing. If I'd been a spectator, I might have too. This sounded so perfect, so sweet, even I had trouble anchoring myself in reality. Gabe appeared to wear his heart on his sleeve and was offering it to me so openly. My body reacted even while my brain tried to stop it, eyes growing hot and damp, little gasps coming to my breath as my own heart hammered in my chest, threatening to claw its way out and jump right into Gabe's extended hand.

The same one that held a small velvet box.

Of course, there'd be a ring. How had I forgotten? And as he opened it and revealed what in fact looked like an expensive engagement ring, I gasped and drew my hands to my face in truth, because holy shit, he was going *big*.

"Gabe," I started, about to reprimand him for spending however much he had on the jewel.

He drowned that by saying, "Catalina, I love you with the entire half I am. Will you marry me and make me whole?"

My brain ceased functioning. I forgot what I was supposed to say here. In a split second, I imagined myself running away. In the next, I pictured a scene where I flung myself into his arms and never let go.

A shout finally tore through my stupor. "If you don't marry him, I will!"

And suddenly there was a fire lit within me that refused that notion. I had the burning feeling to say yes with everything that I was.

So I did. "Yes!"

I threw myself at him, and he caught me. As we collided, we kissed like no one was watching. Like I wasn't the only one being consumed by the emotions that shouldn't be real.

At the end of the night, I had a ring on my finger, a good number of people pissed at me, and a good number of other people—chief among them, Gabe's abuela—wondering if this would now turn into a double wedding. And while the original groom and bride were not at all opposed to the idea, a certain pair of mothers-in-law weren't too happy about it.

Finally, we had succeeded in ruining a wedding. It was time to start planning ours.

CHAPTER TWENTY-FIVE

Monday felt more like a Thursday in my bones as I dragged myself through the office to my desk. Gabe was already at his, sipping coffee from the same mug that had almost burned the skin off my chest. I hesitated for a moment but realized I couldn't do my work while staring at him from a distance.

"Good morning." I plopped on my seat and set up my workstation for the day.

"Buenos días, Gatita."

All at once, a sensation similar to sucking a lemon dry came over me. "You did just *not.*"

"I did just." Gabe continued sipping his coffee, calm as the surface of a lake even though he obviously was holding back laughter.

Glancing this way and that, I scooted just close enough to be in his earshot alone. "Can we not do this at the office?"

"What do you mean?" And because I'd got close enough and sat facing him, his eyes zeroed in on the fact I wasn't wearing the ring. "Oh."

A crease appeared between his eyebrows, and his lips pushed upward. The disapproval confused me, so I explained. "It's just that people will start asking questions—and not the kind I want, when I'm trying to get a job here."

"Of course." Gabe sighed.

He turned away to focus on his laptop screen, and I had the distinct impression that he'd not only dismissed the conversation but he was mad at me.

The reason escaped me. Typically, men didn't wear engagement rings, so he would never have to field any questions unless I revealed to everyone that he was the one who had put the ring on my finger. If that happened, no one would think less of him. But I couldn't help worrying that if people figured out I was getting married before even having a job, then hiring me would be a bad investment if I got pregnant too quickly.

At the core of things, even if I married Gabe, I still wanted to get this job by my own merit. I made a mental note to explain this when we were alone. Like a schoolkid, I grabbed a Post-it, and after jotting down a time and meeting place, I slipped it over to his desk. He picked it up and was about to speak when a different voice sounded behind me.

"Catalina?" I jumped around to find Jeff there. The expression on his face wasn't quite the usual. "Do you mind if we have a quick chat?"

"Yes." I jumped to my feet and immediately amended, "I mean no. I don't mind. What's up?"

A quick glance back revealed Gabe was just as confused. But Jeff just motioned at me to follow, and I did, until he walked us into a meeting room. Usually, if this were regarding any of our projects, we would talk at his cubicle. Meeting room discussions were the kind that people wanted to keep private.

A million thoughts raced through my head about all the things I'd done of late that could get me in trouble. I remembered that a bunch of people had recorded Gabe's proposal at the party on Friday and wondered if somehow that had got around to people here. I couldn't remember a single clause about not dating coworkers. If my heart had been racing as we approached the room, it positively stopped when I saw Macy, our head of HR, sitting at the middle of the table.

"Good morning, Catalina. Please take a seat," she said, and maybe it had been a somewhat okay morning before, but now it was shaping into a nightmare.

I did as she asked, only slightly relieved that Jeff sat next to me and opposite Macy. An unexpectedly optimistic voice in my mind wondered if this was maybe about a job offer, but if that were the case, Jeff wouldn't have appeared so distraught, right?

"Hi, Macy." I cleared my throat. "How have you been?"

"Doing okay, busy as a bee." She smiled at my efforts. "You can relax, this isn't anything too bad."

Too bad implied that there was some bad.

Meekly, I said, "Okay."

"So, um." Jeff was as uncomfortable as I was, sans the shitting-my-pants portion. "Another employee—we won't say who—was reading the news online and claims to have seen you in some sort of riot."

The seconds stretched longer, but all I could do was blink, first at Jeff and then at Macy.

Slowly, I pointed at myself. "Me?"

Macy studied me for a few minutes before reaching below the table. She pulled up an iPad and, after a few clicks, turned it to face us. The picture of Cora at the demonstration in Venezuela was framed in the middle of the screen. It was the one where she'd burned her hands tossing the live tear gas canister. In the background was the blurry image of the Venezuelan tricolor and stars.

Below, in the description of the scene, it read, *Government-Supporting Student Counterprotests Against Opposition, Seen Throwing a Tear Gas Canister at the Crowd.* But in Spanish.

I wanted to laugh. Cry. Scream. I could picture myself grabbing the iPad and throwing it at the wall like Cora had done with the tear gas in the picture. More importantly, I wanted to reach into the picture—into the very moment—and smack my twin sister until her brain realigned itself in the cavity of her skull.

There were tears in my eyes as I said, "That's my twin sister, Coralina."

They both looked at me like I had grown a second head. To my utter embarrassment, a tear ran down my cheek, and I wiped it away.

"And that happened in Venezuela." I closed my fists so tight it hurt, and at least that kept me from crying some more. "Which I haven't been to in years."

Stunned, Jeff asked, "You have a twin sister?"

"Yes. I try not to talk much about my personal life to keep things professional." Hopefully this was a point on my side, but seeing the hesitation on their faces, I pulled up my social media accounts to show them old pictures of Cora and me. A few with Carlos trickled in, but of course they didn't ask about him.

"Oh, that's great." Jeff gave a huge sigh of relief.

"We wouldn't fire you over something like this, but it would make the paperwork for a work permit a lot trickier since Immigration will look at your records and might find something like this." Macy pulled back her iPad and shut it off. "And I won't sugarcoat this, it might still be an issue considering this is your direct relative. They could think your family supports an authoritarian regime."

The floor dropped from under me. Even though they both expressed their pleasure at having cleared up this issue and started discussing how they could play this out if it came to filing for a work permit for me, Macy's words ran in circles in my head.

Gradually, a realization hit me: the reason I'd been denied my OPT extension was probably because of this. Immigration must have found it when they redid my background check. Because of Cora's recklessness. Not only had she got hurt as a result, but she'd also hurt me.

I remained in the conference room alone even after they'd left for their next meetings. Smiling at the conversation had been hard, but I'd managed. I should've told them about the denial to my application. We should've discussed how to address that. But I worried that if they'd found out, they would've decided to not hire me full-time right away because I came with far too much baggage. On the one side, I had a family that supported the government of my country. On the other, I hid the fact that my visa extension wasn't happening.

And what if I followed that up with the fact I'd just got engaged to another of their employees?

Problematic. Unstable. Unreliable. Those would be only the palatable labels they could give me. Cora had ruined my life.

I pulled my cellphone from my pocket and scrolled until I found the chat with Cora. Without thinking about it, I texted her, Estás feliz? Me acabas de arruinar la vida and hit Send.

That was when the tears started coming out in full. I rested my hot forehead against the cool surface of the table, not even caring about germs. That was also when someone knocked at the door, but my throat was too choked up to attempt answering.

"Cata?" The last person I wanted to see right now walked in, but at least Gabe had the foresight to close the door behind him. "I saw them leave, but you didn't—qué pasó?"

His concern only twisted the knife in my heart. I had been wrong about every little thing I'd done, and I knew it, but I also wanted to wallow and lash out. And he was offering himself like a willing sacrifice as he sat next to me.

When he attempted to pull me into his arms, I pushed him away with all my strength because I couldn't do that to him. Not anymore. "No." I brushed my face with the back of my hands. "You can't fix this one."

Before he could react, I dashed out of the meeting room. Gabe knew the usual meltdown places to find me in, though, so I grabbed my car keys and drove to a different area of the parking lot from what my team typically used.

I found a few empty spots and parked there, where only the blue sky and the swaying palm tree branches would witness my complete breakdown. My phone buzzed in my pocket, but I ignored it. I hadn't had enough time with this car to stuff every nook and cranny of it with essentials, and two lightly used napkins were all I had to blot my face with.

I knew there couldn't have been an error in my application. Every section had been perfect when I'd last checked it before submitting it. Using my phone, I logged in on the site where all the information was, including the big, bold word *denied*. I wanted to scream at them that I had everything they wanted from a model immigrant, that they should take it back and give me another chance to prove it to them.

But for the first time since receiving the notification, I sat down and read every word of it. That was where I found a link to something I hadn't found previously. There actually was a process to try again, not through an appeal but by refiling.

A wave of relief hit me when I noted I still had a few days left to refile my application. Except looking at the paperwork it would require almost had me hurling all over the dashboard. Even if the deadline was too tight, I should still try. Shame at having given up so easily consumed me, shame at pinning my hopes on something other than my own hard work.

"A echarle pichón," I encouraged myself. After all, it was me who had to fix this. I had to stop relying on Gabe. If I succeeded, maybe I didn't need to marry him after all.

That thought stopped me short. Every silly plan we had made flashed through my mind, and not just everything we'd already done. This past weekend, we'd discussed things like whether we'd elope or have another wedding or a double wedding. We'd done mental math about my rental contract in the apartment I shared with Maya versus the fact he'd have to leave home, and what moving in together might entail. I'd done a lot of emphasis on no PDA, when it was clear that was all he wanted to do.

And I'd secretly enjoyed all of the possibilities while looking at the ring I wasn't currently wearing.

But wouldn't it be better to walk away from a fake engagement even if it caused public outcry, than to see it through when maybe I could fix this the proper way?

Suddenly, I remembered the note I'd given him with a time and place to chat and knew I couldn't talk with him. Not today. I didn't have a minute to waste if I wanted to get my application back on track.

There were four missed calls from him and five texts. I replied saying I just needed a minute to compose myself. The responses from Cora I ignored.

Instead, I looked up the nearest immigration attorney and drove to meet them, determined to do the right thing even if it killed me.

CHAPTER TWENTY-SIX

The legal fees were staggering, at least for me. That was the biggest takeaway after meeting with the attorney. She suggested I look around at other firms, and if any of them had better prices, she was willing to match them for me.

Because she openly expressed her interest in my case. It wasn't more of the same, and she was itching for a good fight. She was an immigrant as well: her parents had brought her to the US from Jamaica when she was only seven years old. Even now, well into her fifties, she still remembered how harrowing it had been for her parents to navigate the system. That struggle was what had inspired her desire to help other immigrants succeed. Her history gave me confidence that she would do the best she could if she took my case.

After following her advice, I found her fees weren't overpriced—I was just really poor. And if this refiling didn't work, wasting thousands of dollars on a lost case would hurt my finances for a long time. But in good conscience I couldn't not try.

So I hired her. In order to do that, I spent the afternoon going over every asset I owned, from my car to the last stitch of clothing. I could part with most of it; the problem was that everything was cheap and would fetch even less selling it online.

Except for my car. If I sold it, I could meet almost the entire expense. The rest I could manage by replacing my phone with a cheaper one and selling my laptop. Since we were almost done with school, I wouldn't need it much. I could maybe survive on my work computer or by borrowing Maya's.

The next day, when the sky was clear and the sun was out in full force, I found a nice spot on campus where the only backdrop would be manicured gardens and snapped some pictures of the Corolla my friends had gifted me. Selling a gift had to be some type of sin, but I didn't want to burden my friends with helping me on this too. Shame gnawed at me that I'd almost let Gabe fix my visa problem for me.

I wanted to do it on my own now. I *had* to.

With a heavy heart, I uploaded the shots online and set a price. In a matter of hours, I had a reasonable offer. I sat in my room, staring at the message from the buyer and rereading without processing it. They were ready to buy it the next day in cash.

That was the best possible outcome. I could get the cash, pay the attorney, and start the process right away. The sooner the better, because I was barely going to make the deadline.

This was good news. I should be celebrating. It was a small sacrifice, and surely my friends would understand.

Yet my heart was broken. It was hard to meet Maya's eyes the next morning. My throat worked at a lump while I drove over to meet the new owner, an older woman looking for an easy car to drive. We went over the payment and legal aspects together, and by the end of the afternoon the car had officially changed hands.

She was kind enough to offer to drop me off at home. To be safe, I asked her to leave me at a spot a few blocks away. I stared at the rear of the car as she drove off, and maybe it was the balmy afternoon air of the early summer, but it was hard to breathe. I crouched for a moment, just to gather my bearings. It turned out that my blurry vision wasn't dizziness but tears. I picked myself up and walked the rest of the way home.

The apartment was empty, which wasn't inherently bad except that tonight I needed company, someone to tell me I was doing the right thing. I sent the girls an SOS text and sat on the couch to wait. When I'd entered the apartment, I somehow hadn't thought of turning on any lights, and even though it was now almost nighttime, I couldn't muster the willpower necessary to get out of the darkness. If that wasn't a metaphor for what my life currently was, I didn't know what was.

It had been days since I'd last talked with Gabe. The fact that we sat next to each other at work, that we saw each other in class or while working with the senior project team, hadn't bridged the wedge between us. And it was my fault. For not wearing the ring. For running away from him. For being afraid of him—of what being with him meant.

Never had his nickname for me made more sense. I was acting like a wounded cat, afraid of being touched by the hand that fed it and craving it all the same, only able to respond with a hiss to the conflicting emotions. But for both of our sakes, I needed to see if I could fix this without further entangling him in my mess. It wasn't fair to him to continue down that path.

Sounds trailed closer from outside the apartment, the jangle of keys and shuffling feet. Next, the door opened, and Maya asked, "Cata?"

Followed by Taylor. "Are you there?"

I wished I could've had more poise than I showed them. My entire answer consisted of a single sob. They turned on the light, and squinting just sent the signal for my eyes to pour more water down my cheeks.

"Oh, sweetie. What's wrong?" One of them pulled me up against her, and by the smell of nice perfume I guessed it was Maya. Even if I'd opened my eyes to confirm, I wouldn't have been able to. They stung so much from hours crying.

"Guys," I barely managed to get out, "I've ruined everything."

"Shh." Maya rocked me against her. "Calm down so you can tell us what happened."

"This isn't about Gabe, right?" Taylor asked, reaching for one of my hands that had been limp beside me. She squeezed it as if trying to infuse life into it.

"Yes. No." I pulled away when I figured I was probably ruining Maya's clothes. Lifting the collar of my T-shirt to dab at my face, I added, "Mostly no. It's worse."

Maya raised the palm of her hand. "Wait, does this need alcohol?"

"Maybe," I said, swallowing thickly.

"Well, now I'm scared," Taylor said. "Booze me up."

When Maya presented us with glasses of cheap, sweet wine, the general consensus was to chug rather than toast. It was stronger than expected, and the burn down my throat was like a well-deserved punishment.

"Wait a second. This doesn't taste right." Maya picked up the bottle and twisted it this way and that. "What the hell? It's gone bad."

For the first time in days, I wanted to laugh as she picked up our glasses and tossed the rest of the wine down the drain, especially at the crestfallen look on Taylor's face. When my roommate replaced the beverages with beers, we opened them, and I raised my can for a toast.

"Cheers for the friendship we had until I screw it up with what I have to say."

They both shared a look. Taylor said, "Not sure I like where this is going."

Still, we toasted, and I started my tale, all the way from what Cora had done and what that meant for my family. They knew I had a brother named Carlos who had passed away before I came to the US, but none of the details. I needed them to understand why this whole thing was so important. The one sip of bad wine pushed up my throat a couple of times, but it wasn't because of its lack of quality. Recounting the facts had my stomach roiling with nausea. Heat receded from my limbs, leaving me shivering as I closed my eyes, again seeing the scene of Carlos's funeral on the back of my eyelids.

And it could've been Cora's fate too.

Then I told them about my OPT extension being denied. I could've jumped the timeline and told them about the meeting with HR, where I'd learned Cora's picture was the likely reason for the failure—it certainly would've made me look like a better person when I segued into the fact that I'd agreed to marry Gabe so I could stay.

But I didn't. I recounted the facts as they'd happened chronologically, not pulling any punches about my own small-mindedness. They remained silent even as I revealed I'd sold the car and needed a ride to the attorney's office the next day.

Glancing at both of them confirmed they were shell-shocked. They'd become statues that only blinked.

"Guys?" I prompted them.

Maya drew a sharp breath and directed her attention at Taylor. "Do you wanna hold her down and I beat her up or the other way around?"

Running a hand through her hair, Taylor responded, "I don't know. Both roles sound very satisfying right now."

"How about I close my eyes and you can both go at it at the same time?" Squeezing my eyes only made a straggler tear fall. I swiped at it and waited.

"Of course we're not going to hit you," Taylor said with a huff. "Tempting as it is to see if we can smack the stubbornness out of you."

"Girl, why didn't you ask for help?" Maya asked, her voice pitching higher like it tended to do when she was really upset. "Why do you think you need to solve everything by yourself?"

"Yeah." Even Taylor sounded angry, and she'd never even got angry when her ex had hurt her. "Isn't that what friends are for? You know we'd go to the end of the world for you, right? I thought we'd proved it."

I jumped to my feet, propelled by a sudden itch on my skin. It was hard to tell if I could scratch it with my hands or by begging for forgiveness. The latter was probably going to be healthier.

"I'm sorry. It just felt so huge and complicated, and I couldn't think."

"But you're totally okay with using Gabe."

The statement came from Taylor, and it drew me up cold.

I halted in the middle of the living room, gawking at her. If I'd thought I was feeling bad up until now, it was nothing next to what those words caused. The blow was almost physical; I lost my breath and my balance, and the whole area of my chest hurt.

All I could say was, "I—I . . ."

Maya turned to her. "That's not fair. Could you say you wouldn't have acted the same way if the roles were switched and it were Manny offering to save your life? And maybe *literally*, from what we just heard."

"That's not what I mean." Taylor flushed to the roots of her hair. "I'm just struggling with something. A guy wouldn't just make an offer like this to a girl out of the goodness of his heart, especially considering how wrong things could go if word of this got out."

"Which we will not breathe a word of," Maya cut in to assure me. "Not even to our families. Right?"

"Right." Taylor nodded rapidly. "What I mean is, he's probably in love with you, Cata. And if you don't feel the same, no matter what you do from here, you're going to hurt him real bad."

Dios mío.

"Since when do you care about his feelings?" Maya gave her such a look that it made Taylor shrink away. "Wasn't he supposed to learn a lesson about playing with other people's feelings from fake-dating Cata?"

Taylor jumped to her feet. "Yes, but that was when this whole thing was just fun and games!"

In turn, Maya stood up as well and placed her hands on her hips. The I-mean-business pose. "Isn't that better? Because even if the refiling doesn't work, Gabe can still be Cata's backup plan."

"But isn't that cruel? To use the guy's feelings as backup?" Taylor asked, and I flinched.

Maya leveled a stare at me. "I don't care. Our girl's gotta do what she's gotta do. Even if she doesn't have feelings for him, she *needs* him."

Never would I have expected this role reversal, and I didn't just mean Maya and Taylor switching their stances on the topic of me fake-dating Gabe—or marrying him. Mostly, I meant myself.

The argument they had started about the morality of my actions died down as I crumbled until I sat down on the carpet, looking up at them like they had the answers when, in truth, my mind was screaming a big one at me.

Swallowing hard, I said, "Who said I don't have any feelings for him?"

That stopped them both. They glanced down at me with the same level of shock. Which was to say, very high.

There were no tears anymore, but my chest was hollow. There was an empty space where my heart should be. Despite the chaos of my life in the past few months, despite my best efforts, Gabriel Cabrera had stolen off into the night with it.

"Guys." My voice shook. "What should I do?"

All at once, they threw themselves at me and hid me from the world in their arms. I wished I could stay like that forever.

When they eventually pulled away, it was Maya who said, "Do what your heart tells you to."

"Yes." Taylor grabbed her hand and mine. "We'll be here to help you and support you no matter what, okay? Don't forget that."

For the first time since I'd met them, I said, "I love you guys."

And now I had my answer. Just as I'd finally been honest with my friends, I had to be honest with Gabe. It was time we put an end to the farce.

CHAPTER TWENTY-SEVEN

Three shots of cheap rum later, and I still hadn't gathered enough courage. I was sure that had more to do with the quality of the liquor than me. If this had been Cacique or Diplomático, I'd already be feeling like I could flip a whole car.

No, gathering the courage was definitely all on me.

Today was Big Shenanigans, as Ellen called them: her bachelorette party. It was early compared to the wedding date because Ellen had a long business trip scheduled close to the wedding; she had to leave in a few days and would be back just in time for the big day. That meant it had to be very memorable, which was why the event was an all-day and all-night affair that started out at a spa in the morning, followed by brunch at a nice place in Winter Park, and then a scavenger hunt organized by Peyton. The last part saw us traipsing through their old high school and around town.

After the scavenger hunt, the game had us running around Target in search of the outfits we'd wear for the last event, which would merge both the bachelorette and the bachelor parties. Seeing the two fancy girls sneer and gag at all the cheap stuff around the store kept my mind off the fact that I was increasing the debt on my credit card.

The events kept my worries in the back of my mind most of the day. Only when I was alone in the dressing room did my thoughts circle back to the very important conversation I needed to have with Gabe. When would I have the chance? Tonight, during the party? Tomorrow at the hangover brunch? Or Monday at the office or at school?

Now, I sat at a famous karaoke place in Universal CityWalk with Magdalena on one side and an empty chair on the other. I fiddled with my engagement ring under the table, watching as Gabe chatted with Chris on the opposite side during the intermission. Ellen and Chris had already braved the stage with their rendition of the classic duet by Marvin Gaye and Tammi Terrell—and there sure were no mountains high enough for how high-pitched they'd been. But all the tables packed with their best friends and closest kin had broken out in thunderous applause, me included. Their performance had been amazing anyway, because each seemed to have taken it as a challenge to show the other who was more in love.

Gabe kept throwing glances at me that made my pulse spike. If he signed us up for a duet, I would kill him. But then I'd have to talk to him, and I hadn't managed to say a word to him ever since we'd arrived.

"What's up, girl?" Magdalena nudged me with her shoulder, and I turned my attention to her. "All this drinking is going to get you shit-faced quick, you know." She motioned at the three empty shot glasses before me.

I took a shaky breath. "It's just . . . I need to gather my nerve."

"Oh, are you gonna serenade your fiancé?" She wiggled her eyebrows.

"Something like that." Where were the servers? I needed another shot. Or maybe the whole bottle.

"Relax. Even if you sing worse than Chris, Gabe will still love you."

I sucked in air, but she didn't notice. Her husband, Jason, passed Magdalena the sheet of paper with all the song options, chuckling at one of them. Her whole body lit up as they reminisced about the song. I was sure at some point in the night, one of them, if not both, would end up on stage.

Fortunately for me, the place didn't have "Gasolina" available, or the bachata Gabe and I had danced to during Chris and Ellen's engagement party at his abuela's.

Wait, where had Gabe gone?

Someone plopped on the chair beside me, but it wasn't him. Instead, Ellen sipped from a boozy beverage. "So, tell me. Why do you look all panicky even though you're supposed to be having fun? Is it because you don't want to get up on stage?"

"No. Yes." I shook my head. "It's not that, actually."

"Okay, tell your auntie Ellen so she can make it all better."

We had to shout over the club noise and the latest pop hits blasting in the background. I knew no one else would hear a peep of our conversation, and so far, Ellen had proven herself to be a solid character. I really, really wanted to let off some of the pressure in my chest, but another part of me said I shouldn't.

"No, it's okay. I don't want to ruin your night."

Her eyebrows went up. "Oh, now I'm too intrigued to give up."

I gave her a wan smile and twirled my engagement ring some

more, the rock scraping against the side of my pinky finger. It reminded me of what it represented, a wild new plan that was meant to salvage what was left of my original one.

Picturing a life together with Gabe made my stomach flutter as though an invisible cannon were throwing confetti against its lining. But what if that was all a fantasy? One that was likely to vanish after I told him we didn't have to proceed with this marriage now?

All the rum did was give me the cojones to turn to Ellen and ask, "How did you know you were truly in love with Chris?"

Ellen propped her elbow on the table and her chin on her hand. Though she nursed her drink with the other, her attention wasn't on it but on me. "The first sign was that I couldn't keep my eyes off of him. And not in like a creepy way or anything. But I just kept wondering about little things like how he held his pen, how his T-shirt sat on his shoulders, if his steps were longer or similar to mine."

I looked at the pile of empty shot glasses before me and considered the point. When had I started to think about Gabe so much?

My instinctive answer was as soon as he'd proposed his ridiculous plan to make a mess of the wedding, but if I thought deeper, the truth was different. For four years, I'd given regular updates to my friends about him, and looking back on it, the main point wasn't just that I'd been paying too much attention to his every move for so long, but the fact that everything he did caused a visceral reaction in me.

"Then," she continued, not even bothering to hide her amusement, "there was the fact that every time I saw him, I wanted to jump his bones. That sound familiar?"

Even in the poor lighting of the establishment, she must have been able to tell I was growing really hot in the face, because she started laughing at me.

"Wait, wait." She grabbed my arm. "Why are you so embarrassed about wanting to bone your fiancé?"

Oh, shit. I'd momentarily forgotten our public status.

"Uh." Clearing my throat, I said the truth. "We haven't really done it."

The strobe lights flashed off her wide eyes. Finally, she admitted, "Rare, but not a big deal."

"It's just all been moving so fast." I could feel the babbling about to start in full, and I did nothing to stop it. "One second, we were just classmates, and the next I was saying yes to the most beautiful and wild wedding proposal I could've ever dreamed of, and that can't be normal. Everything's happening at warp speed."

"You're scared, and it makes sense." Ellen nodded, taking a swig of her cocktail. "But does it feel right?"

Yes.

Except for the part where it had all started so I could stay in the country.

Would it have ever led to this point otherwise? I didn't know. I probably never would. And I desperately wanted to.

"I don't know," I confessed to her.

"Honestly, if I were you, I'd also be having cold feet. I've been lucky in that I've known Chris for like fourteen years or something. I know exactly who I'm trusting my heart with, and the other way around—and I sure hope you have that level of intimacy with Gabe too."

Flashbacks of every time his arms had been around me came to mind. When I'd needed the most help, he'd been there, with no hesitation. He'd lifted me up, literally and figuratively, when I was at my weakest, even while knowing the worst of me. But it didn't mean it was enough. I didn't know the deepest parts of him, his dreams and fears. Sharing a tender moment of vulnerability while talking about the loss of our loved ones didn't prepare us to be the worthy recipients of each other's hearts.

But I wanted to be. I drank my shot of rum in one go as I realized this. I wanted to be the woman who completely captured Gabe's heart, not out of self-interest, but to learn to care for it tenderly and with confidence.

My head swam a bit, but my feet were steady enough as I stood up from my chair, declaring, "I need to talk with him."

"Go, girl!"

Except Ellen's voice was drowned out by the MC taking to the stage again. "Thank you everyone for joining us tonight! We're going to resume the show with this next song by none other than our hometown boy band, the Backstreet Boys!" Everyone hooted and hollered at that, but I ignored the ruckus while I scooted between our table and another one. Gabe's most likely location was in the bathroom line, which I'd heard was quite long. Otherwise, I could try the bar. And if that failed, I'd call his phone until he noticed the call.

But then I spotted him . . . walking up to the stage.

"Give it up for Gabe, who will sing the classic 'As Long as You Love Me'!"

The live band began the melody just as Gabe grabbed the mic. While everyone lost their minds, as if he were the real BSB and not just a single guy who was only famous on the UCF campus, I stood rooted to the spot. Like magnets, his eyes found mine in the sea of people, and then his voice came out.

It wasn't just that it was all sweet and tender, but he aimed every single word at me. Even as he moved across the stage, even as he hyped up the band like a pro, even as a few girls pretended to be passionate fans in the front row—his attention remained on me. Like this was a love song Gabriel Cabrera meant only for me.

I grabbed my purse, more determined than I'd ever felt, and marched up to the stage while he finished the song. Thunderous applause greeted the end of his performance, but Gabe was hasty in climbing down to join me.

We paused there, staring at each other as if afraid to break the careful balance we'd been protecting all night. But he'd done that with that song already. I couldn't take this anymore or my heart would explode in my chest.

Inhaling the scent of his cologne, I rose on my tippy-toes so I could say into his ear, "We need to have a talk. In private."

Alarm flashed through his eyes. I tried to soothe it by grabbing his hand, and he let me lead the way out. I was aware of many eyes following our moves, and Gabe's friends and family were probably going to think funny things—after all, who wouldn't want to reward such a doting fiancé? —but that didn't matter.

The air outside was humid and impregnated with the smells from restaurants nearby. My sandal caught in a groove on the sidewalk, and Gabe reacted like lightning to catch me. His arms circled my waist easily, and he could probably feel my rapid heartbeat against his chest.

"Thank you," I said, meaning it for more than this catch. But that was nowhere near enough. As I pulled away from his warmth, I tucked my hair behind my ears and said, "Could we go somewhere? I don't—I don't want to do this here."

A small crease appeared between his eyebrows. "Is everything okay?"

"Yes." I forced my lips to stretch into a smile. "It will be." Or so I hoped.

I laced my fingers in his again. We walked like that towards the massive parking lot. He fingered the engagement ring, maybe noting it for the first time tonight. Our hands lingered until we reached his red Jeep, as though neither of us wanted to let go.

"So." Gabe cleared his throat while he started the car. "Was it so bad you just had to whisk me away in embarrassment?"

If anything, I was whisking him away so his adoring fans didn't cinch their claws around him.

"Um, no. It was all right."

"All right?" he screeched. "*All right* is singing in the shower. You can't tell me you didn't feel anything."

I couldn't. Not until I said everything else first.

Changing the topic, I asked, "So, where should we go?"

"Home." The look I gave him tore a smile out of Gabe. "Don't worry, Mom's spending the night at Abuela's. She said, and I quote, the last thing she wanted was to suffer through two drunk idiots. Joke's on her, though, because I'm not drunk, and Chris is spending the night with Ellen."

I wished knowing we were going to be alone didn't have my stomach doing Olympic gymnastics.

To keep things in safe territory, I asked, "How was Chris's bachelor party earlier?"

"Now, *that* was just all right," he said, sighing. "It's not like I wanted to go to a strip club or something, but did they really have to spend the entire afternoon shooting darts like it's a professional sport instead of something to do as you wait for another drink?"

I bit my lips not to smile. "What would've been more fun instead?"

"Being with you." Gabe tore his eyes from the dark road ahead of us for a moment, long enough to sweep a glance over me that raised the temperature in the car. "But listening to what you have to say will be just fine too. I assume this is about why you've been avoiding me for days?"

I licked my lips. Maybe I needed more liquid courage.

Still, I said, "Yes."

We drove in silence until he pulled up at his house. Even with the light traffic at night, the drive had felt like an eternity. As we walked up the lawn and he opened the front door, I wished desperately to go back in time to the calm silence we'd shared just minutes ago. There would be nothing calm about this conversation once I set foot in his house.

"Want a drink?" Gabe removed his blazer on the way to the kitchen. The tight black shirt stretched in areas of his back that were all sinewy muscle and what I now knew to be soft skin. I fisted my hands to stave off the itch to reach for him.

"Sure. Make it stiff."

That made him glance back, eyebrows raised. "Careful what you wish for, Gatita."

Wasn't that the moral of the story?

Still, he poured us two rum and Cokes, adding lime for garnish. After a quiet toast and a healthy swig, Gabe said, "Okay, I'm all ears."

As I sat across the kitchen island from him, I was at a loss where to start. Where had it gone off the rails?

Then I remembered. It wasn't because of the conversation with HR and what had happened from there on, but minutes before that. When my lack of engagement ring had shut off his smile.

"I'm scared," I admitted, the sound of my voice echoing in the quiet.

Gabe lifted his eyes towards me, a shocking amount of hurt in them. "Of me?"

"No, of myself. Of all of this."

I paused. The next words lodged in my throat, choking me. I had to make sure to get the hard part out of the way first. It was the right thing to do for him, in case he'd only been doing this out of some sweet but misguided sense of obligation.

"I hired an attorney to refile my visa application. We may have a chance, and if we succeed, you won't have to marry me." I swallowed thickly and dropped my eyes to his hands resting on the counter, to the long fingers that had held my hand so securely and caressed my hair as he had kissed me. "Win-win, right? It would piss your mom off even more than she already is, and you won't need to be shackled to me. You can keep on dating, and I'll stop bothering you."

Absolutely nothing followed that statement. The air conditioner and the distance from him chilled me. I rubbed my hands up and down my arms, and when it wasn't enough to warm me up, I took a bigger gulp of the cocktail, hoping the alcohol would do it.

"I'm glad about the visa stuff. Maybe I should've thought of that earlier." The way his voice was clipped around such heavy words settled on my shoulders like the weight of the world. I could already feel pinpricks in my eyes. I closed them.

"No, I should've thought about it myself. Then none of this mess would've happened."

"Is that what you think this is? A mess?" Gabe sounded closer, and when I opened my eyes, he was right next to me, leaning on the countertop as though this was a casual chat. Except there was nothing casual about the thunder in his eyes.

My mouth was dry. I knew this would make it worse, but I had to finally be honest.

"Yes, it is." There was no change in him except my own

increasing awareness of the space he took, of his nearness. Gathering all the strength rum could provide, I said, "It's not a lie. We wouldn't be engaged if it weren't for this visa issue. As soon as we fulfilled our deal, we were supposed to go our separate ways. And maybe that's what needs to happen now."

"Is that what you want?" Gabe's voice was so low I barely caught the words. When I did, my wits scrambled away. He tilted his head to regard me better. "And what if it's not what I want?"

"I, uh." I swallowed thickly. "What?"

"I have a very different view of this whole thing." Gabe turned my stool around until I faced him. With how close he'd got, he was able to nestle between my legs and push me up against him. He looked down at me from his vantage. "Remember what I said to you when I gave you that ring?"

No. Right now I couldn't even remember my own name.

The corners of his lips drew up. "None of it was a lie, Gatita."

The sharp breath I drew left me dizzy, and he steadied me with his hands. "That can't be true. You said . . . you said outrageous things. About looking at me and—dijiste que me amabas. And that can't be true."

"It is—sadly, since you don't love me back." One of his hands tilted my face back, caressing the edge of my jaw with a hot stroke. "But if *you* want out of this engagement, I'll back off. If you want me out of your life, I'll leave."

I grabbed two fistfuls of his shirt, blinking back tears. "I—I just don't want to keep using you."

"Use me." The timbre of his words carried a growl. He drew me right up against him until I was on my tiptoes and my nose bumped against his. "Use me when you need help, when you need a laugh. Use me when your body itches for my touch. When you're bored and scared or sad and lonely. Use me as a pillow or as your personal chauffeur. Catalina, I want to be there for you. I want to be *with* you."

"But am I what you need?" And there it was, the ugly truth that had been haunting me. I couldn't possibly tell him I was head over heels for him this way. A tear rolled down my cheek, and Gabe wiped it with a tender swipe of his thumb. "Am I *enough?*"

Gabe shook his head softly. "No, you're not enough. You're stubborn, hardworking, sweet, angry, beautiful, intimidating. You're everything I ever dreamed of and more."

The breath I released was shaky. "Oh, Gabe."

"So, what is it going to be?" His lips were a hair's breadth away from mine, and I smacked his chest softly for the manipulation. He pulled back, his eyes twinkling but an uncertain smile on his face. "Do we break off the engagement, or do we try to see where this goes?"

"What if everything goes wrong?" I whispered, and he cupped the back of my head in his hand.

"It won't, because I'm in love with you, and that's not fake." Gabe's smile returned in full. "And hopefully, before tonight is over, you'll love me back just a little."

He had already accomplished that even before swooping down to kiss me.

The first thing I noticed when I woke up the next morning was the heat. And the second thing was that I was mostly wearing a sweaty bedsheet and a whole man half on top of me.

"Gabe," I choked out, pushing him off. My head was breaking into two, and my mouth tasted like it was stuffed with cotton— and not the candy variety, but cotton that had been in a bottle of really gross medicine. Moreover, he was heavy, and I was having severe trouble breathing. "You need to move."

He finally reacted to the rasp of my voice. With a groan, he rolled onto his side. I gulped for air and tossed the bedsheets away so the steam could escape. Then I made the mistake of turning my head.

Gabe rubbed his bleary eyes and then pressed his temples. The fact we shared a hangover after what we'd done last night wasn't the most concerning part. What *was* concerning was that in my haste to cool down, I'd discovered he was only in underwear. His boxers sat way too low and skewed on his lean hips. His pectorals, abdomen, and the V down his hips were so well defined they rippled as he moved. And down there was ample evidence he'd been enjoying the heat we'd created under the bedsheets.

The next mistake I made was looking down at myself. Seeing I was still in my underwear offered little relief. I snatched the bedsheets back up to cover myself. Then I tossed my mane of tangled hair away from my face.

Gabe was now fully awake, his mood bright after what he'd just seen. "Did I die and go to heaven?" was his greeting.

I rolled my eyes. "Can you please go out so I can dress?"

"Why dress when I'll want to undress you right away?"

I nudged his leg away from me with my foot. "I'm serious. Maybe your previous girls were all comfortable in their skin, but I'm not."

Gabe rolled onto his side and propped up his head on his raised hand. It didn't matter to him that this further highlighted the situation below his waist. "Why not? Your skin is beautiful, from what little I saw."

I knew he was baiting me, and I still blushed to the roots of my hairs. Clearing my throat, I said, "Oh, you saw plenty more than I expected to show, trust me."

Gabe smirked.

Last night's kiss had started like any of our kisses, suffocating in its intensity and the desire we shared to get even closer. When that hadn't been enough, Gabe had wrapped my legs around his waist and carried me up the stairs into his room, somehow managing not to break the connection for long despite the jostling. Fortunately, once he'd got us in his room, he'd tossed me on the bed and climbed on top of me, where it was easier for both of us. It was like it had been on my living room couch, except amplified by the fact we'd drunk a lot of rum downstairs and, in my case, at the nightclub.

I wished I could've blamed him for what happened next, but the fault was all mine. As he'd trailed hot kisses punctuated by swipes of his tongue down my neck, as he'd sucked the sensitive skin at the base of my throat, as one hand had pushed the hem of my dress all the way to my stomach, I'd pushed him away with all my strength—just so I could tear open his shirt, until he got the hint of just doing away with it.

That was all he'd needed to grow bolder. In short minutes, we were down to our underwear, and that was when I'd realized the dizziness wasn't because of him but because of the booze. As Gabe had started to work his way down the uncharted territory of my chest, everything I'd drunk earlier had rushed upwards. Only thanks to extreme willpower had I managed not to become a human fountain.

I'd ended up dashing out of the room and into the bathroom, where I'd proceeded to ruin the rest of the night.

Now, facing him in the morning, I couldn't help but hide my face in my hands.

That wasn't all. Gabe had held my hair as I'd emptied the contents of my stomach and handed me towels afterwards as I washed my face. A while later I was woozy but with medicine and a sandwich in my stomach, and he'd tucked me next to him in his bed, where we'd fallen asleep.

"I thought you were wearing pants last night," I said, as though that were the most important topic here.

He shrugged. "It wasn't comfortable, so I took them off."

I was thankful. But also not, because now I knew what I was missing out on.

"Gabe," I started, tucking the bedsheets under my armpits, "there's something very important you need to know."

"I'm all ears." And then he made a feeble attempt at tugging the bedsheets away from me, which I didn't allow. "And eyes."

"I'm a virgin," I declared, which effectively shut him up. "And I don't think I'm ready to change that status."

Gabe cocked his head a little. "Está bien."

"Are you sure?" My eyebrows went up. "Because you're, uh, very active in that regard as far as I know—and can see." Here I didn't even bother hiding that I referred to the massive boner in his boxers.

"I respect you," he said simply. Something warm expanded in my chest that had nothing to do with the overwhelming heat in the room. "Doesn't mean I'm not going to dream about making love to you every night until you're ready, but I'll respect your wishes."

I didn't know whether to laugh or cry, so I settled for, "Thank you."

"Guess I'll go get some breakfast started." He scooted away until he sat at the edge of the mattress and gave out a huge yawn. At the same time, he stretched his arms upwards. The play of muscles in his back made my heart beat in a staccato, but I held my hands firmly tucked away. He pushed to his feet and shuffled towards the door.

"Um." My voice caught his attention again. I made an eight in the air with my finger. "Aren't you putting on any clothes?"

Gabe looked down at himself. "I'm wearing underwear."

"More clothes, I mean." I gave him a deadpan look.

He appeared to consider it before shrugging. "Nah, I'm good." With that he turned away and headed downstairs, leaving me gaping after him.

A few seconds later, after clearing my head, I jumped out of the bed and looked around for my dress. It was bizarre being in his room while I wore so little, but even more that this was my second time in such a state. The last thing I needed was for his mom to walk in wielding her chanclas again. Where the hell was my dress?

I didn't want to hang around like this any longer, so I opened Gabe's closet, grabbed the first T-shirt and shorts I saw, and put them on. They were huge on me, which definitely provided coverage.

Downstairs, I said, "I can't find my dress."

"Good," he said by the stove as he cracked eggs on a hot pan. "Let it stay gone forever."

"Too bad for you I put on some of your clothes." I slid onto the same stool as last night and pushed away the glasses that had been filled with our cocktails. He'd found a hair tie somewhere and made a messy bun at the back of his head. It was doing things to me as he made a quick breakfast.

Another thing that did? When we were eating a few minutes later, and he leaned on the counter like last night, except this time he wasn't wearing a shirt.

"So how come you're a virgin?" he asked conversationally, which sent scrambled eggs down the wrong pipe in my throat.

I took a big gulp of orange juice. When I was able to breathe again, I noted he was serious. I pushed around the food on my plate, debating whether to tell him my reasons. I didn't have to, and if I said as much, I was sure he'd respect that too. But now that we were officially and truthfully boyfriend and girlfriend, I didn't want to start off with omissions or deceptions.

"I haven't thought about it much because I've never had a boyfriend." Shrugging, I lifted my eyes to him. "But I don't think I'd like it to be just something I did while drunk one night."

To my surprise, he nodded. "So is it something you'd like to wait for after marriage?"

That stumped me. My eyebrows lowered, and my eyes settled on his empty ring finger.

Just like I'd never pictured myself wearing a wedding gown, because I'd never been counting on a future involving such a commitment with a man, I had also not given a lot of thought to sex. It didn't mean I'd never been curious about it or that I'd never fantasized about a guy—including the one before me. I'd just been busy with so many other things instead.

His question made me reflect on the fact that, yes, I didn't want a milestone like that to mean nothing. I wanted it with someone I was secure with, that I trusted, that I loved. And who did so in return. That was what felt right to me.

"I think so, yes." I watched out for any signs of disapproval. Instead, he gave a big grin.

"Then when are we getting married?"

I expelled a huge sigh. "Like I said, we don't need to—"

"But I still want to." He said this with seriousness back in his expression.

"Um, if this is only because I'd rather wait after marriage to have sex, you may want to reevaluate that."

"No, that's not it." Gabe reached up to scratch the back of his head. "I don't need to keep looking. It's you I want to spend my life with like this. Having breakfast half naked—fully naked would be preferable—talking about any and everything. Every morning for the rest of our lives."

That almost sent the world to a tilt. He destabilized my views every time he opened his heart so fully like this. Huffing, I tried to bring him back down to earth. "Look, it's just too quick, and there might not be any need after all. I promise you that if you stay a good boyfriend for a while, I'll consider it again."

"And how long is a while?" The smile was coming back, so I braced myself. "A couple of days? Weeks? Surely not two whole months."

"Gabe!"

He reached forward and grabbed my hand, the one with my engagement ring, and kissed it. "I'll support you in anything you need to make the refiling successful, but when I proposed I was serious. And trust me, I was pretty surprised by it too."

"You're crazy," I whispered, turning my hand to grasp his.

"Yeah, for you." Gabe raised his eyes to meet mine again. "I'm serious. When do you want to get married?"

I bit my lip. When it was clear I didn't have the answer, he pulled his hand away, but only so we could finish breakfast. After putting the plates away, Gabe asked, "We don't have to decide now, but how about we start by looking up what we need to do in order to get married, just in case?"

"Fine, but before that please put on some clothes."

He groaned.

Later, we sat on the couch, dressed in matching comfy shorts and old T-shirts. We propped our legs on the coffee table, and he drew me against him with his arm around my shoulders and fired up his laptop.

As I watched him navigate the browser with one hand, he casually said, "Since we're in the mood for sharing some hidden truths, I wanted to say one more thing."

"Uh-oh." I twisted enough to glance up at him. Whatever was on his mind couldn't be terrible, because there was a little smile playing on his lips.

"So . . ." He typed *requisites to get married in the great state of Florida* in the browser's search bar. "Remember when I first asked you to ruin the wedding, and we made the deal? I might have not told you the full truth."

"Gabe." There was a warning in my voice, and I stiffened. If anything, his smile widened, and he hit Enter. A short list of requisites popped up atop the results.

"And remember you asked me why I'd give up the possibility of the full-time spot at Metal Systems so easily?"

All the options I'd conjured up in my head vanished. I didn't understand what other truth he might've possibly withheld about this particular point.

"Um, yes?"

"Well." He looked down at me, his eyes glinting like thick honey against the morning sunshine streaming through the living room windows. "That's because I had already interviewed for a position at a different company, and, uh, I just got the offer yesterday."

"Gabe." This time his name tumbled out of my mouth like a surprise. I sat up straight.

He raised his hands. "And for the record, that was before we even made our deal. I started looking for another position because I'm pretty sure Metal Systems is going to hire you. The role was going to be yours all along, on your own merit." Seeing that I was absolutely speechless, Gabe drew me back against his side and kissed the top of my head. "So don't feel bad for me, okay? The other place is going to pay better." He chuckled.

"I hate you."

"I'm sure you do, and that's why you're considering marrying me, huh?"

I sighed and snuggled closer against him, completely surrendering to him. "Ya cállate y miremos la lista."

For the next hour or so, we pored over the requisites. We discussed the legal and church wedding options, and since we both practiced the same religion, we decided on a wedding with vows in front of God rather than just marrying with a license.

"But let's not invite my entire family," he begged.

I shrugged. "It's okay, I don't even have any family to bring except Maya and Taylor."

"We can have a small wedding by the beach," he said, and the fact I oohed sent us down a search spiral for a venue with a decent price. The last thing we needed to pin down was the date, but that would have to wait on whether my refiling was successful or not.

When his mom walked through the front door, she caught us in the middle of a phone call with Chris and Ellen's wedding priest to schedule a premarital course with him, which staved off her desire to beat us up. She eyed the way we were dressed, drew her own conclusions as she crossed herself, and ultimately left us alone.

Gabe turned to me with a barely contained smile and said, "Bienvenida a la familia." And as I laughed, he kissed me.

CHAPTER TWENTY-EIGHT

That walking on sunshine song had always annoyed me—its peppiness felt so artificial—yet that was how I felt on the morning of our senior design presentation.

We had survived the final exams and papers of the last semester of school, which in my case was a miracle. For the first time in my college career, my personal life had got in the way of my studies. Gabe hadn't struggled with his academics as much as I had, which was only a tad annoying until he'd offered to study with me before exams. That was what people called a double-edged sword because while, yes, we covered a lot of ground more easily, our hands also wanted to cover each other's grounds.

But that wasn't the only reason I was happy. Yesterday had been my *formal* job interview for the full-time position at Metal Systems. And the emphasis on the word *formal* was entirely theirs. In fact, at the end of the interview, Macy had said, "We just have to follow the process at this point, but we're so excited to bring you aboard!"

After that, I'd marched right out of the meeting room, grabbed Gabe by his wrist, and dragged him into an empty meeting room, where I proceeded to give him a mouthful about my well-deserved win—and by mouthful I meant I made out with him. In the office. Who had I become?

A happy person, that was what.

If that weren't enough, I'd woken up this morning to a notification from my attorney saying my case was being processed already.

Now all we had left was this presentation and we would be ready to graduate, and I looked forward to good things after that. Hopefully, my refiled application would be successful and I'd be able to accept the full-time position at the company without a hitch. Then there was the wedding to look forward to—Chris and Ellen's, to clarify. All of which would make the summer something to look forward to. For the first time in months, I saw the light at the end of the tunnel, and it looked like the same kind of sunshine as the song.

And then there was Gabe. Maybe he was the sunshine itself.

Now that he knew I was again without a car, he picked me up before going to school. We were supposed to meet up with Taylor, Brandon, and Tom to go over the finer details of our project at the shop. They were already there, crouching over the vehicle. Taylor went over the wiring, Tom made a final pass of polishing the fairings of the vehicle, and Brandon went over a checklist we had prepared to make sure we had everything ready.

It was the latter who, upon looking up at our entrance, said, "Good. You're driving the car, Cabrera."

"What?" Gabe reeled back a little. "Why me?"

"Dude, you're the shortest and slimmest of the three of us," Tom said.

Taylor stood up from her crouch with thunder in her face. "They don't want to let me drive it because I 'could get injured.'"

I made a move that prompted Gabe to grab my hand and hold me back.

"What if *I* get injured?" he asked them. "Besides, I don't want to, and if Taylor does, she should."

"But she's a girl," Brandon said, shrugging as though he wasn't showing his ass with his words. "She's probably a terrible driver."

My best friend and I exchanged a glance.

However, she appeared as determined to be the pilot as I'd seen her when she'd resolved to break up with Amber, and again when she was getting ready for her second date with Manny. Like she knew, beyond a shade of doubt, that she was right.

So I lied for her. "As a matter of fact, Taylor is one of the best drivers I've ever seen."

"There." Gabe raised his hand. "Everyone in favor of Taylor driving say aye."

Three to two, we chose Taylor as the pilot.

After everything was triple-checked, the guys picked up the vehicle and loaded it in the back of Brandon's pickup. He and Tom drove off to the track the teacher had prepared in a closed-off parking lot on campus. The race typically attracted a lot of people from other years and even from other programs. Some went as far as making banners to cheer for their favorite teams, and there was a lot of heckling involved, especially if any vehicle failed during the race. We hadn't brought any cheerleaders, but I wasn't worried about that; we'd done a stellar job with the design and manufacture. Now everything rested on Taylor's shoulders.

She rode in Gabe's Jeep with us as we followed Brandon's

pickup to the site. I twisted to look at her from the passenger seat. "No pressure, but you better not drive like you actually do."

Gabe flashed a glance at us. "That bad?"

"Worse," I confirmed.

"No worries," Taylor said with a terrifying grin. "We're getting full marks on the design and manufacture, and what we need to win the race is someone reckless. Therefore, I'm the bisexual for the job."

I sent a prayer to the heavens and wished for the best. The entire grade for the class depended on this race.

It took a good ten sweaty minutes to haul our creation to our place at the starting line. The course looped into the corners of the parking lot and back around in a misshapen circle that had been outlined by myriad traffic cones. After giving Taylor a four-person pep rally, Gabe and I waited by the starting line with our hands clasped together. This seemed to capture people's attention far more than the teacher's speech did. I tried to tug my hand free to see if the stares would shift away, but since Gabe didn't let me off the hook, I couldn't test the theory.

"Let them stare," he whispered in my ear.

I turned to him. "Is this what life is going to be like from now on?"

His answer was a huge shit-eating grin. The words he'd been about to say died on his lips as the teacher blew the horn and the competitors took off. The entirety of my class erupted in cheers.

Taylor floored the engine from the get-go to take the lead. The next vehicle tried to overtake her, and she slammed the side of ours against it. Our rival careened off to the side. Someone smashed directly into one of the traffic cones lining the course, and the plastic made their wheels catch until one of them came right off.

Taylor raced away, taking a corner with such speed she had to angle her body against the momentum to not lose control.

"Está loca," Gabe said only to me, and I nodded.

My new crappy phone started buzzing in my pocket, but I ignored it. There was no way I'd look away from the train wreck. Or car wreck, I thought as a second vehicle dropped out of the race because its chassis had torn apart at the midway point. The driver dashed away in time to not be run over by another competitor.

Gabe shook his head. "Yeah, I'm so happy I didn't drive."

"Me too, but I'm glad she has insurance." A fact I knew after she'd been in multiple small traffic accidents over the years.

I pulled my phone out of my pocket, since it wouldn't stop shaking, and wasn't surprised to see it was Mami calling. I let it keep ringing but put it on silent. I would call her back after the race.

Taylor was coming back around towards the finish line, still leading the pack. I caught a flash of glee in her face as she made every other driver eat her dust. When she rushed through the finish line as the indisputable winner, Gabe and I jumped and shouted in joy, smacked a big, wet kiss on each other, and ran over to my best friend.

"That was wild!" I shouted.

She threw herself at me, and we barely managed to not come crashing down. Next to my ear, she shouted back, "That was amazing!"

"Holy shit, you rock!" Gabe also shouted.

Taylor shook her fist at Brandon and Tom, who stood slack-jawed beside us. "Take that, suckers!"

Rather than being offended, the two big guys started laughing. Next thing, they lifted her up on their shoulders and paraded her around the track, even in front of the teacher, who was busy grading every group on a chart. I pulled out my cellphone to snap a few pictures to send to Manny and Maya. Once that was done, I saw eleven missed calls from Mami. She could sometimes get intense if I wasn't on the phone right away, but I didn't recall ever having this many missed calls in the span of like ten minutes. No, I confirmed after checking, just five.

"Ya vengo," I told Gabe, heading towards an empty spot where the noise wasn't so loud. I called her back, and she answered on the first ring.

Except it wasn't Mami but Papi, and he was crying.

The sunshine that had been bathing me vanished just like that.

"Papi!" The word tore out of my throat, feeling raw. "Qué pasa?"

Everything around me faded as I concentrated. He'd started yelling, not at me but just using anger to get the words out of his chest. All that registered was that something had happened to Coralina. They hadn't seen her in days. She wouldn't pick up the phone. Mami had gone around asking her friends from university, but they also didn't know what was going on. Papi had gone to the police, which led nowhere. He suspected it had something to do with Rodrigo, Cora's boyfriend, since they couldn't find him either.

I closed my eyes and swayed. The pitch of my body was stopped by another, and I vaguely registered arms closing around me.

In a daze, I asked Papi since when—since when was Cora missing.

Four days.

After the first day, they hadn't thought much of it. She'd sent them a text saying she was with her boyfriend, and they were already tired of telling her that premarital relationships were a sin and having her ignore them. After the second day, which included no responses to their texts and calls, they began to worry. On the third day, they started calling all of Cora's friends. This morning was when they had gone to the police.

Papi had decided to call me then. Mami had passed out on her chair as the detective pretty much said there was nothing they could do if this was a domestic issue, which was in his opinion what was going on. He even had las bolas to suggest that maybe Cora and Rodrigo were eloping.

"No," I said to Papi. "Ella no haría eso."

I knew this for a fact. While Cora and I were vastly different, I knew her like the back of my hand, and I knew she was all about the telenovela. No one could pay attention to her if she simply disappeared from the screen.

Something was truly wrong.

Gabe moved around to face me, holding me up by my arms as I spoke with Papi, listening to half of the conversation. Gabe's expression was heartbreaking, as though he were also about to cry. But then he started wiping my face, and I realized that I was the one crying.

"Help me. I need to go home," I told him, and Gabe bundled me in his arms and carted me away to his Jeep.

As we headed over to my apartment, Gabe didn't have much to say, but I did. I started out by calling my sister every horrible name under the sun that dared to keep shining above us. And then I realized that the last time I'd had contact with her, I'd blamed her for getting my OPT denied and ruining my life. In my heart, I had wished we didn't share the same face. That we hadn't been born together.

A cry tore from my chest when it dawned on me that I could lose her. That I might have already lost her. That I would be alone forever if both of my siblings went ahead of me. Gabe's hand drew my head between my knees to help me breathe, but that wasn't enough to ease the ache in my chest.

Maybe only my parents could. Or maybe I was meant to do that for them.

I had to go to them right this moment, but how?

CHAPTER TWENTY-NINE

I was walking underwater. Everything I saw and heard was muffled. I moved in slow motion, and it was hard to breathe.

The apartment was empty since Maya was in class, but a few minutes later, Taylor arrived. Once it was clear I had to go back home to my parents, she and Gabe helped me see if any flights were available. The cost was astronomical, nothing I could afford even if I maxed out my credit card. That made me cry again until Taylor shook me by the shoulders.

"No more crying! We're here to help."

She escorted me to my room and helped me pack for a trip I couldn't book. Going through the motions started waking me up. Taylor pulled my suitcase from the closet, and I said a backpack should suffice. I could only bring the basics to not catch the greedy eyes of anyone looking to repossess my valuables.

I found the shoebox where I'd stored all my things from back home. The old, barely smart cellphone I'd arrived with, my house keys, my passport, and my national ID. Taylor collected a few toiletries from the bathroom and brought them over. Where was Gabe? But I didn't think about it further as I picked the most threadbare T-shirts and underthings I had and stuffed them in along with my wallet.

"It'll take days to drive there," I suddenly said to Taylor. My neurons had taken a walk and weren't quite back yet.

"You're not driving to Venezuela," she said with a firmness that shook me. "You're flying."

"But how?"

"Ready?" Gabe popped his head in. Before I was able to ask him for what—an emotional breakdown? I was there already—he said, "Let's go. We have to get going now."

They ignored me after that. Taylor spoke to Gabe, adding, "Okay, be safe. I'll talk to the school, but don't forget to call you guys' boss."

"Yes, ma'am." He saluted her before extending a hand towards me. "Ven conmigo, Gatita."

By force of habit, I grabbed his hand. "Where?"

"We have to get to Miami tonight," he said as he gently pushed me towards the apartment door. "Or you'll miss your flight tomorrow morning."

My eyes welled, and I clung to his arm. "But it was so expensive."

I felt him kiss the top of my head. "No importa. Me importas tú."

We drove in silence for hours. My head jumped from one horrible scenario to the next, and I prayed more than ever that I wasn't returning to Maracaibo for another funeral. When we made it to Miami, I immediately told him to get home safe. Gabe flashed me a look like I was out of my mind.

"I'm not leaving you alone."

My heart couldn't take any more of this. My face was tired

from crying so much, and I just rested my forehead on the cool pane of the window. "You don't have to do any of this."

"The hell I don't." His voice was calm, but his eyes blazed even in the night that encased the car. "This is when you need me the most."

He'd rented us a room at a hotel close to the airport. Sleep evaded me the entire night, but Gabe held my anxiety at bay as he cradled me in his arms.

Later, during the night, when his breathing had evened out, I snuggled closer to him and whispered, "I don't deserve you."

He shifted, and as I glanced up, I found him as wide awake as I was. Gabe asked, "What do you mean?"

I thought back to all the times I'd been mean to him, both to his face and behind his back. Tears came to my eyes as I confessed every petty thought I'd had of him, all the ugly things I'd said thinking they didn't matter and that now made it so clear that, in fact, he was too good for me.

"Guess we're two peas in a pod, then, because I'm no saint either," he said, tucking me against his shoulder again. I found his eyes, and a small smile stretched his lips. "Everything I did was so you would fall for me, you know? Teasing you, convincing you to be my fake girlfriend, asking you to marry me. I wanted you to look at me and only me. To think of me. To fall for me. Just like I fell for you."

That made me sit up. The bedsheets fell away from me, and the cool air attempted to bring my temperature down despite Gabe's words heating me up from the inside.

With a shaky voice, I asked, "So your ex was right? You had a crush on me?"

"Huge, flaming torch, more like," Gabe said with a sad little laugh. "She was right to be angry at me. I shouldn't have dated her or any of my previous exes when I'd had my eyes set on you since, like, freshman year."

I bit my lips hard as if that could hold the waterworks back. No surprise when it didn't work. Gabe pulled me back against his chest, and soon after, his breathing evened out. Exhaustion weighed heavily on me, sapping the last remnants of the energy I'd had this week. I gnawed at my lip while I watched the contour of Gabe's sleeping face in the dark. If it weren't for him and the girls, I'd probably be stuck in my room crying my heart out, frozen in that state, unable to do anything or ask for help. I had to produce the willpower I needed so their efforts wouldn't be in vain.

In the morning, Gabe woke me up from a short and restless sleep and made me have a banana for breakfast. I watched him fuss around the hotel room, picking our things back up. There were dark circles around his eyes, as if he too hadn't slept well at all.

This wonderful boy whom I'd once detested deserved better.

Tears spilled from my eyes as he drove us to the airport. My chest squeezed harder and harder throughout the check-in process. When it was time for me to go, I looked into his eyes, darkened by worry, and I steeled myself to do the right thing for him.

"Gabe." My breath hitched as he stroked his thumb across my cheek, wiping a fresh tear away. I held onto his hand for a moment before removing it from my face. His warmth lingered on my skin, making me long for him even before I said the words that had been constricting my lungs. Finally, I let them out. "We need to break up."

"What?" He reeled back as if physically struck.

"I—" My voice broke off. I dabbed furiously at my face,

trying to get rid of the proof of how hard this was. "I don't know if I'll be able to come back." My application was in process; I didn't even know if leaving the country would nullify it.

Gabe tried to hold my hand, and I pulled away. "Cata, I'll wait for you. As long as it takes."

"But that's not fair to you." I hugged myself, my voice barely a whisper amidst the noise in the terminal entrance. "You deserve someone normal. Someone who can be with you without any gimmicks."

Gabe closed his arms around me, lowering his face to the crook between my neck and shoulder. His hold was the only reason my knees didn't buckle as he said, "Well, I love *you*. I want to be with you."

"So do I," I admitted for the first time, sobbing, clinging to his clothes, wishing I didn't have to do this. "Gabe." Gingerly, I held his face away from mine. He blinked fast, as if holding down tears. "I've never said this to you before, but . . . you're the best thing that's ever happened to me."

"Cata—"

"No, listen." I took a shaky breath and stepped back, looking up at him. "I'm not saying this because you've helped me through all my darkest moments, including now." I offered a watery smile. "You've been my ray of sunshine; you've brought out all the best parts of me I didn't even know I had."

Gabe had made me laugh, he'd made me want to fight, he'd made me love. None of that had been fake. I loved him with every fiber of my being.

"You reminded me of what's truly important." I sniffled, my chin trembling while I fought back the sobs lodged in my throat. "F-family. You'd do everything for yours. Now I have to do the same. And I don't know what I'm going to find. I don't know how long I'll be away. Or if I'll be able to come back. Or how this will change me. And—"

"I'll go with you." Gabe grabbed my hand, tried to tug me closer. "I'll get another ticket."

No, I mouthed the word. Then I said, "I would never put you in danger. I would never take you from your family." By this point, my entire body was shaking with the strength of my grief. "The best I can do for you is set you free, Gabe."

Rising on my tiptoes, I placed one last kiss on his cheek.

"Cata, don't—"

I didn't wait for him to finish his sentence. With a burst of energy, I threw myself into a big group of people heading for the security line. Their chatter drowned out Gabe's final words for me. Only once I was safely on the other side, after completing the security check, did I glance back.

Gabe's lone figure stood outside the gate. His eyes were still fixed on me, and even from this far I could tell he was crying. Knowing I'd put that pain in his face cleaved my heart in two, and unbeknownst to him, I left one half with him.

The flight was bumpy, but I spent the entire time asleep. Once, the person sitting next to me woke me up with a jolt when my head had rolled over their shoulder. I settled against the window on my other side, back into nightmares.

Clapping woke me up. Disoriented, it took me a while to understand I was in a plane. People were already standing up in the aisle, speaking loudly and predominantly in Spanish in the cadence of different Venezuelan accents.

Welcome home, I thought to myself.

We must have been stuck on the tarmac for an hour, filled

with complaints that nothing ever worked in this country. As soon as we were released from the plane, people broke out into something like a stampede to make it to passport control. I wanted to follow the rhythm of the crowd, but my feet were heavy. The delay had me waiting in line for three hours until eventually it was my turn. I kept my eyes down, hoping to not invite any interest. The security agent asked me why I was coming back to the country in a way that wasn't quite welcoming, and I told him that it was a family emergency. He turned this way and that to look at what I was wearing and my luggage before letting me go.

The air was hot and humid when I made it out of customs, like the air-conditioning wasn't working. I looked down at my feet, standing over Cruz-Diez's mosaic. Tiles had been ripped out here and there, a perfect metaphor for a people who had lost the screws in their heads a long time ago. Everywhere I turned, people regarded each other with suspicion, as if any of us could be a thief or a murderer, and sadly, I picked up that habit as if I'd never dropped it. The hairs at the back of my neck rose every time someone glanced my way. I countered with my self-defense mechanism, glaring harder than they did, wishing it were enough to keep anyone with bad intentions at bay.

I elbowed a guy out of the way who tried to sneak up on me and take my place in line at the counter of the airline that flew to Maracaibo. When I was finally able to talk with an agent, and once I finally managed to slur my words enough for her to understand me, she confirmed the price of tickets and that the next flight was scheduled for tomorrow afternoon. That was a whole thirty-plus hours away.

I couldn't afford it anyway, so I shuffled out of the line and walked over to the area where I could ask about bus rides. Those were more accessible, but the next bus to the western part of the country was leaving two days from now.

I sat on the floor in a corner between a vending machine that had stopped working in the '90s and a door leading nowhere that had been sealed shut with tape. It was a metaphor for Venezuela as a whole.

Hugging my backpack against my chest and raised knees, I dropped my face against it and just faded away for a bit. I didn't sleep, I just let my mind drift until eventually a thought reached the forefront. Checking that no one was paying attention to me, I reached into my backpack for my old cellphone and plugged it into the electrical socket by the vending machine.

It worked. For the first time in a day, I felt a small spark of hope.

I called Papi. He was stunned when I told him the news and didn't scold me, like I had expected. Instead, he told me to wait and that he'd call me back after a bit. When he did, it was to let me know he'd bought a ticket for tomorrow's flight under my name.

"Hay noticias?" I asked him, hoping for any good news.

"No," he confirmed. Silence fell between us. There was so much to say, and yet nothing came out. He added that he was trying to find a hotel room nearby for me, and I said I'd rather wait at the airport than have to find a driver back and forth. Not to mention I didn't have any Bolívares, and what dollars I carried would barely cover a meal.

Later, during the night, I found a small restaurant in the airport where I ate an arepa. The receipt claimed the restaurant had free Wi-Fi, and I tested it with my American phone. It was patchy at best, but I managed to send an update to the girls. I caught the two check marks in the corner that said they'd received and read it, but I wasn't able to get any texts in return, no matter how much I fiddled around with the Wi-Fi. My finger hovered over Gabe's contact, but I clicked away from the messaging app instead.

Every muscle in my body ached the next morning. There was a foul taste in my mouth as I lined up for the plane back to my hometown. My heart hammered in my chest as though it wanted to run on ahead and return where it came from.

This time, I drifted into such a heavy sleep that it took a flight attendant shaking me to snap me out of it. I jolted awake because, in the thickest maracucho accent, she announced we had arrived a while ago.

Forever and a half passed until we were able to deplane. I ran through La Chinita airport with more energy than I'd thought I had. When I finally made it through arrivals, there they were, mi papi y mi mami.

I slammed into their waiting arms and clutched at them as if they could evaporate from my grasp. The three of us dissolved into tears, the kind that were loud and ugly and sloppy and had everybody looking at us.

My energy began to ebb away, and they practically had to carry me to the car. The same one they'd used to cart my siblings and me to school, to our friends' houses, to church.

"Cora?" I asked them, my head lolling as Mami buckled my seatbelt. She shushed me, saying we'd talk once we got home.

The daylight sky beyond her struck me as too blue, too bright, when it had no right to be. I squinted against the harsh sun of my homeland, and when I blinked again, my eyelids weighed a ton. I whispered Cora's name again, part cry and part prayer that I could see her again. That I still had a chance to make amends, to hug her, to scream at her. That I hadn't lost her like I'd lost Carlos. That it wasn't my fault too. And then I faded away.

CHAPTER THIRTY

Twenty-four hours passed before I was able to lift my head from a pillow.

It was bizarre waking up in my childhood bedroom after years away. Not much had changed in it. The bunk bed Cora and I had covered in stickers was still there. The walls were the same faded pastel peach, adorned with discolored Backstreet Boys, One Direction, and Britney Spears posters that still hung on for dear life. Both our desks by the windows were covered by Cora's things, from textbooks to makeup items and balled-up clothes. The only striking thing about the room was that I was alone in it.

No sounds came from elsewhere in the apartment. A wave of nausea hit me as I shifted up to sit. Could someone get jet-lagged when there had been no time difference from point A to B? But then I remembered everything that had happened in between—no wonder I felt like a truck had run me over.

Choosing to drink some water rather than hurl, I shuffled my way to the kitchen. Mami was there, sitting by the table, staring at a family picture she kept on the fridge.

It had been taken six years ago during Christmas. We were all dressed in festive colors and waved sparklers in the air. Back then, Cora and I had looked identical. Same haircuts and same clothes, which had been incredibly offensive to us at the time. But all three of us had dressed as Mami saw fit. Carlos's face gleamed with sweat because he'd been forced to wear a knit sweater that had cooked him in our thirty-degrees-Celsius winter.

Papi and Mami looked so happy in the picture. The shutter had caught her in the middle of laughter, her eyes closed to the world as she looked only at the joy inside her. Papi seemed almost twenty years younger than now, in comparison. They had aged drastically since I'd been away, not just because of the lines in their faces but because of the heaviness in their eyes.

Mami's were vacant now. I cleared my throat, and she called out Cora's name. When she realized it was just me, we both dissolved into tears. She held out her arms, and I burrowed between them. I rubbed her back, and she patted my head.

"Estás muy flaca," she said in between sobs. "Te voy a hacer unas arepitas."

"Dónde está Papi?" I asked her as she fretted about the kitchen, setting out to make arepas. The quiet in the apartment meant Papi was out, and I desperately craved news.

Mami said he'd left at the crack of dawn. Operations at the company were halted until we found Cora, and everybody was spread around the city, searching the way the police should be doing. The case had gained media attention, which was good news for a change. This time I didn't care if my face was plastered everywhere, as long as it helped find her.

As Mami beat the dough, I grabbed my old cellphone and sent a barrage of texts to my high school friends. Half had moved abroad. Most of the ones who remained in the city were already aware of the situation but had no info.

Seeing me fiddle with the phone, Mami said, "Tu papá nunca cortó la línea, por si volvías." I never thought it would happen, and yet here I was, thankful Papi had kept my phone working in hope of my return. And that reminded me that neither he, Mami, nor I would ever lose hope for Cora's return.

Didn't people say there was supposed to be some telepathic link between twins? We were identical—shouldn't the connection be particularly strong between us? I'd never felt it, but right now, more than ever, I desperately wished I could know in the deepest part of me that she was fine. But all I found inside was heartbreak.

Late in the night, Papi returned home. The weariness in his eyes didn't bode good news, but it also didn't suggest the worst. I hadn't found any leads from any of my or Cora's friends. We sat together for a simple meal where none of us ate much. My phone pinged with a couple of messages, just generic greetings from old friends and good wishes for Cora's safety.

After dinner, I turned on my American phone and tested the Wi-Fi connection from my room. It was slow and patchy, but eventually some fifty messages loaded up. Most of them were from Gabe. I hugged my pillow tight against me, wishing it were him.

Breaking up with him was still too raw, and I didn't have any more energy to cry again. I muted his chat and checked out the one with Taylor and Maya. I caught them up on the non-news, and they sent back gifs portraying hugs and offers to help any way they could. I honestly couldn't think of a single thing other than thanking them for everything they'd already done for me.

Graduation is next week, do you think you might be back in time? Taylor asked. Her three dots appeared again, and it took a moment for the new text to come through. But just in case, I explained everything to the school counsellor, and we'll figure something out for you.

My vision swam with fresh tears. Thank you. I love you guys.

We love you too, responded Maya.

The conversation reminded me that graduation was essentially the expiry date of my current visa. I gathered enough energy to write an email to my attorney, explaining everything that had transpired in the past few days. Then I copied more or less the same information in a different email for Jeff. It was a last-ditch attempt at holding on to the American Dream that now faded with every ticking second. If this didn't null my in-process application, if it didn't cost me the full-time position I'd bet my life against, I'd consider it a miracle.

I sent the emails and left it all to fate. Funny how every plan I'd carefully orchestrated had crashed down, and it didn't even feel like the worst that could happen.

Once that was done, I collapsed back on my childhood bed on the bottom bunk. I was drained of energy even though all I'd done all day was mope around the apartment, looking at the mementos of a past lifetime that reminded me of when we'd been happy and just didn't know it.

There was a soft knock on my door, and Papi popped his head in. We stared at each other without knowing what to do. I broke the tension first, waving him over.

Slowly, as if uncertain, Papi sat on my bed beside me. "Cómo has estado?" It was the first question he'd asked me, about me, in years. I had to bite my lip hard to not cry out from the ache in my chest. I hadn't known how much I'd missed him until right that second.

So I told him everything. From the moment I'd decided to leave and why, going over every major milestone in the past four years. I mentioned my friends, the fun we'd had, every time things had got tough and we'd been there for each other. I talked a fair bit about my grades, about how I was the best welder in my class—even over the guys. A twinkle came to his eyes then, no doubt proud that the special skill he'd taught all his kids growing up had led to this accomplishment. I told him about my intern position and the possibility of making it full-time. And I told him about Gabe. All of it.

He listened in silence as I explained the nightmare of the visas, what Gabe had proposed to do for me. How in the end I'd been trying to fix it the right way, sacrificing possessions and comfort so I could do it by myself.

"Siempre fuiste una luchadora," he said, his gruff voice cutting at parts. He reached out and hugged me tight. "Pero todo lo tuviste que hacer solita porque te abandoné. Perdóname."

I clung to him, burying my face in his chest. How wrong we'd been, driving a wedge between us by ourselves and blaming politics for it. We had all this love that we'd lost track of, and because of our pride, we'd now wasted four years of our lives not talking to each other. If Papi had died suddenly, we would've never had this chance.

I asked for his forgiveness too, because I'd had more part in this rift than he had.

Eventually, we calmed down. We chatted about my plans for the future. I talked as if everything would work out, as if I'd get exactly what I wanted. Gabe's name did quite a bit of featuring in my responses to his questions. In turn, I asked him if they'd consider leaving the country as well. He said only if . . . And neither of us needed to fill in the blank.

Our conversation was interrupted by a sudden ping. Papi pulled out his phone from the pocket of his shorts and stared at it. When there was no reaction from him for too long, my heart began beating against my ribs with violence.

"Cora?" I asked, snatching his phone. There, in the chat between him and Cora, was a single message showing a location on a map.

We sprang into action, shouting for Mami. In seconds, we were rushing down and out of the building, taking the stairs because the elevators didn't work. We got in our car, not even thinking about calling for help.

The location pin sat directly atop the most famous motel in town.

As Papi drove us over, none of us dared voice our worst fears. A million scenarios ran through my head, churning the contents of my stomach violently. I wished we'd brought a weapon or an army of people to back us up. What mattered, though, was getting to the place as soon as possible. The streets of Maracaibo seemed darker than usual. The lights from lamp-posts and speeding cars weren't enough to dissipate the fear riding with us in the car.

We arrived at the motel, a seedy version of Aladdin's castle that fooled no one. Papi had barely parked the car in the busy parking lot before he was running over to the reception. My eyes stung from the lights weaving through the cheap plastic palm trees at the front. Or maybe because I'd never been so worried in my life.

Mami and I held each other's hands tightly while Papi demanded answers from the receptionist. The attendant claimed confidentiality at first, but then her eyes widened when she saw me, clear recognition flashing through them.

"Por favor." I latched onto her arm before she could react. "Díganos dónde está mi hermana."

Her manager came out, and the scene turned into a shit show where everybody shouted epithets. Papi was about to come to blows with the manager, and as Mami tried to hold him back, I picked his pocket to get his cellphone.

While they fought, I'd go hunt for my sister.

Zooming in to the map, I got a sense of where Cora's cellphone signal came from. I followed it out of the building and into the parking lot. My heart picked up speed with every step I took. I started calling out Cora's name, which must've caught Mami's attention, because the next second she was with me.

"Qué ves?" she asked, and I told her I wasn't sure. We ambled around the parking lot in the dark, not even caring for our own safety when Cora needed us.

Then we heard it, a sound clearer than any map. It was Cora's muffled voice.

We took off. My feet ate the pavement faster than Mami's. My breath sliced my throat like knives as I pumped my legs. It was nothing compared to the panic skewering my heart. I didn't dare to call out her name anymore, in case she wasn't alone.

But there she was, finally. Crouched between two beat-up cars, alone, trembling and wearing only tattered underwear. She clutched her phone in between bloody hands. When I appeared in front of her, the light behind me made me cast a long shadow over her. Cora flinched and made herself even smaller.

"Soy yo," I said, barely recognizing my own voice. It was so raspy and unstable she probably couldn't recognize me. "Es Catalina, tu hermanita."

"Cata?" Hers was even smaller when she spoke.

I threw myself around her to shield her from the world and cried out for our mother. The scream behind me told me she'd seen us. The three of us embraced so hard that no one would be able to pry our arms from one another. Mami thanked the Lord over and over, while all Cora and I could do was cry.

It would take several hours until we would be able to go home, and days to learn a partial picture of what had happened.

The motel manager had called the police on Papi. When they got there and heard what was going on, one of them decided to be a good cop that day and investigate if Papi's claim had any merit. In walking the perimeter of the hotel, the cop found Cora's now ex-boyfriend, half naked, with bloody scratches on his arms and a gun in his hand. He'd been trawling, trying to find Cora. She'd managed to find an opening and had escaped the room he'd kept her prisoner in during that long week.

According to the police statement, Cora had tried to break up with him, and he wasn't having it. That was why he had kidnapped her and . . .

We didn't know what else because she wouldn't talk to anybody.

The next day had gone by in finding a hospital that could take her in and run some tests. Whatever the results had been, they'd made both of our parents cry. They refused to share them with me, which told me everything I needed to know.

All throughout, I held Cora's hand. Even if she was shell-shocked, if I tried to move away, she would cling to me. I took strength from who knew where to not break down in front of her. I didn't think it would help her much if I did.

For days, I talked nonstop about nonsensical things like television shows, movies, or something Maya or Taylor had said. I even shared the news I got from Maya that my refiled application had been approved two days before my graduation. The relief left a bittersweet taste in my mouth.

On the day I'd have walked up on stage to get my diploma, Cora and I sat together on my bed and watched the ceremony live via a YouTube feed my friends had set up for me. My heart squeezed as I saw Gabe on stage, and I had the impression he'd lost a little weight from how the robes sat on his shoulders.

Cora squeezed my hand really hard, almost as if to give *me* comfort for missing out on the milestone. I didn't care. What I cared about was that she was safe. But looking at her sometimes vacant eyes, I wondered if I was telling myself that for my own comfort.

I didn't talk about Gabe with her. The last thing I wanted was to bring up the word *boyfriend* in any of the languages we spoke. Not saying his name aloud helped me pretend the longing I had for him wasn't as real as Cora's hands in mine. Not knowing if I would see him again was only my second concern after her.

A few weeks later—and the day before our birthday—Papi stepped into our bedroom and announced that el hijo de puta had been locked away for good and would never hurt our family again. I didn't know how reliable the prison system was in a country notorious for its criminal activity, but I didn't have the heart to argue.

Later that day, though, Cora's tears started to fall for the first time. As if she finally realized it was over.

That was the mood that sucked her in for days. One night, after she'd drifted off to a restless sleep, I slipped into our parents' bedroom and woke them up.

"Cora se tiene que ir de aquí," I told them.

There would only be reminders of what she had lived through if she stayed. Not to mention that, with Rodrigo's ties to powerful people in politics, I doubted he would stay in prison long.

Cora deserved better. She deserved healthcare that could take care of her needs, and I mostly meant the psychological ones that we wouldn't be enough to help her with. She deserved a clean slate, a new chance, a different life where nothing reminded her of the deranged criminal her high school sweetheart had become.

I remembered the turtleneck sweater she had once claimed was all the rage here. I recalled her strange attempts at contacting me and then pulling away for days. In her way, she had been trying to tell me what was going on, and I had failed her.

I wouldn't fail her now.

It took me a day to convince Papi. He, Mami, and I sat around the kitchen table while Cora napped. We had left the bedroom door open so we could listen just in case, and we kept our voices hushed to not disturb her. I explained that the US would most likely not be a possibility for Cora. My attorney had confirmed in a quick email to me that the odds were high that Cora would be perceived as a partisan of the government and would not be allowed an asylum claim.

We searched online for other options, similar to what I'd done not long ago for myself. One country was discarded for not having a good record on women's safety, another for an economic downturn, three for publicly telling Venezuelan immigrants to stay away.

I had a bit of a wildcard idea that I didn't share right away. Both of my parents focused mostly on neighboring countries that would be easier for them to visit. But eventually I asked them, "What about Canada?" The thing was, Cora and I had been practicing our English together for years, and she had an even better accent than mine. The skill should open doors for her, right? Especially now that she needed those open doors more than ever. Plus, the universal healthcare was a big deal.

Convinced, my parents and I prepared the paperwork for Cora's asylum application to Canada. I had six months from my visa approval to go back to the US, and with Jeff kindly agreeing to push my start at Metal Systems until after the summer, I was able to focus on the task. We got the paperwork ready in record time and filed the claim through the office in Bogotá, Colombia, and a true miracle happened. Not even two months after I'd arrived, the four of us were driving to Bogotá for Cora to fly out to Canada.

Our parents would take us all the way to the airport, where Cora would embark on a new life, and I would return to the one I had paused. During the many hours of the drive, I traced the scars in the palms of her hands with my fingers, drawing hearts over them so she knew I loved her. I also told her, in case she just needed to hear it.

She startled me by looking at me for the first time, *truly* seeing into my eyes. "Yo también te amo."

None of us had a normal reaction. I guessed that we'd grown exhausted by our tears, and instead, we broke into cheers and laughter. Mami and I clapped like people in Venezuela did when a pilot kept everyone alive by successfully landing the plane.

Color rose up in Coralina's cheeks for the first time. I wished this had happened earlier and not hours before we had to part ways. I jerked her against me and clamped my arms around her.

"I missed you," I whispered only for her.

"Ya volví," she whispered to me. Her voice hadn't recovered the strength and buoyancy I'd known for twenty-two years. I hoped one day it would.

"You know where we're going?" I asked her.

"Away. Very far away," Cora said, looking out the window.

She would travel by herself. The original plan had been for all of us to get tourist visas to join her, but we hadn't got them in time. We'd found a social worker in Canada who could pick her up at the airport and help her figure out the arrival process. Papi also had a former employee in Alberta who'd offered her help; she was an engineer who had moved to Canada thanks to a job offer in the energy industry. So that was where Cora was headed, at least temporarily.

The next morning, the day of Cora's departure, I woke up with a vivid memory of Carlos. He had said he would go out to be my champion so I could have the life I deserved. I wondered if somehow that had come true, if in everything that happened after his departure, he had somehow saved my life from what it could've been.

Had I been too late for Cora?

I watched her as she slept beside me before the alarm rang and woke everybody up. I hoped I could live up to Carlos's memory and be *her* champion.

A few hours later, at the airport, I faced the hardest farewell of my life. As the four of us parted ways in three different directions—our parents back to Maracaibo, Cora to Canada, and I back to Orlando—I hoped this was the right thing for all of us, that I hadn't just broken up our family and made everything worse.

CHAPTER THIRTY-ONE

Waking up from the nightmare took twenty-six hours after Maya picked me up at the airport. That was what almost two months back home had felt like. There was no relief when I opened my eyes and set them on the ceiling of my room in the apartment I'd shared with my friend for two years. Only guilt waited for me. And so much anger at myself and the world.

Why had my twin had to go through something like that, whereas I got to come back here and keep on as usual? Everyone would keep riding the roller coasters in this town, and I would tag along, appearing as though I were enjoying the ride. But on the inside, I wasn't the same. I would forever carry disgust at myself for the way I had treated Cora when I was angry, for how easily I had turned my back on my family years ago, for how easily I had become a *me-first* person.

Who was I, after all this? I knew with certainty I couldn't stay the same.

The first change I needed was in the status of my smell. I shouldn't be this rancid. The sun shone bright through the blinds, which meant it had to be early. How early, I didn't know. Of which day, I also couldn't gather enough wits to remember.

I plopped back on the couch after my shower, wet hair dripping over the ratty sweatshirt I wore, and stared at the black TV screen as if willing it to turn on and show me what I was supposed to do with my life after this.

The thought came to my mind unbidden—*Maybe talk with Gabe.*

I fired up my American phone for the first time in too long. Hundreds of notifications greeted me from several apps, but my eyes fixed on the date. Today was Chris and Ellen's wedding.

My absence was probably not enough to ruin it. Maybe the Cabreras' mom was running her mouth all over the place, souring Ellen's day. Or maybe by not being there, I was only wrecking Gabe's mood.

Oh, I missed him. I placed a hand over my chest, surprised it could still beat this hard without him.

There was a racket outside the door. I moved like an old lady from the couch and peeped outside. Maya and Taylor were talking in hushed voices in the hallway, and Maya had a bag of groceries in hand. I opened the door, and they recovered quickly.

"Welcome back!"

"How are you doing?"

"Have you talked with your family since—"

"Do you need any help?"

The worry in their faces tugged at my heart. I debated between hugging them and staying in their arms all day or asking them for help to do something else.

For once, I went for the latter.

Taking a deep breath, I said, "Yes, I need your help to get to a wedding."

"Yes!" Taylor gasped dramatically. "Then there's no time to waste!"

"You took a shower, good." Maya put the shopping on the kitchen counter. I could practically see the mechanisms in her brain turning at full speed. "What do we have to work with?"

"Not much." I motioned at myself. "I didn't have a chance to buy the bridesmaid dress. Not that I'm still a bridesmaid after my absence."

"No matter, I'll make it work."

Taylor was on her phone as she said, "We still have lots of time to get ready and have Manny pick us up." Then the line must've connected because she shifted her focus to it, giving her new boyfriend a whole list of instructions.

The two tag-teamed their efforts, with Maya as the lead aesthetician and Taylor as her assistant. If, by any twist of fate, they didn't see success in scientific research and engineering respectively, they could make this a full-time gig. As one pulled at my hair and the other stabbed my eye with mascara, they turned me into a final product they could be proud of.

I didn't recognize myself in the mirror. The mauve dress I'd borrowed from Maya hugged every curve. My hair was styled into an arrangement that was half atop my head and ended with waves loose around my bare shoulders. It was pure art.

Then I saw my face. The fact I looked like Cora just six months ago threatened to make me ruin their hard work.

"No crying now!" Maya screeched and shoved me out of my room. "Cry later when you see your boyfriend."

Except I didn't have a boyfriend anymore, did I?

Not if I didn't win him back.

"Change of plans," I announced to my friends as they too got dressed to the nines. "I'm going to this wedding not to ruin it but to get Gabe back."

Taylor paused while dragging a cocktail dress up her legs to pump her first in the air. "Aw, yeah!"

"Atta girl." Maya grinned at me through her mirrored reflection while she applied mascara. "That's the Cata I love."

Minutes later, Manny appeared at the door. He was dressed so smart he looked nothing like the sweet mechanic in dirty overalls I was more used to seeing, but rather like the kind of guy who'd appear on the cover of a novel about billionaires. Taylor messed her lipstick kissing him for long enough that Maya and I finished getting ready.

We finally bundled in Manny's car. I was thankful he was the one driving and not Speed Racer, who sat beside him in the passenger seat. They exchanged cute little glances every so often, holding hands every time we caught a red light.

Meanwhile, Maya wasn't here for that. She shoved me aside so she could poke her head between them. "Floor it, the ceremony already started!"

Manny did not, in fact, floor it. He followed the speed limit and all the rules of the road, and that was how I knew he was the perfect match for Taylor.

I settled back in my seat and looked out the window, which started to help me get my bearings. It wasn't just that I recognized the streets of the city I now called home. We passed the school I had technically graduated from, the company I had so desperately hoped to join. We drove by the McDonald's where Gabe had bought me ice cream, and my stomach rumbled. I hoped the dress was stretchy, because I planned on attacking the buffet. The more we drove down roads that hadn't changed in my absence, the closer we got to where Gabe was, and the more I began to pray that *he* hadn't changed. That he still felt the same way about me. That he was still willing to put up with my bullshit and tease me and kiss me and hold me and . . .

By the time Manny pulled into a parking lot near the church, I'd worked myself up into a bundle of raw nerves. "Maybe we should just go directly to the reception," I told them as we walked to the front door of the church. "Or at least find a side door."

"Nonsense," Taylor said, huffing. "Since everyone's facing the altar, no one will notice us come in from the front door."

That said, she offered no time for me to prepare and just opened the door. A hinge that needed lubricant croaked, the sound echoing across the walls of the church as we'd come in precisely at a praying pause.

Every single person turned to look at us.

Taylor whispered to us, "Oops."

For the first time in what felt like an eternity, a rush of emotions bubbled up my throat. I wanted to laugh, apologize, scream, and smack her upside the head. Even more, I wanted the earth to swallow me whole.

What happened instead was that it grew hands and clawed at my feet, keeping me rooted in place as a commotion started all the way up at the front, and a voice I knew very well asked, "Gatita?"

"No . . ." I dragged the word out in a groan.

"C'mon." Taylor pushed me. "We'd better sit down so the ceremony can resume."

The four of us tried to duck our heads out of sight as we headed to a mostly empty pew in the back, but people's attention was still on us. A kid straight-up pointed and said we were being rude at church. There was some healthy irony there, but I couldn't disagree.

When I sat and faced forward, I was able to see Gabe. The commotion had been him, breaking rank with the rest of the groomsmen. He headed for the center aisle at a jog, passing by his mom, who tried to grab on to him and failed when his abuela blocked Mrs. Cabrera's way. The feint he did to avoid her hands was on par with some of the best soccer players.

I shook my head at him, mouthing that we could do this later. This was not the right time or place. I sneaked a glance at Chris and Ellen and was struck by the gleeful smiles on their faces. As if this were totally part of their dream wedding and not at all a disaster.

I wished I'd got the memo that we were still going forward with Gabe's silly plan so I could have opted out of it. The only responsible thing I could think of was leaving the way I'd come, so I shot to my feet and fled out of the church. The door squeaked once more, but it didn't remain shut for long. Gabe pushed open the doors all the way, sprinting behind me.

My brains were still lost in baggage claim because I shouted, "What are you doing?"

"I'm not letting you go again," was his response.

People streamed out of the building, the better to peer at the scene.

Since it was clear that he wanted to make one, I figured I could mitigate it by letting him catch up to me and then dragging him away from prying eyes. The idea became even more solid as I spied his mom heading down the aisle with the same expression she'd had on her face the day she threw her chanclas at us. A quick glance down confirmed that if she had the same idea right now, her heels would cause a lot more damage than the Havaianas.

"Gabe," I said, about to warn him of our impending demise.

Instead, he reached me, and the world spun—because he pulled me by the arm until I slammed against him, wrapped an arm around me, and pivoted me in a way that tore a squeal out of me. Then he planted a big, bold kiss on my lips.

For a second, I wondered if this was part of the plan all along, or rather, the culmination of it. The grand moment of wedding ruination to preserve in the history books of his family and Ellen's.

But then I felt the tender way he cradled the back of my head, how he held me tight against him, the way his lips coaxed mine open with a desperation so sweet I grew boneless in his arms. Gabe broke away for a second and whispered, "I missed you, Gatita."

I felt the first tears form in my eyes, but I kept them closed to the world and wrapped my arms around his neck, pulling him against me again. His warmth seeped into my body and reached my heart in a way none of the conversations I'd imagined between us could have.

"I missed you too. I didn't know if you'd take me back."

There was a smile in his eyes. "I never agreed to break up with you, did I?"

A thud finally forced us to break apart, followed by a series of gasps. I remembered Gabe's mom and wondered if the sound had been her shoe hitting him in the back of the head, but he looked fine as he pulled us back together. More than fine. His honey eyes twinkled down at me as he said, "I can't believe you're finally here, where you belong."

"Where is that?" The question came out as a whisper.

Gabe held me tighter and rested his forehead against mine. "In my arms."

"Well." That was Taylor's voice without a doubt. "So that happened."

Confused, Gabe tore his eyes away from mine to glance back, releasing a curse that should have sent him straight to confession. I peeped around his arm and nearly made the same mistake. Right at the entrance to the church, his mom lay prone on the ground.

Gabe and I glanced at each other. Had we just killed his mom from shock?

As people swarmed around Mrs. Cabrera, the bride, the groom, and the priest headed towards the commotion. Ellen instructed people to clear the way. She didn't care that her dress was white as she knelt down to check up on her almost mother-in-law. After a few tense moments, she stood up.

"She's just unconscious, and it doesn't look like she hit her head very hard."

The relief that hit the congregation resulted in applause. As one, Gabe and I also knelt down to check on his mom. The poor groom finally made it through the growing crowd and did the same.

The next person to join the party was Magdalena, who, upon seeing the mess, started laughing—just straight-up cackling like a hyena.

"Well, little brother. You sure outdid yourself with your plan."

I made eye contact with Chris across his unconscious mother and noted with equal parts horror and amusement that he could barely hold in his laughter. If a groom getting his big day torn to shreds by a mischievous brother like this weren't bizarre enough, then there was Gabe. Today marked the first day I had ever seen him blushing.

As he fretted over his mother, he whispered, "This actually wasn't on purpose."

His mom groaned, coming back to the land of the living. After a moment, she said, "The hell you didn't, muchacho malo! Ven pa' darte."

Gabe leaped out of the way, pulling me up by my arms. "Vámonos, o de verdad nos va a matar."

Gabe's abuela, his siblings, and the bride thought him running away from his mom was the height of comedy. As they doubled over, the poor priest started ushering people back into the church to resume the ceremony.

Gabe held my arm and flashed me a boyish grin that induced a heavy sigh out of me. It was too late to avoid any damage, but I followed him at a brisk pace. Without context, we almost looked like newlyweds happily walking away from the church to embark on our new lives.

And although it was unorthodox, that was exactly what we did. Together.

EPILOGUE

TWO YEARS LATER

I looked at myself in the mirror, hardly believing its reflection. My face was obscured by a delicate lace veil that streamed down to my chest. I clutched a bouquet of white roses and pale pink peonies, their scent permeating the entire room where Mami and my closest friends fussed about me. Mami stretched out the train of my dress, and behind her Ellen snapped pictures with a professional camera.

"Se ve tan hermosa," Mami said, dabbing at her eyes with a tissue in an attempt to not ruin her makeup. Although this would be the fourth time she'd done that already.

Behind me, Maya grinned. "I think Gabe's going to die the second you walk down the aisle."

"Hopefully not," Taylor said with a laugh. "We don't want Cata to become a widow before actually getting married."

I rolled my eyes, which unfortunately they didn't see.

The mermaid cut was similar to the dress I'd tried on years ago at the dress shop with Ellen. It highlighted every curve and even made me look taller, but it was a bit uncomfortable to move in. I was so graceless while turning around that I probably looked like a penguin. "Did Cora dial in?"

"Let me check." Ellen crouched down level with the laptop resting atop the hotel room vanity. She clicked around until Skype came up on the screen and dialed my sister. We'd made a few attempts earlier, but either her connection or ours was spotty.

Cora's face appeared on the screen. "Finally," she said with a grunt. "Wait, I can't see squat."

"One sec." Ellen maneuvered the device around so the camera was squarely on me.

My twin gasped. A silent moment followed as her dark eyes roamed up and down my frame. Then a little wrinkle appeared on her forehead, and she ran a hand over her new buzzcut. "Wait, all I see is fancy fabric and not my sister."

I snorted.

"Hold this." I passed the bouquet to Taylor—whom I planned to throw it to later—and lifted the veil in jerky motions. "How about now?"

"Va va boom." Cora whistled. "Gabe's going to lose his shit!"

"Exactly what I said," Maya agreed.

I knew the dress was pretty, with a tight bodice made of lace and delicate pearls that enhanced my assets and left my shoulders bare. The professional makeup made my face look like Cora three years ago, not at all like she or I looked like now on the regular. How I wished she were here to tease me in person. But all that mattered was that she was on the mend. Not doing well yet, but getting there.

A knock on the door preceded Magdalena. She popped her head into the room and, after what I'd been learning was the customary gushing over the bride, she announced it was time to head over to the church for the ceremony.

"Love you, sis," I told Cora.

She gave me a small smile. "Love you too. Now go get your man."

As I bundled into a limo with my bridal party, I couldn't help thinking how I'd never imagined I'd one day get married. Or that my siblings wouldn't be there for the big day. Their absence made my chest squeeze so hard, there was no room for nerves.

I sent a silent prayer to my big brother in heaven. I hoped he knew Papi, Mami, and I were okay, safely settled in Orlando. And that Cora was slowly picking herself back up in Canada. That he was proud of who we had become. I hoped he knew we would never forget him, that we had learned from him to enjoy every second we got, and that just as he'd been my champion, I would honor his memory by loving the people around me with all my heart.

A smile bloomed on my face as I glanced at all the women in white. Each of them, including Mami, wore dresses in all shades from mother-of-pearl to the starkest white. It had been Ellen and Magdalena's plan to so-called ruin this wedding. Mrs. Cabrera was still so pissed at this deviation from tradition, she'd spent the whole day hurling insults at the bridal party rather than at me for stealing her last baby. The fact she'd driven over in a different car made the plan a success already.

Amidst laughter and champagne flutes, we reached the same church where Ellen and Chris had tied the knot just a couple of years ago. We filed out of the limo, and I couldn't help laughing when the photographer got confused over who was the actual bride.

And then I found myself holding Papi's arm. His countenance was serious, but there were sparks in his eyes as we began the march down the aisle. The way he glared up at the front made me want to laugh. He also hadn't yet forgiven Gabe for stealing away his middle child.

As we walked by the pews, my boss, Jeff, and his wife waved. A few other coworkers watched with the same kind of sappy smile on their faces as I no doubt had.

Finally, I set my attention forward, my eyes on my future husband. Even through the sheer mesh of the veil, Gabe was the most beautiful sight as he stood tall in his black tux, his jaw-length hair tucked behind his ears in just the way that irritated his mother. That beautiful, mischievous man was no longer the Campus Babe but my heart and soul.

Papi handed me off with a grunt, but neither of us paid him much attention. Gabe pulled the veil up and away from my face and froze. Air rushed out of his lungs, and it took the first few words from the priest to reanimate him. Gabe picked up my hand, his eyes sweeter than honey as he broke protocol and kissed it.

The rest of the ceremony wasn't the rebulú the last wedding I'd been to with Gabe had become. Despite earlier threats, his mom did not object to our union. The priest declared us husband and wife and, as the congregation cheered, Gabe pulled me up against him.

"Al fin eres mía," he said, his voice low and only for my ears.

The corner of my lips went up. I braced my arms around his neck, accidentally messing up his hair with the bouquet. "Please, don't make it sound like this was your plan all along."

"Oh, but it was."

He pressed his smile against my lips, officially making us one. That was when I realized I'd made my American Dream come true—I'd finally found the happiness I'd been longing for.

Now, if only Cora could find her own happily ever after, and if Gabe's mom could stop stabbing the back of my head with her laser eyes, I would want for nothing else.

ACKNOWLEDGMENTS

I always read the acknowledgments section first, before reading the actual book. Weird, I know. But I like to see who the author is before I get to know their characters! Now I get to write my own and show you a glimpse of the village that made this bookish dream of mine possible.

First and foremost, thank you Lord. Contigo todo, sin ti nada.

Heartfelt thanks to the Backstreet Boys; you helped my mom and I keep our spirits up during those first months of the pandemic. You were the exclusive soundtrack as I wrote the first draft of this book in April 2020. Please sign my book?

To my friends Nicole Bea, Tamara Lush, Avery Keelan, Cayleigh Kennedy, Rodney V. Smith, Gerardo Delgadillo, Kate Marchant, and Simone Shirazi—thank you for believing in me before I did. And for patiently listening to my periodic, unhinged rants. Y'all are the MVPs.

To Gloria Chao, I can't believe I got to share the experience of my debut book with you!!! Sometimes life is just magical. Thank you for all your guidance and cheerleading.

To Aimee Crouch. Bet you're regretting becoming my friend when it meant teaching me English grammar for, like, fifteen years, huh?

To Anita, Gris, Nati, Ivan, Alex—thank you for supporting my writing career even when it meant I couldn't hang out because I was on a deadline. Party in my backyard!

To Irina Pintea, you're the first person at Wattpad who believed in this book and I'm so happy to have you in my corner. To Margot Mallinson, how lucky that I got you as my debut editor? I'm still pinching myself. To Andrea Waters, Eva Joti, Suzanne Sutherland, Lauren Dick, Sarah McDonald, Xavier Garcia-Gallardo, Fiona Simpson, Deanna McFadden, Alessandra Ferreri—without your support, this wouldn't have been possible. Also thanks to the Watty Awards judges who selected the first draft of this book for the 2021 win, you visionary geniuses, you.

To my Wattpad readers. Did you think I forgot you? *Never*! Seeing you fangirl over the #campusbabe has been my joy (especially chaoticbei and randomsweetstuff, your screams are my fave). As long as you love me, I'll keep writing.

Last but not least, *switches cassette* mil veces gracias a mi familia. Siempre me apoyaron incluso desde la época en que nada de esto parecía tener sentido. Aunque estamos separados, papá en el cielo y ustedes a través del océano, celebramos este logro juntos. Los quiero como perro caliente de puestico.

ABOUT THE AUTHOR

Marianna Leal taught herself English by writing anime fanfiction—while studying Mechanical Engineering in her hometown, Maracaibo, Venezuela. Now she resides in Florida (after a brief stint in the Midwest that was preceded by Scandinavia), and works for an engineering company that cares about the environment—while also writing books that represent her gente in both English and Spanish. She loves bunnies and em-dashes.